Running Wild Anthology

of Stories

Volume 6

Edited by Benjamin B. White

Running Wild Anthology of Stories, Volume 6
Text copyright © remains with the authors

Edited by Benjamin B. White
All rights reserved.

Published in North America and Europe by Running Wild Press. Visit
Running Wild Press at www.runningwildpress.com Educators, librarians,
book clubs (as well as the eternally curious), go to
www.runningwildpress.com.

ISBN (pbk) 978-1-955062-39-8
ISBN (ebook) 978-1-955062-40-4

Contents

Life Lessons.. 1

Shells A Mel Vans Mystery 9

Shared Endorphins.. 49

Committed 53

My Fire On Your Cutting 71

The Mole Catcher.. 73

The Justice of Dust 87

Lost and Found... 97

Gun Love... 129

Mystic.. 153

Killing Slugs with Salt 175

Henry, Kabir, and That Little Book........................ 181

Shark Tooth... 189

The Science Project 199

How to Act 215

The Edge of Things.. 225

Follow Me... 245

The Cure 265

Life Lessons

Kali Metis

This world wasn't made for me. I've known this since mom first took me out. Outside our home. Outside my safe place. That's when I knew I wasn't like others.

The first time my mom took me among the living, those without limits, I was five. Yes, you read that right. I was five. She carried me out our front door to Old Faithful, *Pop's favorite car, and down the road. Along the way she told me to mind myself. To not be rude to others. Make friends. "And if someone has something rude to say, you be good. No fits."*

I stared out of the window, nodded like I was paying attention. I was good at that, even at the age of five.

We stopped at a corner store. She told me to sit still and that she would be back in a minute.. Folks stared in at me, like they never saw a child before. Mom came out of the store hollering. Told them to leave me alone. I stayed good though. No fits. Mom got back in the car, all teared up. I didn't ask what was wrong. I knew what.

We pulled up next to a cottage with overgrown trees and bushes like something from a storybook, a Grimms storybook. A wooden sign that must have been a hundred years old read, "Happy Hanna's Kindergarten. All welcomed." The smiley faces were worn so the mouths were missing. The yellow faded to almost nothing. Only the eyes seemed bright.

Mom picked me up and out of the car and then put me right inside the door. She kissed the top of my head and left like someone was chasing her. She didn't bother looking up to see where she was putting me. This was the start of my first trip.

"Last call for boarding. Train number 333. Gate 6. Track 8."

I've been traveling ever since.

I stand here for what feels like an eternity. The walk from the bus to this gate takes me a solid 45 minutes. Just to board a train that'll last another hour to get where I'm going. Can't imagine how long it'd take me if I walked it.

I had looked around to see who I could play with. Find out who would take care of me. Mom never left me like this before. She never left me alone and I had never been outside our home, even if Pop had said he wanted me out sooner than later. I didn't know what that meant back then.

"Ma'am, you need to go down there to board." The trainmaster points down six car lengths, which feels like six football fields away. I sigh. I've stood at this entry for the last 15 minutes wishing there was some place to sit. Hoping someone would open the damn door. And now, I have to walk six football fields to wait again. I do all I can so I don't give her the stink eye and start forward. Others pass me with ease. Piled on with their luggage, my backpack miniscule in comparison. The straps worn. The zipper's teeth hungry. My cane propels me forward.

From the dusk of the darkened room, a room that stunk of cigarettes and sadness, came a woman with a face folded by wrinkles, her back hunched, her stride short, her hickory cane keeping her upright. She reached out to me with a sinewy arm that stretched halfway across the room. She helped me sit up proper on that stained rug. Said she'd show me something. Something that'd make me all better.

I don't bother looking at my watch to see how long it took me to get to the new entry. The new way of things. I simply stand and wait for someone to open this one. After letting in the other passengers, the conductor comes over and flicks a switch to let me in.

The old woman pointed to me and told me to get up. I did my best. Lifting myself up by my arms. Do it, she said. I almost cried. My arms used like legs, no one had ever told me to stand up all the way. Not even Pop. That's what I thought, she said. She motioned for me to follow her. I drug my cramped legs behind me, the way I'd always done. She looked behind her, eyes black like night, face stern. Don't know why I wasn't afraid. I should have been. She made her way to a doorway. The beaten white door had been closed. Locks lined the outside door jam. She clicked and clacked each one open. She motioned for me to follow her. Down the stairs to the basement.

"You're gonna hafta sit upstairs. If you can't make it then go to the other car." Oh no. I can make it. Make no doubt about that. I slide my cane into the side loop of my backpack and make my way up the steps. When I was younger I'd rush. Embarrassed that I'd make someone else wait. Fuck that. They can wait. I can feel the people behind me as they shift. Their anxiety elevated. Their breathing audible. I turn and smile. Wave. One of those shy, "Oh I'm so sorry you have to wait. I'm such an asshole," kind of waves. I give them what they expect and continue forward. I slow down a little. Their bitching gets louder. I gave them what they wanted so now I do what I want.

I had thumped my way down each step. Doing as I was told. Made it all the way down to the dirt floor. The old woman told me to hush and stay there. My eyes didn't need to adjust much since the basement was about the same light as the rest of the house. I dug my hands into the loose earth and noted its odd dampness. The scent of metal and iced sweat. Scent of fear and power. In the corner I heard a murmur. Like someone trying to talk. As a kid, I thought she had the TV on. But then I looked where the sounds came from.

I pick the closest seat to the stairwell. The thought of going farther exhausts me. I take my time shifting off my backpack, unlooping my cane, I put them on the seat closest to me. My backpack ruffles, shifts, needs. I pat it, caress it, let it know it's okay then shuffle to my seat. I smile, apologetically waving at the others as they hurriedly plop down into their seats.

In the farthest corner from me there was a cage. I thought I hadn't seen it right. Inside, it looked like a big old lump. But then it moved. Moved the way Pop moved when it was night and he came in all late and he stunk of dollar-store whisky. The same way he moved as Mom tried to get him to bed so there'd be no fuss. That slow, staggered, lost move. As it unfurled, I could see its arms, its legs. It stretched out to the form of a man. His clothes ragged. His hair matted against his head. Covered in dirt. The dirt from that floor. I gasped. Started to cry. I wanted to get up and run. I wanted to cry out for my mom. Something inside me told me she wasn't there. Wasn't going to come back. The old woman looked at me with those black eyes, raised a long finger, and told me to shush.

The drunks downstairs in the café car order their gin and tonics, their starter beers. The workaholics get out their laptops. The lovers call their others, tell them they'll be home soon. I smirk. The train car fills. I wonder if this'll be another train so full that folks are standing. I hope it is.

The old woman came over to me. I thought she'd hit me. Her eyes were deep, endless. She had moved with thought, intention. She reached over me to a shelf. Pulled down a worn, oversized, tan leather bag. Like one mom asked dad for. He called it a hippie traveler's bag.

I picked this train because I knew it'd be full. I knew it'd help me feed the hunger. These people, they have too much anyway. Time to share. The conductor checks my ticket then leaves me alone. Folks look at me like they're going to sit next to me, but don't. One guy comes over and insists I move my bag. I shrug and put it on my lap. It whines at first then calms, realizing it's closer to me. Feeling my warmth.

The old woman mumbled something under her breath. The man in the cage coming to. Like whatever had him messed up was wearing off. Like he remembered the meaning of life. She lifted the bag over her head, kept on mumbling. I tried my best not to cry, not to scream, not to yell. I couldn't stop shaking though. I couldn't stop shaking.

"What you got in there." He must be one of the drunkards. His breath reeks of stale booze. He's been hitting it since early. Probably started at lunch.

"Nothing of significance," I say.

The man banged against the bars. The old woman chanted louder. The words from some other tongue. The man started yelling at her. Called her names. I could see his strength. He wasn't a small man. He was bigger than Pop. She kept going like she's not with us. Like she was a spirit. He looked up at her and started to scream. I wanted to scream with him.

"It better not be a pet. They don't allow pets on these trains." He feels up his pockets like he's looking for something. Probably cash or a cigarette. Yup, cash. I pet it to stay calm. It'll be fed soon.

"No, sir. Not a pet. Just one of those new electronic games."

The old woman opened the mouth of her bag. Right at the man. He shook like he was seizing. Like I did when mom forgot my meds. Like Pop when he'd been drinking for days. Mom called it a bender. I covered my mouth. I couldn't help but scream, but I had to do what the lady said. Mom said to be good and not have a fit. I needed to make mom happy.

"Can I see it?" He asks. He pulls out a few bills, leans into me. I want him to go back down to the café car.

"Oh. Nah. It's nothing special."

He insists. I tap my backpack readying it. I put my fingers on the zipper tab.

"The café car is now open and serving. Welcome aboard," the announcer says.

Then the man dropped. The woman stopped chanting. The room filled with my muffled cries. She turned to me, wild-eyed. I stopped screaming. She stood up straighter. Her stance filled with power. The kind of power on those TV shows with superheroes but this was real.

He's distracted by the announcement and taps my shoulder. I cringe. I didn't invite him to touch me. He'll be the first. It knows. Yes, he'll be the first. "I'll be right back," he says and stumbles his way over to the café car. The train's motion nearly makes him fall over. I look at my watch. We should hit the tunnel any minute now. My backpack shakes as if it knows. I comfort it, shush it, let it know it's coming.

She turned to me, and there's something more. Something different. Her back was straighter, her eyes glistened with life, her gnarled hands youthful. Her face smoother. Her cane, lonely in a corner. Her need for it gone. Stand! she commanded.

The whine of the train heightens as we are swallowed into the tunnel's void. Laptops, phones, everything flickers. Connections lost. I pull the zipper's tab and let it free. The hunger audible. The cravings deep. The screams tangible. I taste the passengers confusion just like it tastes them. When I was younger, I didn't think it'd finish in time. But as the light of day breaks through the tunnel, I can feel it cuddle onto my lap. It curls up and purrs. Its renewal is mine.

My legs unfurled. I found my way to a new height, a new strength. I looked down, amazed. I stepped forward and then again. I laughed. A laugh from deep inside. A laugh of joy, of freedom. She smiled and motioned up the stairs. Go, she said. I'll show you more tomorrow. For now, go.

Light floods the car. The smells of fresh sweat and fear tinge the air. My favorite flavors to end the day. I get up and rehook my cane to my backpack. I jog the aisle to see the remains. All that's left are husks of travelers. Their eyes milky, void of comprehension. Their mouths agape, unable to sustain life. In the corner is the shell of the drunkard. Fresh bottle in hand. Didn't even get the cap off. I hop off the train and run down the tracks.

Shells
A Mel Vans Mystery

Andy McQuestin

Showdown at The Rum Club

I found him there, in the dim din of The Rum Club. He was sitting alone amidst a gathering of mismatched furniture, all strewn with cushions of silk and wool. The club's opulent den added to his dilapidated aura. He was in the body of Bassam 'Bazza' Talib, a popular local crime figure. But I wasn't hunting him for Talib's various alleged crimes, I was hunting him because inside that body he was forty-five-year-old tram driver Ian Alcott, a scabmite.

I did my usual trick, straight to the point, call them by their real name.

'Hello Ian.'

He raised his eyebrows in a silent admission. They were much bushier than his previous ones, the thin reddish blond ones I'd seen on his discarded shell, being sustained now at the Royal Mercy, only a few blocks from here.

'I'm terribly sorry,' he said, 'Do I know you?' I almost laughed at this, so unsuited were his manners to the scratched, threatening voice of Talib.

'No. I'm Mel. I've got to bring you in, Ian. Time's up.'

No answer. I continued, small hand movements, placatory gestures. Textbook. 'Don't panic – we're in no rush. We can have a little talk first. But I will have to take you in. Best to accept that now.'

A smile. Nothing in the case file suggested Alcott was a particularly dangerous proposition, but he'd chosen Talib's body for a reason. A part of him had to relate to Talib, to fancy himself as a tough guy.

He said, 'Listen, Mel. The fact you're here alone tells me you're not a cop. And I don't know you, so this is not an intervention from someone who misses Ian Alcott – because there's no such person, not even me. So you're a PI.'

'Congratulations. You could be one yourself with those powers of deduction.'

The smile soured, faded, returned a little twisted.

'Tough and smart, I see. And cute. And, being the nature of your trade, available for hire. Why don't you sit and have a drink, on me? We can talk business. As you can probably imagine, I have access to quite sizeable funds these days.' As he talked, he shuffled about on the couch as though seeking a more comfortable position, but his real discomfort was in the fact his sidearm was tucked into the back of his belt, which was sinking into the pillowy depths of the couch. He couldn't access it easily without standing, or else getting me to sit too.

I needed him to relax. 'Just business?' I asked. 'I like business, but I'd have thought Bazza Talib had more to offer than that.'

Now a wide, reptilian grin. 'Of course. I'm still getting used to the body, to be honest. But it brings a few, let's say, enhancements.'

'I can imagine,' I said, my tongue ever so lightly skirting my bottom lip. Like I said, textbook.

'So what will it be?'

'Spiced rum, double, neat.'

He called to the bar staff and I waited for his attention to return.

When it did, I slowly removed my trench coat and let it fall on the nearest couch. He sat back on the cushions with his arms spread-eagled. He let his eyes fall to the fitted white top, like a second skin. You can count on all men to pause at the chest, and I had mine pressed out for inspection. They never look quick enough to the waist, where my gun swings out like the big cock they wish they had.

The smile gone, he rolled hopelessly to the side to retrieve his own gun. By regulation, I needed him posing a threat to bring him in the silent way. Eventually his fingers grasped the handle of Talib's Glock. I let him straighten up then fired a stun round into his chest. The second one hit his groin, the pain registering just before he passed out. Not quite textbook. But fun.

Scabmites

I had to get the body of Talib to the police station in the inner-east for processing, then they would take it to Royal Mercy to undergo the process to unite Ian Alcott with his discarded shell. Talib, then, would slowly regain possession of himself. Moving the body alone was not plausible, even for a woman of my strength, so I called Commander Dean Knowles. He said he'd send a car immediately. I checked Talib's pockets for prizes. Found a jewel encrusted pipe in his jacket pocket, but nothing crystal to smoke with it. I kept it all the same. I put my coat back on, eager to cover up. The tight top was a costume for the job at hand, not usually the way I liked to roll. I stared at the young bar staff until they pissed off to the far end of the club and kept their pretty faces to themselves.

Alcott's mother was the one who hired me. I guessed she would be...happy? Who knows? There wasn't a lot of love or even desperation evident in our sole meeting before I took on the case. A little anger, perhaps. The disappointing son who'd found a new way to be a disappointment. I could see it from Alcott's perspective: becoming Talib was a significant upgrade. But I never let myself extend my empathy beyond that. I hated each and every one of the selfish fucks. Scabmites.

Scabmites. The name, I remembered, was a shortening of scabies mite, the only skin-burrowing bug. One of those deer-in-headlight scientists made the comparison on current affairs television and the online press ran with the abbreviated term, scabmites. The comparison was a fair one: The entering of another's body, consuming their flesh, assuming their life. Scabmites were parasites, only their takeover of the host was total, more akin to an emerald cockroach wasp. I'm guessing you haven't heard of it. It paralyses cockroaches with a sting, then injects a serum of neurotransmitters allowing it to control the living cockroach's mind. It chews off the antennae to remove that final aspect of independent instinct. Finally, it drags the cockroach to its nest and lays its eggs in the cockroach's abdomen. The cockroach is physically able to leave, but it isn't in control of its own interests, so it lets the larvae eat it alive until one life is swapped for another and the larvae burst from the cockroach's remains.

…It's more like that. So, yeah, I hate scabmites.

At the Station with My Man, Commander Knowles

Dean, or Commander Knowles for those who buy into that chain-of-command bullshit, was waiting in his office. We high fived to mark the successful retrieval of another scabmite and we even threw in one of those one-arm hugs. We liked all that old-fashioned men's stuff.

'A toast to you, Mel,' he said in that calm, gallant voice that, blindfolded, you might find sexy. He poured sparkling water from a bottle he seemed to have at hand specifically for this occasion, and we clinked glasses and drank. 'How many now?'

'Total?'

'Yeah.'

'Seventeen for me. Four this month.'

'A record of some kind, surely.'

'Team effort, Dean. Couldn't do it without you.'

'Modesty. No wonder you don't see a future with the force. It's politics and self-advocacy all the way in here.'

'Always was Dean, nothing new.'

'No, I guess not.'

My coat was open and I saw him glance down and back up from my tight white shirt, but it was more the look of a discomfited parent than a sleaze.

'Just a prop, Dean,' I said, opening the coat wide and turning side to side to get it over and done with. 'The case background indicated it might be effective.'

'And?'

'Good enough. Probably didn't need it in the end.'

Dean grunted, and, as he took another drink from his glass, I swiftly belted up my coat.

'Any cases you want me to look at?'

He tilted his head, curious investigator mode. 'Now why would I want that Mel? I'm happy to help you pursue your case work, god knows there's enough work out there for us and another dozen of you, but I'm not your employer.'

'Thanks for the lesson, Dean.'

'Is there an issue? Lack of work?'

'It's a trickle not a flood, that's for sure. Bad press after that PI stunned the wrong person. Hit a normal, mistook them for a scabmite. Did you see that?'

'Yep. Not good.'

'Amateur hour. And now it's fucked things up for all of us.'

Dean nodded and looked down, studying the carpet. Publicly, state and – especially – federal police were critical of PIs getting involved in scabmite hunting, but people like Dean, on the frontline, were grateful for a lightening of their load, allowing them to resource other problems like the unprecedented upsurge in petty crime, which coincided with the unprecedented upsurge of homelessness throughout the city. It just cost too much to live indoors, too much to eat, and nobody would pay the price to treat the cause or the symptoms. So the public paid the price crime by crime, and the police, often inexpertly, pursued the perpetrators, the secondary cause of the crimes.

But Dean wasn't thinking about that at all. Because he said, 'Of course, Mel, there is that one case you could go after. You know we haven't got far ourselves. And I've heard nothing from that PI who took on the case, at your recommendation, am I right?'

I snorted a yes. 'I'll leave that with you Dean, if you don't mind. I like to keep things professional.'

Did he have to bring it up? I placed my glass of water, bitter now, on his desk.

'I'm off.' A fist-bump, my heart not in it, and out the door, out of the station, into the two a.m. streets. Only the cokeheads shuffling past in their shiny shoes, the alleys and lanes silent with the tension of sleeping bodies.

Two to Tango

You can't just roll out of bed and decide to be a scabmite. From what little science has been able to discover, we know that there is a connection between a neuro condition and a paranormal phenomenon, to use the old language, where a depression-like state of desperately wanting out of one's own life, own body, precedes a realisation of the possibility of doing just that. Accounts from the few scabmites who have returned to their shells in full health and (the fewer still who) have recounted their experiences, tell us their identification of new hosts is akin to instinct. They just know who they can and cannot penetrate. In other words, a scabmite needs a receptive host; there is a symbiosis at play.

Of the science behind what makes a host a host we know even less. Profiling has shown that each and every host has, at the time of takeover, been experiencing an intensified period of anxiety, stress, shame, or other neuro-emotional state that has made them, in simple terms, wish they were someone else. Not suicidal, not necessarily clinically depressed, but wanting to not be themselves for a time, like the scabmite, but with less conviction. Cases have ranged in extremes from the terminally ill to people about to speak in front of small groups. Whatever the cause, the scabmites detect the signals. From there, the future of the host is determined only by the scabmites. The scabmite elects to take over or they don't. When they do, the scabmite's body, if they are their original selves, collapses, like a bird falling stone-dead from the sky. The paramedics can usually diagnose them as a shell on arrival. They go to a hospital to stabilise. After a while they can be taken home to be cared for. The doctors think familiar settings might be good for the resting subconscious, despite precious little sign of mental activity, even as compared to a coma patient. I think they are just freeing up hospital beds. Fair enough.

When the scabmites move on, the old hosts regain their independence and withdraw into a temporary remote state, similar to shock. Once they recover they seem to remember all of their actions, but can't explain the thinking behind them.

What freaks me out is how many close calls could be occurring every day. You wish you weren't going to that baby shower this weekend and – boom – you're a host. The government tells us the best defence is to try and stay positive. Good luck.

Him

Each year I learn a bit more about myself. It's the one aspect of aging I enjoy. I calculate by the time I'm one-hundred and thirty-five years old I will have worked out who I am and drunk over five thousand bottles of top shelf liquor, if I ease up a bit after I hit three figures. Despite being an on-and-off hard-drinking PI with a shitty home life, I still pride myself on avoiding clichés most of the time. But alas, there is a Him. Was.

I met Roderick 'Roddy' Stevenson Ballycastle through a friend who thought he'd appreciate my direct manner of talking, even if nobody else did. Fortunately for both of us, nobody made too much fuss about the coming together and we were able to meet over a drink at a casual house party, so we could keep the date to under five minutes without being impolite. I don't know what it was I liked at first. Prospect of a fuck, probably. It certainly wasn't that ridge in his nose that made kissing him like climbing through a car window. It wasn't his stuffy name, because I always saw myself ending up either alone or with a Raul, Constantino, or Idris. It wasn't his stupid boys' nickname, Belly-o, which I banned in the apartment we would later share. Like I said, I don't know. He was nice, always nice. He laughed when I said honest things. He told me I was as smart as the internet, and for a year I mistakenly thought that was a compliment. He made me feel like I was making someone happy.

That was Him, this was now. There was still time for sleep, before the sickly lemon Sun would be up and clawing at the corners of my window.

Move Towards Safety

Some mornings, like this one, I woke up with my arm across his chest. His body cool through the gown. They say you shouldn't sleep beside them; you might disturb… something – they don't know shit, really. But I've got one bed, and I'm not sleeping on the floor just because Roddy was a selfish arsehole. So he has his side and I have mine, like a real couple.

Sometimes I say good morning, a little joke I have. Part of the whole staying positive thing. This day I said nothing. I checked the readings. I'm expert at what all the numbers mean now. He was fine, for a shell. He was nobody. I moistened his skin with the sponge. I moved out of the bedroom, away from danger, or more importantly, like they teach at protective combat, towards safety. Coffee.

My machine poured me a sustainably sourced one, so it's expensive and crappy. I leaned against the kitchen sink and had my planner read out to me. The bones were bare. I called the office, heard John's sweet voice asking how he could be of assistance.

'Anything new?'

'Mel! How did you go last night?'

'Good. Got him.'

'Fantastic! Well done you.'

'Not so fantastic. Should've drawn it out a bit. My planner is looking light on for the next month.'

'Time for a holiday, perhaps?'

'Gee, John, an unpaid holiday, that sounds grand, just grand. You'll have me homeless in a fortnight.'

'Oh, sorry.'

'And you, with me. We could be each other's blankets.'

'Mel, that's insensitive.'

'Sorry John, you're right. Listen, do we have anything new.'

'No scabmites, but we have some stolen cars from a yard in –'

'That'll do, John, thanks.'

'Mel,' he said, sighing deliberately into my ear.

'John.'

'It doesn't have to always be scabmites.'

'I know that John, but as long as there are some, they'll be the priority.'

'Well there's always one. You know his sister will pay you to investig–'

'Bye, John.'

I spent another coffee brooding over the fact John was right. And Dean was right. And if that wasn't bad enough, I had time. Time to pursue a personal case, time to find Him.

Digging up Dirt from the Grave of a Ghost

To begin with, we did things *I* liked. Got coffees, went out for breakfast, a few gigs, boozy arvos in the inner suburban pubs, the good ones, where the chairs were vinyl and some rooms still had carpet on the floor. When that went well, and the sex was good, we started doing Roddy things. Driving out of the city for little bushwalks, nature trails, talking as we walked, all that. I started to like Roddy things, too. This is the first warning sign of a thing becoming a Thing: The dreaded 'common interests'. We were finding them with ease.

Sometimes after our little walks, a conversation would continue in the drive back to the city, Roddy becoming increasingly passionate about the topic, which was usually human rights and more often than not the homeless crisis in our city. Roddy's major gripe was that the general 'everyone' were ideologically supportive of every good cause you could think of but didn't act on the big issues in their own backyard. I agreed with him, mostly, but without the same fervour.

I pointed out that people had busy lives, that just getting by was its own cause sometimes. That pissed him off, but we never argued.

Roddy said, 'People have this mentality that the problem is beyond them. That it's too big for them, or that it's someone else's responsibility, like the government's.'

'It more or less is, isn't it?'

'Let's say that was true. What if they don't do anything, like they haven't done anything?'

'I...don't know.'

'Yes you do, Mel. Yes you do. You do something.'

'Okay. But again. People are busy. And there's a lot of problems in the world. Not just this one.'

'That's another part of the problem. We need to do one thing at a time, and do it well. You don't service all the parts of a car at once. You do the oil and water, the brakes, then the tyres and steering.'

I laughed at that, the thought of Roddy trying to service a car.

There was probably a change happening at that precise moment, or maybe it had already happened. I was so lost in the feeling of being happier than I'd ever been, I didn't see him sliding toward the abyss. I didn't reach out to catch him.

So he did something. He looked into how he could help out. We made some donations. He started working at the community kitchen, serving food, cleaning. If he found it rewarding, it didn't show when he came home. He would be polite, quiet, stand in the corners of rooms. He was a wave from a lone sailor on a passing boat. And I was floating on a raft with no sails, no sign of land. I started putting more energy into my work, finding the scabmites, the good I could do for the world. Never thinking, not once, what if?

When what if happened, when they found his shell unconscious on the floor of the community kitchen, the cops had no chance of guessing who the host was. There was no registration required to get a meal there. No last known addresses, no names, no one.

So I made some inquiries, nothing much. Hung around the kitchen, meeting some of the regulars. Many were the newly homeless, the hopefully-just-between-homes sect, disconnected from the rest, they knew nothing. Eventually I was pointed down some paths. I spent an early morning amongst a large group of people, all ages, who huddled together for company and security. They slept along the river, near the aquarium, where weekly incomes can be spent gawking at the passing bellies of caged sharks.

Had anyone been acting strange?

Plenty.

Had anyone passed out suddenly?

Yes, a few. What's new?

The trail was cold before it ever got warm. On my suggestion, Roddy's sister, Judith, hired a PI from the northern suburbs with an okay rep. I passed what I knew to him, told him to let Commander Knowles know if he found him. Asked him to bring him in the loud way, unharmed. Then I went back to work, visited the hospital after hours, drank a few extra each night and, when the time came, took Roddy's shell home. So began our second life together. That was a year ago, today. Happy anniversary, arsehole.

A Sniff

There was a new joint two blocks from me, in the old sushi place, that sold Portuguese tarts; as good a place as any to sit and stare at my phone, waiting for my nerve to climb over the hill of my better judgment and call the PI. It took three tarts, a coffee, and a few rotations of the pipe in my hand, sniffing it in the hope of catching a trace of something alien and deep. I considered a fourth tart, but the two women behind the counter were too thin to understand, I didn't want to frighten them.

The PI's name was Regio, something Regio. We made small talk. We'd heard of each other.

'Nothing useful,' he said, in answer to my question, 'It's more or less cold for me. I took Judith through what I have last week. I spent a good six months trying to piece things together around the homeless crowd, you know, down near the aquarium?'

'Yep, I know.'

'That was no easy task. He moved through a few different hosts, of that I'm sure. I've spoken to three confirmed cases. It won't surprise you to know there is no shortage of folks down there who wish they were someone else from time to time.'

'Smorgasbord.'

'Exactly. So I can't be sure I got them all. But in any case, I lose the trail there.'

'Maybe he's still there.'

'I thought that too, but I don't think so now. That community keeps a pretty good eye on each other. They noticed the changes in one of their number each time they hosted your boy.' I winced at the remark. 'I'm pretty sure I've I-D'ed the last host from that crowd.'

'Tell me.'

Regio explained how his interviews found that each time Roddy moved into a host, the person was observed to be more talkative than usual, more active, very interested in others, but also more skittish, especially at night. He was probably frightened out there, in the cold, in the dark.

'Was there a pattern, in the hosts he selected?'

'Too few hosts to say for sure, but he seemed to move progressively to more, how would you describe it…at risk people. A teenage girl, a mother with two children, a chronic meth user on his last legs. He sat that one out, at least two months, the longest the guy had been clean since he was seventeen.'

'Two months in the one host?'

'Yeah, but I learned this after. He would have been in that host when I was first interviewing around the community. But that guy, his name was Brenton, he was himself again by the time I met him. Only clean.'

Roddy, the bloody do-gooder, I had to laugh. A rare, good deed from a scabmite. 'And was he the last?'

'No, he went on a little sprint after that, three, maybe four hosts in the matter of a few days, if their accounts can be taken at face value. It ended with one of the veterans of the community, an occasional patron of the kitchen. But when he came back from the kitchen that day he was himself again, he just couldn't explain why he went to the kitchen, he had no interest in politics.'

'Politics?'

'Right. A few state pollies and welfare advocates were speaking at the kitchen that day. Bit of press, a big crowd.'

'Fuck, Regio.'

'I know, Vans, I know. You're gonna say that's where he changed hosts. That much is obvious. But where the hell do you look from there?'

It hit me. 'Wherever he could make the most difference.'

'Come again?'

'Regio, would you mind if I make a few inquiries of my own? I have no interest in taking the contract, you keep the cash and any credit if I find him. I just want a run at it.'

'Be my guest. I've stopped charging Judith anyway. Like I said, it's gone cold for me. But if you find something, you've got to cut me in, okay? I don't wanna look amateur here.'

'You have my word.'

'Good enough.'

I put the phone down and let the buzzing of my blood quieten until it was just me and the foil shells of the tarts. The few people I knew in politics learned long ago to turn their backs when I approached. But Judith...

Judith was always icy with me, but when I told her I was going to break all my rules and work the case, and – more importantly – that I had a lead, she was so energised she worked the phones for three hours straight and called me back with a name.

'George Bakirtzis, security manager, Premier and Cabinet. Very concerned about the risk of scabmites around parliament. He can see you tomorrow, Parliament House, oh eight thirty. Just ask for him at the front desk, I'll text you his number.'

'That's great Judith. More than I expected. Thank you.'

'You're welcome.'

'Okay, bye –'

'Mel?'

'Yeah.'

'Good luck. Please.'

David Bowie Songs

Sometimes it is not you but the days that are tired, and they rub off on you. It had been an abrasive one, I felt lesser from the skin loss. I couldn't go home and face what was left of him. A drink, then, in public for a change. I walked into the north east of the city where the small bars cluster and conspire like thieves. No security guards on the door here, no need. You won't see a fistfight here unless you start one, and I wasn't in the mood that night.

I took the lanes there, shortcutting the busy street corners, avoiding the tourists. There was fresh street art everywhere, the brightest of all voices yelling into the wind. In the doorways of the emergency exits, in the sunken alcoves, evidence of street life; a blanket, wrappers, ciggie butts, a filthy, wet pink rabbit. This is a home. They were out at that moment, working, searching.

Approaching one dead-end alley a man appeared suddenly, everything about him dirty and non-descript. He halted, alarmed, then limped away, muttering curses. I looked into the alley, saw a young man, also in a cap, cleaner, looking down at his hands before pocketing whatever was in them. He saw me looking. Good, I wouldn't startle him. I walked into the lane.

I bent at the knees and leaned to one side in a non-threatening posture, all soft edges, like asking for directions at a bus stop. 'Sorry, excuse me. I was wondering if you could help me?'

He stared at me. When his voice came it was deeper than I expected. 'Wid what?'

I pulled the pipe from my jacket. 'I need something to smoke in this.'

'Piss off.'

'Come on, please. I can pay overs.'

'You're a pig.'

'Like hell. Listen, I know you're not a dealer or anything, I was just hoping you might be carrying something I could buy.'

He considered this, hand twitching in his pocket.

'Quartz?' He asked. An ancient term. Crystal meth. Maybe *he* was the cop.

'Perfect, thanks.'

'Turn around.'

I did as the kid said. I wasn't armed, so he wouldn't find anything alarming if he patted me down or felt me up. 'One fifty,' he said, 'On the step, there, weigh it down with that little rock.'

'A gram, is it?'

'A hit.'

'Steep, mate.'

'Is what it is.'

I wanted it enough. 'What do you want it in?'

'Food or liquor.'

With the death of cash, gift vouchers were one of the common currencies for deals between unfamiliar parties. Jewellery was another, blowjobs, so long as the dealer can then cover the cost of the score themselves. Once known to each other, a customer and dealer will keep it civilised: Drop accounts, tap and go. I took my vouchers from my inner coat pocket, picked out the food ones, made up the rest with liquor. I placed them on the step, slid the little rock over them.

He walked over quickly and I felt his fingers in my jacket pocket. He retreated. I slid my hand in and felt a single shape, like a loose knuckle. I left the lane.

The best bars don't have signs. They still have names, this one was called Cracked Actor and it was small, dark, perfect. Old records played all the way through at moderate volume, Talking Book, Marquee Moon, Imperial Bedroom. I drank gin in a corner until I began to feel less self-conscious. Then I took my jacket off and sat at the alfresco bar, dying for a smoke but not willing to die for them. I talked to the woman behind the bar for a bit, taking my mind off the days to come. Then it was time for the ice, so I returned to the streets.

In a lane not far from the bar a woman of indeterminate age asked me if I could spare any warm clothes. I couldn't, I only had my jacket over a shirt. In the end it was her who helped me, she recommended a quiet spot for my smoke.

I took the hit quickly. Fingernails running down my throat, warm blood coursing down into my stomach, congealing there, forming a second heart that started pulsing, spreading air that cushioned my organs, my bones, my brain. I rose a few inches from the ground, and started walking around that way, going lightly, unhurried. I walked a few blocks, looking for significance in the display windows and late-night takeaway food stores, not worrying if I didn't find any. I lost my way for a moment, which made me laugh given I know the city like I know my own face, but then again, even my face looked different in the dim reflection of a shoe store window, which was kind of funny too. I got warm. I walked back to the lane to give the woman my jacket but she had moved on. I carried it in my arm instead, until a chill came and I put it back on. I felt the air going out of my cushion. I found a bar that used to be called Under Pressure. I went in.

An hour later I was talking to a man going by Leo or Leon. He wore a wool jumper and I liked the coarse threads. I touched them occasionally. He kept craning his face towards mine, obscuring my view of the jumper, but he told some good jokes so we persevered in each other's company. I asked him if he knew the name of the place we were in.

'Yeah, it's called Candlestick. Dunno why. New name, same look. I knew the previous owners, back when it was called Sound and Vision.'

I groaned in acknowledgment of the passage of time, its rapidity. 'Sound and Vision, the Bowie song.'

'I didn't know it was a Bowie song.'

'It is. Same as the name before that, Under Pressure.'

'Oh yeah, I remember that one. I didn't come here then.'

'I did, we sat in that corner over there. He wanted to go dancing, but I wanted a quiet night's drinking. So when a song he knew came on he would stand up and make these little dance moves. Just to move his body. That boy.'

Leo(n)'s eyes drew away, I registered a look of concern, or frustration. I didn't give a damn. 'Maybe I should be off,' he said, and he was off.

The Red Room

I felt like roadkill in the morning but at least I hadn't spent all night thinking about Roddy and in no time I was up, showered, armed with a coffee and catching the train into the city, bound for the state Parliament House.

I walked up the steps that used to host protests until they were moved into the streets to avoid becoming eyesores. If you stand at the top of the steps and look down on the passers-by you can simulate the experience of being an elected official.

At the front desk a tall man found my name in his planner. 'Ms. Vans, follow me.' The antiquated gender titling was still acceptable here, apparently. I don't take offence easily. I quickened my steps to match his long paces and followed him through doors of ancient, lacquered pine, service staff nodding at us from every direction. We walked some carpeted stairs and across an open walkway that overlooked a library dense with thick books you wouldn't wish upon your shadow minister. Finally we entered a windowless room furnished with a ring of red leather chairs with individual blackwood tables beside each.

'Please, take a seat,' said the tall man.

'Any of them?'

'Yes, any.'

I studied the old colonial watercolours on the walls, ghost gums by the river, far-off aboriginal clans at leisure, until a knock on the door toned like a xylophone, and a shorter man entered, wearing a grey three-piece suit.

'Mel Vans, I'm George Bakirtzis.' His hand reached out, straight and sure, a comfortable grip on mine. He quickly signalled me to sit again and sat across in the chair that best faced me. 'Apologies for the formal atmosphere in here. Funnily enough it was designed as an

27

informal setting, back in the day. Anyway, we can talk freely in the red room.'

It was then I registered the slight humming above our heads, the heavy-duty locks. It was a speakeasy, a vault for secrets.

'Thanks for meeting me, um, George?'

'George is fine. You're welcome Mel Vans.'

'Mel is fine.'

'Very good.'

'Well, I'll get right down to it, will I?'

'There's no better way, Mel.'

A man who spoke my language, nice and direct. I liked him from greeting to goodbye. I liked his comfortable seniority, his grey hair, his beard holding a touch of its former black lustre. I could imagine him tolerating all manner of pretension from the pollies, holding steady in a crisis, or bouncing a squadron of grandchildren on his knee at Easter. We got down to business.

Transcript of conversation between George Bakirtzis and Mel Vans, date withheld.

MV: Righto, George. I'm not sure what you've heard, but I hunt scabmites. Right now, I'm looking for one in particular. Someone known to me, actually. I have reason to believe he may have passed through this building in one body or another. I'm told you're the man to speak to.'

GB: Yes, insofar as the scabmite can be seen to represent a security issue. Criminal matters remain the realm of the police, so if I found something, I'd report it.

MV: Of course, no doubt. But let's face it, there's certain sensitivities involved. You'd need to be certain for one, and there are careers at stake, public confidence, breach of need-to-know, that sort of thing.

GB: I took you for a direct talker. If you are insinuating that I am aware of confirmed cases of scabmites in the Cabinet you should say as much, and I'll deny it.

MV: Time out.

GB: Time out?

MV: Nobody is questioning your integrity, George. I like to think I can pick an honest person right off the bat. I don't doubt for one second that you would report a confirmed case to the police, but I know from experience that confirming a case is not that easy. Also, you have an employer to consider, and that employer is the Premier. So the stakes are fucking high, excuse my language.

GB: All true. Are you making a point?

MV: Apparently not. My point is, I want to talk openly about not only what you know, but what you suspect. You have my word that anything you say will only be used to help me find the scabmite I'm looking for. I'm not a journo. I'm not after a scoop.

GB: Your word, then?

MV: Yep, it's yours.

GB: And while I'm always happy to help, my time is in high demand unfortunately, so is there something in this for the Premier and Cabinet?

MV: I'm not sure yet, I think so. I think this particular scabmite is coming for you guys. I think they're looking to have an impact.

GB: I see. What is their name?

MV: That's out of bounds, sorry George. Everything else is fair game.

GB: Very well. So, time back on, is it?

MV: (Laughs). Yes. Have you ever seen symptoms of scabmites in this building or anywhere you've observed parliamentarians?

GB: Yes.

MV: To both questions?

GB: Yes.

MV: None confirmed, I know, but have you ever been almost certain.

GB: No.

MV: No?

GB: No.

MV: Okay, given your expertise, I imagine your threshold for concern is relatively high. How would you describe your highest level of concern, or suspicion, when you have observed scabmite symptoms, what did you observe, when was it and who was it?

GB: How many questions was that?

MV: I think you can handle it George, I'm saving your Premier's time.

GB: At most I was conservatively alarmed, enough to brief the Premier. I observed a staffer speaking out of turn, uncharacteristically, suggesting meetings that should be made, publicly pushing courses of action. This was only a couple of months ago. They're fine now, back to normal.

MV: Who? What staffer?

GB: I have boundaries too, Mel.

MV: Can you tell me which minister they worked to?

GB: No.

MV: Can you tell me if they worked for the Minister for Housing and Community Welfare?

GB: I can tell you it wasn't that portfolio, but I won't enter any further into a process of elimination.

MV: Thank you, George. Any other cases that stand out, particularly in the last eight or so months?

GB: There was a cleaner. Rana. Worked here for years and years. People started reporting unusual behaviours. Aggressive speech, prying. We fired her. They were strong symptoms, but I put it down to a mental breakdown of sorts. Why would a scabmite want to be a cleaner?

MV: They have access to much of the building, right? Don't draw much attention. I'm sure you're familiar with the idea of leap-frogging, where a scabmite uses one host as a stepping stone to another.

GB: I've heard of it. But in Rana's case the behaviour continued until she was fired, so if your scabmite was using her to leap-frog, they failed, because she took them with her when she left.

MV: Any others?

GB: Recently, I've noticed a lot of…I don't know, I might be paranoid in my old age.

MV: I don't believe it.

GB: Plenty do.

MV: What sounds like paranoia to them, George, is years of relying on gut-instinct. Can you tell me what you've seen?

GB: I've felt like some of the senior staffers and ministers have been behaving erratically. Nothing major, just changes in attitude, forbearance, body language, even.

MV: That's a big symptom in my experience. Muscle memory is strong, but soon enough the scabmite will accidentally bring new physical habits to the host. Could be scratching, picking, touching a certain body part, using the hands more, or less, when they speak.

GB: That's exactly it. Why haven't I heard this, why isn't it advertised?

MV: The government, the police, they don't want to create panic.

GB: (Throaty, grumbling sound)

MV: Can you tell me more about these recent instances?

GB: Very little, I'm afraid. The behaviours change, a few days, maybe more, I don't see everyone day to day. If we're not sitting, I wouldn't have a clue. A senior adviser to one Cabinet minister returned after a month away and seemed a completely different person to me. But the next day, back to normal.

MV: When was this?

GB: Three weeks ago.

MV: That precise?

GB: Parliament was sitting.

MV: Oh, right. Would you say this was about the time you started observing all these staffers and ministers with changed behaviours.

GB: Yes, I would… Jesus.

(Breathing sounds, a pause)

MV: I think we're thinking the same thing here, George.

GB: Maybe. I'd guess you're thinking the returning staffer was a host for the scabmite, and ever since parliament returned he's been hopping from host to host.

MV: Spot on. Best way to stay incognito. Stick and move. Like boxing.

GB: (Whispering) Could be…

MV: Would you say there are many staff or ministers in this government who are susceptible to becoming hosts?

Who might wish they were someone else, from time to time?

GB: You have your bad days, that's for sure. Depends on the threshold.

MV: With a scabmite this driven, I'd say the threshold is pretty low. A couple of days wishing for a different life would do it.

GB: Then I'd say our defences are completely fucked, if you'll allow it, Mel.

MV: (Laughter. Sighs.) Have you spoken to any of the possible cases? Interviewed them?

GB: I asked. The Premier wouldn't allow it.

MV: Might be time to ask the Premier again.

GB: Yes, I think it might.

MV: George, I know this person – this – scabmite. He has an axe to grind. I can find him, with your help.

GB: Let me speak to the Premier, make some inquiries. If I can pinpoint the most recent suspected host, I'll call you.

MV: Call me regardless.

GB: Very well. Give me two days.

MV: George, you're a gun.

GB: You young people and your sweet talk. Your word, remember, Mel.

MV: You have it George, I swear.

Transcript ends

Shell Preservation and Restoration

You go home. You shower, cleanse. Disinfect. You dress in loose clothing. You wear gloves so you don't scratch the skin. You set up the bed barriers, roll it to one side. You change the top sheeting. You remove the gown and wash the back with a sponge. With care. The arse, the backs of the legs. You apply the protective oil to the skin. You roll it onto its back again. Wash the armpits, chest, genitals, thighs. Take off the compression stockings and wash the feet. Put on a new pair. You get a second cloth, the nicer one. You wash the face, stroke the eyebrows. You moisten the lips. You look away when the eyes flutter.

You wonder how much you ever really know someone, beneath the surface of their shell. How much of what you know was just this, the visible person? A shell changes but can always be recognised by its owner. But beneath, with the electric pulses and all the as-yet-unknown chemistry of the brain, all the fear and desire, wanting, comparing, wishing…

You make sure the face is dry before you apply the moisturiser. You soak the hair in warm water, apply the shampoo, comb it through. You rinse and you dry. You check the charts, twice. You know the numbers.

All this time, you are never you; you are her. You are Yesterday. The woman who loved him. Then you sit in the kitchen with your feet up on the sink. You are you. I am me. A meteor aflame as it enters the atmosphere, hurtling towards its target, never blinking, hell-bent on hitting its target with catastrophic impact.

I still love that shell, but I hate that motherfucker out there on the loose, I hate him with all my love.

No Escape

I took a long walk in the morning, toward the city. I skirted the Garden, up past the old church precinct that once was the hub of the city. Inside the arched gateways they were giving away coffee and soup. People shuffled in and out like they were walking inside sleeping bags.

I should have turned back then, instead I turned west into the city, right into the throng of peak hour arrivals, pouring out of train stations, ears plugged, faces closed. The coffee shops flashed the news on big screens. News is everywhere. There is no escaping the noise. The external seeps its way in, burrows, like the scabmites. We are all just hosts, carriers of the world around us. Promulgators of headlines.

Today's headlines: Feuding talk show hosts, anticipation high for the Pies against the Dees, China denies fresh accusations from the UN and, in politics, several allegations of 'severe misconduct' by federal Minister for Social Services, the honourable Christopher Fielding.

Nothing honourable about him. I thought of Roddy, he'd always hated Fielding. He'd be loving this, seeing him under the pump, fronting the press, wishing he could crawl back into the hole he came from...

Oh, shit.

Clusterfuck

Things that happened:

I called George Bakirtzis to tell him my hunch. He was out at the opening of a new park, keeping an eye on the Minister for Sport and Leisure. 'We'll talk in the red room. Fourteen hundred and thirty.'

I called Regio and left a message, 'Call me back, re the Ballycastle case. Big U urgent.'

On every screen in my house, the headline, *PM backs embattled Cabinet Minister.* No plans to stand down Christopher Fielding, good news for Roddy, I guessed.

I started packing a bag, just in case this was heading towards a couple of days in the capital.

Regio called back. I told him I had a hot lead, minimal details until I confirmed a few things. I needed his case funding, I was strapped.

'Sure thing,' he said, 'There's about five k left in the tin. But once it's gone, it's gone.'

'Thank you, Regio.'

'Just one condition Mel.'

'Name it.'

He named it. I agreed.

I called Judith, she was working. 'Can I meet you there? I've got a bite.' She gave me the name of a café where we could meet.

I took a car there. The driver was talking about the news, 'They say they're backin' him because he's got a radical piece of legislation he's been working on. They need him to table it.'

'Sounds unlikely. Sounds like cover, don't you think.'

'Yes, usually I would say the same. Say bullshit. But they are saying it's really big. Really something.'

So I wasn't the only one getting busy. It seemed Roddy was making his move.

Judith was waiting in the cramped joint she'd chosen. I ordered sandwiches for both of us just to make the staff go away. I told Judith the lead. Told her it was just a hunch, 'Don't get your hopes up.'

'You got a car over to meet me. My hopes are up a little.'

'Like I say, just a hunch.'

She reached out and grabbed my forearm, I was alarmed. 'Mel. Don't hurt him, okay?'

'Judith, you have to know this has no perfect ending. Becoming a scabmite is highly illegal, now this, if I'm right. It's not good.'

'Just don't hurt him.'

'Righto.'

I had an hour before meeting George. I took a car to the Diplomat's Daughter, just over from Parliament House, and ordered a scotch and coke. It was a small crowd for lunchtime, I gathered close to the screens on the far wall and listened.

The Prime Minister was calling for media restraint.

I know, I understand, that there are serious allegations about the conduct of the Minister for Social Services. I understand the Minister may have made comments suggesting some of the allegations are true. If the allegations are indeed true, you can trust my Government will act swiftly and proportionately.

However, I ask for your restraint at this important time. I say important, because the Minister and his staff have been working for some time now on a critical piece of legislation, which I think could be the beginning of a long-overdue solution to the rise in homelessness, the cost of housing, and the income gap we are experiencing.

What the hell was this? Since when did the PM care about this issue? I doubted there was any revelatory thinking behind the bill, just moving the money from causes that increased the wealth of the wealthy to a cause that was morally right, but economically disadvantageous. Why would this man, the next in an endless line of well-off white men with multiple houses and future-assured children, be so excited by legislation this humane? It could be a distraction to mask something else, but there were much easier ways to distract the public than promising imminent legislative change. Dig up some dirt on a shadow minister. Talk about terrorism. Boat people. Could it be blackmail? I had no idea. Politics was not my specialty.

The tall man was at the front desk again, but George met me there and we walked briskly to the red room.

I told him my hunch. That the scabmite had found his way to Canberra, possibly through access provided by this state parliament. That he'd taken on a new host. Maybe the Minister for Social Services straight off, maybe one of his staff, but in any case, he was the Minister for Social Services now. The Minister's alleged behaviour was probably true, but never was a minister so eager to confess their wrongdoings as this one. But he was pushing his legislation first. The bit that didn't click was how he'd got the PM and the rest of Cabinet to agree.

'Is blackmail a possibility?' I asked.

'Always a chance. But I don't think the PM alone would be enough in this instance. Unless he's got dirt on half of the Cabinet. Wouldn't be hard I s'pose, once you had the access.

'But wouldn't they just deny it? One man making claims about a whole Cabinet. It would be easy to, y'know?'

'Discredit him. Yes, it would.' Bill looked at the watercolours, a light caught his eye. 'Unless…'

'George?'

'It would be harder to discredit him if all the dirt is on *himself*. You cover yourself in shit, it will stick. And the smell will hang around the Cabinet for months.'

'And he wouldn't care. Because he's not really the Minister.'

We sat quietly for a time. Two professionals, pretending to be calm.

'Mel,' he said, 'How confident are you that your scabmite is the bloody federal Minister for Social Services?'

'More confident than I'd like to be. The thing is, I know the scabmite really well.'

'You've said that before.'

'No, George. *Really* well.'

So I told him. About us, his passions, his sense of right and wrong, how he started out as a scabmite in the homeless communities, how he likely swung into a suit the day some of the pollies visited the community kitchen in the city's east. How the PM's announcement on the type of legislation to be announced was the final piece of evidence. How I was almost certain. Sickeningly, painfully certain.

'Well,' said George, leaning forward on the leather chair, 'If we're going to brief this up, we need to piece it together first.'

Partial transcript of a second conversation between George Bakirtzis and Mel Vans, date withheld.

MV: We need to try and pinpoint when and how he made the move to Canberra.

GB: At the time of your call this morning, the last person I had identified as being a bit off was Sue Devine, Senior Advisor to the Minister for Housing and Community Welfare.

MV: Fuck.

GB: Right.

MV: And before that?

GB: Another of the Minister's staff. And another before that.

MV: Roddy.

GB: Sorry?

MV: Our scabmite, his name is Roddy. They were him – he was them, whatever. It all fits. Who else?

GB: Before that was a few of the treasury advisors, one of my staff, and before that, the one I told you about, who returned from the break a changed person.

MV: Their role?

GB: On the staff for the Minister of Education.

MV: Education...Could be...Wait, had they always worked for that minister.

GB: No, they moved over in a bit of a staff swap with the Minister for...Bugger.

MV: Housing and Community Welfare, right?

39

GB: Right.

MV: Roddy again. Do you know which staff were at a press day the government had at the community kitchen, city east, about eight months ago?

GB: That's beyond me, sorry. Might be recorded somewhere.

MV: Do you know if any of the Minister's staff were having a particularly challenging time? Illness, that sort of thing?

GB: Yes, one. Young bloke. Hamid, maybe. Took stress leave eventually. Young people, always heaping pressure on themselves.

MV: That's Roddy too. That's where it started for you George. The first suit.

GB: Okay, so he went to this event and – how do you say it? – Became Hamid. Then he hung around, doing what?

MV: Researching I would say. Working on the policy.

GB: This makes sense.

MV: I know.

GB: No, listen. The word out of Canberra, just this morning, is the PM is pissed with the Premier. Seems the legislation the PM is so excited about came as a bit of a surprise to him, and a lot of it was formulated at the state level, right here, by advisors to the state minister of the hour.

MV: All of them Roddy. Hamid, the Education Minister's staffer. The treasury guys...

GB: Critical for any bill, the treasury.

MV: The last few from the Minister for Housing and Community Welfare, obviously. All Roddy.

GB: And Rana, the cleaner?

MV: I don't think so. That breaks the chain. Like you said, she left. Could be a scabmite, but not this one.

GB: And I have your giant leap, Mel.

MV: Do tell.

GB: Just under two weeks ago, the Minister for Housing and Community Welfare and her Senior Advisor met with the Federal Minister for Social Services and his staff, in the capital.

MV: George, you really are a gun. It's a guess, but I think Roddy got busy up there too. He found a host on the Minister's staff, either discovered or flat out fabricated some of the claims against him. Went on the record to a journalist.

GB: That would explain why the young staffer is now backing away from her claims.

MV: Yep, she can't explain why she made them.

GB: But other staff have not withdrawn their claims.

MV: Probably because they're true.

GB: Ninety-nine times out of one hundred, I've learned.

MV: So Roddy created this climate around the Minister, until he wished he was anyone else on the planet, I suspect.

GB: Then moved in, started redecorating.

MV: There's your brief, George.

GB: (Pause) Mel, they'll want this quiet. Do I still have your word?

MV: Of course.

GB: Alright. I'll brief the premier and, I imagine, the PM shortly after. You better get ready for a flight to the heart of the nation, Mel. I'll call you with your flight details soon.

Transcript ends

On the way home I put in a call to Commander Dean Knowles.

'Knowles.'

'Dean, I have one, from your jurisdiction, but he's interstate.'

'Go on.'

'Can't really. There's complications, hush-hush.'

'Intriguing. Not usually your style.'

'Rest assured, it's killing me.'

'So I can't brief up?'

'No.'

'Down?'

'No.'

'Thanks for the call, Mel.'

'Dean, you get the man though, when we bring him in.'

'I'll take the stat. Thanks.'

'Can you do me one favour?'

'Go on.'

'I can't carry my gun and stun rounds across the border. Can you have a piece waiting for me.'

'Where?'

'Canberra.'

'Sheesh. Big time. Sure, text me your flight details and someone will help you out at the airport. Wait, it's not, y'know?'

'Bye, Dean.'

At home I finished packing. It was ridiculous, but I wanted to look good for this. I packed black things, my good eyeliner. I walked around the house like a dog that can't decide whether to stay in or go out. On my screens the PM was scrambling to show he understood the new bill in sufficient detail. He kept saying 'a suite of reforms'. There was an asset tax, focussing on owners of multiple properties, including businesses and families, the cutting of all funding to exclusive private schools, greater regulation of the property market, real estate, and construction industries. He winced as he announced these things, as though he couldn't believe the words coming out of his mouth. Then George called to say he was on the way over, where the hell did I live?

We landed in Canberra, a little airport for a little city. George slept on the flight, I guess he really was calm in a crisis. I was strung tighter than my crystal meth come down. A man with no name met me at the airport, handed me a parcel. *Thank you, Dean.*

I had a car waiting for me, an assistant behind the wheel.

George retraced the key points of the brief he whispered in my ear before the flight took off: A small party function at The Dominion, a marble and glass joint over the lake. The Minister for Social Services was there. The bar was closed to the public and the Minister was told to wait, the PM wanted a private chat around closing time. He'd probably smell a rat, but he'd have to stay. It was the PM after all.

'No cops?' I asked, triple checking.

'No cops. No press. You and him. Confirm. Confession. Bring him in.'

Before I got into the car, George said, 'Be careful Mel. If he's desperate, he might try to take you as a host.'

'No chance, George. I'm too bloody happy to be alive.'

Showdown at The Dominion

I walked in, the place was empty but for a single waistcoated bartender and the Minister for Social Services, slumped forward over the bar. The scene needed a western soundtrack, high noon, instead it was that sexualised teen pop from the past, "Genie In A Bottle," ugh.

I said, 'Hi.'

He looked over, then straightened up slowly. I saw him wonder for a moment if I knew, then realised of course I knew, because I was here.

'Hi. Hi Mel.'

I stared at him. Stayed near the door.

'Mel, far out. Finally you've found me. I've missed you so m–'

'Don't, you bastard.' The words coarse and quiet, like distant footsteps on gravel. *Don't.*

'Okay.'

I didn't have anything worked out. I decided to wait for him.

'Will you come closer?'

I took a few steps. A few more. Stood at the bar, the far end from him. 'I'll have a spiced rum, double, neat. And some privacy please'. The bartender made my drink in quick time. He looked at the Minister who signalled with one finger and the bartender topped his glass of Riesling and abruptly headed off for the kitchen.

'Mel, I want you to know –'

I said, 'don't. You want to talk, talk, but don't talk about us.'

'Okay.'

'Talk about this,' I said, waving towards his suit, his face, the detestable Christopher Fielding peering at me with bloodshot eyes. 'What the fuck are you doing, Roddy?'

'You know what I'm doing.'

'It isn't going to work.'

'Isn't it?' It was harsh to hear his emotion filtered through the sneering, arrogant voice of Fielding. 'I think it already is. The bill is being prepared, everyone is talking about the issue, taking it seriously. They can't back away now. It's front and centre, where it can be focussed on. Do one thing at a time, properly. Do you remember that?'

'I remember.'

'But I don't want this skin to get all the credit. Once the bill is passed, I'm taking this host to disgrace.;

'Oh yeah? Gonna sexually assault some girls are you Roddy?'

'Nothing like that. Just reveal the racism, the bigotry. Get drunk, say some things publicly. Admit to everything. Maybe record some conversations with other ministers who think like this one, leak them, take a few down with him.' The fury in his voice, fiercer than the nice person I once knew.

'You think they'll let that happen?'

'The PM already has my word. I'll resign within the next two weeks, sign their statement, protect the party.'

'And will you?'

'I'll sign it. But that's the Minister, not me. They don't have my word.'

'And what then? What happens to you?'

'I don't know. I can't keep it up. I don't want to take over an innocent host. I guess I'll let you take me in.'

'Let me? Roddy, do you think you are still making the decisions here? I'm taking you in when I decide to take you in. Could be then, could be now.'

The Minister smiled with a softness I'd not seen from that face before, a fraction of Roddy peeking through.

'Do it then, Mel. The project won't be complete, but I will have done enough.'

'You think? As soon as they know Fielding was only a host they'll scrap the bill. Hell, they'll probably spin it to say all his misdemeanours were you.'

'I can accept that. I don't really care what happens to him after, that was just dessert. As far as activism goes, it's been a pretty good awareness campaign don't you think? I think people will look at homelessness through a more proactive lens, now. Some good will come of it.'

'And you'll be reunited with your body until you're well enough to go to prison. They'll neuter you, too, take away the capacity to scabmite again. There's a process now. It's permanent, Roddy, you'll be slower.'

He nodded at his wine, said nothing for a while. Eventually he looked straight ahead and said, 'I don't care what happens to me. You don't get here from wanting to live your life.'

I tried to relax, lean on the bar, stick to the game plan, but a pain was searing through my chest.

'Why did you leave, Roddy? How could I have made you so miserable?'

'Mel,' he said, soothingly, and for a moment I thought I heard my name spoken in his old voice, 'You never made me miserable. You were the light. I wanted to say before, when you first walked in: You need to know I gave up on me first. You were a side effect. I'm sorry for that. I didn't think enough about you, couldn't. I felt so helpless, meaningless, in the face of everything we couldn't prevent.

'You *were* helping, Roddy. More than most.'

'It wasn't enough.'

'And this? Is this enough?'

'It's better.'

'So if you had the choice again, would you do the same?'

'Mel…'

'Easy question, Roddy.'

'It isn't like a choice, Mel. It's a consumption.'

'Would you?' I repeated, teeth clenched.

He sighed. The lines on the Minister's face straightened in defence, as if speaking to the press. 'Yes.'

I don't know what I was expecting from him. It wasn't that. I was expecting more from myself, too. I was meant to seek and destroy, like my vision the previous night, me as a meteor, coming for his

Earth. But it was Roddy who was the flaming mass of destruction, set to drive himself into the heart of the world as it is, as we knew it shouldn't be.

'Will you come in willingly?'

'No.'

'I can't shoot you.'

He shrugged, turned away.

I said, 'Soon, you're going to be taken down. You'll wake up in your skin at the Mercy Hospital. I'll be by your side. That's when I'll say goodbye.'

I don't know what he said then, I was walking away as soon as I finished speaking. He was just the Minister for Social Services now.

Outside, beneath the limitless black sky of the capital, Regio was waiting for me beside the car.

'He's yours,' I said, 'Take him.'

Shared Endorphins

Emily Castles

I was out on a date with a man who had an insomniatic parasite. He was very embarrassed by it all and had leaned in to tell me within the first ten minutes, 'I think you should know; I have an insomniatic parasite.' Charles was a Cambridge boy with shoulder-length blond hair, pushed back in a way that seemed to defy gravity. He was *so* clean-shaven, that I wondered if he had, in fact, ever shaved, despite being in his early thirties. I had scouted him out on Bumble, as a talent agent does a Hollywood actor or cruise ship entertainer. While not my usual tortured-poet type, my housemates had persuaded me to come out with this slightly older, corporate sort. 'What have you got to lose?' They had said.

'A what?' I remarked, sipping my cranberry and vodka, which had cost £15 for the privilege. He went on to tell me a little, but not a lot, about the parasite that inhabited his mind, and how it tortured him every night with sleeplessness.

'I didn't know parasites could cause insomnia.' I stated, inquiringly.

'Oh yes.' Charles nodded, enthusiastically. 'It's the worst sort of insomnia imaginable. Completely debilitating.' He then pointed at a small cut on his cheek, just below his eye, that I hadn't noticed before. 'This was from the beast, during a midnight brawl.'

***

I met the insomniatic parasite a few weeks after. I lay awake next to Charles because Charles was restless, and I could never sleep next to someone who was restless. All of a sudden, Charles let out a massive snore that made me jump. He was *asleep*. I turned my head towards him and met the insomniatic parasite, strolling out from under Charles' ear and across the pillow towards me.

It wasn't quite like how I'd pictured. It looked like a caterpillar, but with yellow, marble-sized eyes on the end of its antennae, and bat-like wings that were folded into its sides. Slithering across the white bedding, it left a trail of slime behind it, glistening in the moonlight that trickled through the crack in the curtains. It was all very *David Lynch*.

It looked inquisitive for a moment, smiled briefly, and then swiftly launched itself towards me. I had barely a chance to breathe, let alone move, when I felt the slithery demon wiggle into my ear, down the ear canal, and into the auditory centre of my brain. Here, I felt it set up camp, promptly beginning its work.

For several unrelenting, torturous hours, I was at the mercy of my sadistic parasite. I lay awake, but with my eyes closed and unable to move. My body burned as the parasite engulfed it in flames, the skin melting away from the bone, dripping onto the cream carpet like an accidental fondue. Bald vultures flew through the open window, landing on my paralysed face and pecking ferociously at my exposed eyeballs, eyelids long flaked off.

Body still burning, and vultures still pecking, masked soldiers stormed the doors and began their gruesome tactics. They ripped off my fingernails one by one, they broke my bare bones as though they were candy sticks and they launched rats upon my decaying carcass to mop up the remnants of my fried organs. I was awake for it all. I felt it all. It was the insomniatic parasite, playing with my mind, but it was real. And it was hell on Earth.

The following morning, I woke up. I was confused and surprised, as I hadn't remembered falling asleep. Looking over to Charles, who was shaking and sweating, I realised that the parasite had evacuated my body during the early hours, returning to its former host and leaving its holiday home to collapse with exhaustion.

'I feel amazing.' Charles beamed, munching down his bacon and eggs while I scowled at him, nursing my woozy head with cheap instant coffee. 'Okay, hear me out, hear me out.' He continued. 'What about if we shared the parasite? Every other night, we'd take turns. Then we'd both get at least *some* decent sleep. And I tell you, after last night, it's totally worth it.'

I stared at him in disbelief.

'Charles, before last night, *every night* was a decent night's sleep for me. This is *your* parasite, don't bring me into it.'

At this, he scoffed and shook his head, but then the conversation was over, and we moved on to discussing Artsakh and global politics.

I didn't see Charles the following night. I was out for a friend's birthday. Over more vodka mixers, I dished the dirt on my parasitic night to my dearest girlfriends. They empathised with Charles' situation as well as mine. 'How terrible for him,' they remarked, 'dealing with that every single night.' They all understood my unwillingness to share parentage to the creature, 'You've only been dating for a few weeks, far too soon to take on that sort of responsibility.' I left the bar feeling secure and proud of my actions from the previous evening, but with a renewed understanding and pity for the tortured soul of Charles.

I returned to his flat the following evening and we had a wonderful time. We ate and we laughed and the insomniatic parasite didn't come up in conversation even once. I forgot all about it, which was a mistake.

I woke up in the middle of the night tied to the bed, with Charles looming over me. To the right of my head was the sadistic beast, salivating over my untouched dreams. Before I could speak, Charles did.

'Look, I'm really very sorry to do this. But I've had to put up with this for almost ten years, and it's really not very fair. You don't understand what it's like.'

'Ch-Ch-Charles.' I whimpered, pulling at my hands and feet, which were strapped firmly down. 'What are you doing?'

'It's hell, it's complete hell. And what wouldn't *you* do to escape hell? This isn't my fault. It's, it's that *thing's* fault. I haven't slept in a *decade.'* He rubbed his hair, troubled and panicked.

'Please, whatever you're doing, just stop, just stop.' I cried, pulling hopelessly at my heavy limbs.

'I've made a bargain with the insomniatic parasite. I've made a bargain with the devil. My own body, for yours.'

I cried, because I had no words left.

'Unfortunately, the parasite wanted a better deal. Something more exciting to make it pack up and leave it's faithful old home.' He sat down next to me. 'You see, it's been rather kind to me. Letting me go about my daily business, only plaguing me in the solitude of night. But it's lonely and gets bored during the daytime. Understandable, right? And so, I've promised it residence in your brain, day and night. There'll be no break, as such. I'll keep you here, tied up, so the parasite may thrive as I've promised. You needn't worry, you won't get ill or die or anything drastic like that. I'll snap you into consciousness for feeds, for showers. I'll look after you. I promise. It's the only way I could persuade the *thing* to leave me. You see, it's really not that bad. And just, I really just need this, you know?'

Before I could say another word, the insomniatic parasite launched itself like a rocket, straight down my ear and into my brain. And my hell on Earth, the hell that existed in my brain and my brain alone, began.

Committed

Lauren Lang

I've always loved women, the curve of their breasts, the fullness of
their lips, the way their long legs swish their skirts as they walk down
the street. Their smiles have always been my light in dark times. Even
when I was small, standing in the bread lines, it was the other little
girls and their grins that made the cold and the hunger rumbling in
my belly tolerable. We compared flour sack dresses and the size of
the holes in our too-tight shoes to pass the time. It was as if we had
known each other all of our short lives, even if we never saw each
other again. No one knew when our daddies would be able to go back
to building cars in the years before the unions and the war brought
Detroit's great automobile manufacturing plants back to life.

We women went to work together to support the war effort. I had
never seen so many gorgeous girls as I did at the Ford motor plant at
Willow Run. There were gritty, sweaty ladies of every size and color
riveting together B-24 bombers in their pants and low-heeled shoes,
hair held in place by carefully chosen handkerchiefs. They were
beautiful in a different way; their strength and determination to
contribute to the war effort made them formidable in a fashion I
didn't know women could be. These girls were fearless. They left the
comfort of their homes for the noise and the clamor of factory life
without a second thought. They were dedicated. It was as if every

rivet held the entire war effort together.

I respected them. I wanted to be like those women, but I also wanted to lie naked in bed with them and use my calloused fingertips to trace my way down their newly formed muscles and worship their strength with my body.

It was easy to pretend then that I wasn't what I was; easy to get close to the girls. No one questioned us when we leaned on one another for emotional support. I helped the other women write letters to the newly-minted husbands they hoped would come home. I was a shoulder to cry on when they found out they had been widowed at the Battle of the Bulge or at Okinawa.

When they asked me where my sweetheart was serving, I was vague. If they pressed, I blushingly admitted that at 18, I hadn't found a man to marry. They encouraged me, told me that they were sure I'd be clobbered with some soldier or swabbie when the boys came home. I don't think any of them suspected.

Though I was close to everyone, I still had my favorites, but I didn't pay special attention to any one girl over the others. Melody, shy and sweet, with her porcelain complexion and dark, unruly curls, held my affection for months. She wore rouge she didn't need, blushing at just the mention of her name. Sharon was her opposite, boisterous and loud, she commanded attention wherever she went. I longed to run my fingers through her flaming red hair and reduce her to speechlessness with my thighs. I fantasized for months about watching the back of her head bob up and down between my legs.

I had never done such a thing or allowed such a thing to be done to me, but the married girls talked. They twittered in low voices about the things they missed, answering unspoken questions for those of us who didn't yet wear a ring. It was the type of conversation we couldn't have with our mothers but might have had with an older sister if we were lucky. I, being the oldest, had nowhere to turn for such intimate knowledge. My mother would have slapped me silly for daring to broach such a lewd topic. The forbidden conversations set my imagination on fire, though the girls I worked with didn't realize they played the starring roles in my daydreams.

Those wishful thoughts died with the end of the war. While the other women whooped and celebrated in the streets, I shed crocodile tears over the victory and plastered a fake smile over my sorrow. I loved my country but mourned the friends I knew I would lose to their husbands and the babies they would soon bear. I was alone in my grief, isolated by my lack of love for men.

Sweethearts saved me. I found my way to that bar one evening at Alice's urging. Widowed at Iwo Jima, she couldn't afford to quit her job on the meager pension her husband's demise provided her. She needed to remarry, and Sweethearts, she promised, was an excellent place to meet men. They came for the "show," she told me cryptically. She didn't provide any details, and I didn't ask.

The building looked normal enough from the outside. Crossing third street in downtown Detroit, our Mary Janes clomped against the pavement, and the fabric of Alice's full, billowing navy skirt made a satisfying swish as we hurried towards the door. She had a thin waist accentuated by the tapered cut of the dress, and her bust was shapely, bulging against the fabric. The V-neck cut of her blouse showed off the tops of her breasts. Wartime had meant sacrifices for everyone, and I was glad to see the utilitarian garments we had all worn, so reminiscent of uniforms, give way to more feminine shapes again.

For my part, I'd chosen something more conservative. My tailored, bell-shaped plaid skirt fell just below my knees, and the square cut of the matching jacket revealed little about my trim figure. I wondered if I should have worn something dressier, but I was not chasing the prize Alice longed to win.

As we crossed the threshold, I wondered about what Alice had hinted at earlier. The front room was like any other establishment. Couples drank together on stools in front of the bar or in booths along the wall. Everything was dark, polished wood lit by small, round chandeliers that threw jewels of yellow light against the ceiling. The cash register clanged in the background, ringing up sales of Schlitz and Ballantine. Thirsty men chugged from cold glasses while the ladies looked on, sipping martinis and gin rickeys.

Conversation flowed through the room, but I noticed men glancing toward the door near the back. The gaudy steel pane did not hint at what it concealed, but every eye in the room locked on anyone that moved towards it. I stared as well, wondering what lay beyond that barrier, so reminiscent of a bank vault.

We ordered drinks, a rum sour for me and sidecar for Alice, and chatted aimlessly for a while. Finally, Alice, bolstered by the alcohol, spoke up.

"Should we?" she said, nodding her head toward the doors.

"What's back there?" I hoped to salvage this rather dull evening.

"Why, the show, of course," Alice said. "Haven't you heard of this place before?"

"No, I haven't. What kind of entertainment should I expect?"

"Homosexuals," Alice whispered.

"What?" I crooked a skeptical eyebrow.

"I know," Alice said, leaning closer to me, "I heard there are rooms back there full of kikis. The men come to watch them dance with each other."

"And that's who you want to meet?" I said, eyeing her. My heart pounded, and my palms began to sweat. I'd worked so hard to avoid being identified as deviant. This one evening might ruin years of work. I forced myself to breathe slowly and kept my face blank.

"Well, not the girls," Alice said, laughing. "But I wouldn't mind introducing myself to a few of the boys they attract. None of the women back there will take them home, but I just might under the right circumstances."

"Alice!" I exclaimed, "You're drunk!"

"I can't stand going home to an empty house one more night, Vera. You wouldn't know. You have your parents and siblings to keep you company. The loneliness is killing me." She stood, steadying herself against the bar. "I have to at least take a look. Come with me. You need a man as much as I do. You can't live with your mother and father forever. You'll be an old maid if you don't find a husband soon."

"You sound like my mother," I told her. It had been getting harder and harder to justify my lack of interest in dating. We were a large family in a small house, so little was private. My siblings wanted my room, and my parents couldn't understand why I didn't crave a home and family of my own. In the Old County, where my grandparents were from, children were the lifeblood of the agricultural families, so women started bearing early. I was already older than my mother had been when she birthed me.

I feigned resistance, but as terrified as I was by Alice's suggestion, I had to know. Were there really other women like me so close to where I lived? The possibility was more intoxicating than the drink in my hand.

I promised myself I'd be careful. Long practice hiding my interests would protect me now.

I stood without haste and followed my friend as she tottered away from the bar and towards the forbidden.

The door swung open easily, revealing another world. The space was larger than I'd expected. It was divided into several different rooms, though it was hard to see into them through the mass of bodies and the thick cigarette smoke. In the low light, women clasped women, men hugged men, and mixed couples clutched one another, dancing a frantic jitterbug. Those that weren't dancing held a drink in one hand and their partner's fingers in the other, not caring that everyone could see whose company they preferred.

I was enthralled. I was repulsed. I would not admit my longing even to God. I knew reprisal – both His and my parents' – was guaranteed. The pastor had made it clear: our kind is an abomination. The newspapers were even saying we were akin to communists. My father, listening to the nightly radio broadcasts, believed the same.

There was nothing political about the way I felt. Watching the girls flaunt their feelings in public was a heady cocktail, equal parts terror and desire. They reminded me of the strong, brash women at the factory. Yet their bravery, though laudable, was also foolish.

Alice knew the danger we were in, so it surprised me that she had brought me here considering what type of place it was. Her brother-in-law, a soldier like her late husband, had been accused of homosexuality during the war. He was court-martialed and discharged. Once he got home, he continued to associate with men. Eventually, one of the neighbors reported him, and he was arrested and committed to a mental asylum. According to Alice's mother-in-law, who looked in on her from time to time, he had been released only a short time ago. There was nothing left of him but a slobbering mass of what used to be a man. He had undergone a new procedure called a lobotomy after electroshock therapy couldn't change his inclinations. The procedure was supposed to cure him, but it had left him unable to feed or dress himself much less work or live alone. Alice's mother-in-law had taken over his care, changing and wiping him just like when he was an infant.

The papers reported another man recently charged with sodomy, afraid of being condemned to the same fate, had leapt to his death from atop police headquarters after being arrested in a raid at a bar just like this one.

It was just as dangerous for women to be in places like this as it was for men. Sex between women was declared illegal in 1939. My longing for the same human connection these women enjoyed made me a criminal.

I watched in horrified awe as two women kissed. It was swift, but I caught it like a flung bouquet as I drank in every detail of the place. I wasn't the only one that saw. The men Alice was so eager to meet leered in the couple's direction. They stood in groups, pointing and laughing, crass, vulgar creatures emboldened by alcohol and contempt.

A woman gyrated towards us, moving to her own beat rather than the music. She was flushed, though I couldn't tell whether the color in her cheeks was from drink or exertion.

"Can I have a dance?" she slurred at Alice, who looked horrified. I'd been so busy taking it all in that I had forgotten her. Her made-up complexion went white.

"No...no, thank you," she stammered, unsure how to respond. The woman shrugged and moved on, her feet and arms flailing to her inner rhythm.

"Do you want to look around?" I asked Alice. She ignored me and gaped at the scene. In truth, I was afraid that if she heard the question, Alice would make us leave, and I would be unable to invent a reason to stay and see more. I grabbed her arm before she had a chance to answer and pulled her through the writhing throng towards the room to the right of the dance floor. There, men, seated in front of a small bar or at tables crammed close together, drank and laughed.

These were not the people either of us were looking for, so I pushed back through the crowd seeking the room on the left of the dance floor. I never let go of Alice's arm, and she neither protested nor resisted.

We found the kikis in their own small room, secluded from the prying gaze of the men on the other side of the wall. The opening was large enough to be inviting but did not give the impression that the place could accommodate all interested parties. This room was furnished with booths and had a more intimate feel. The lighting was lower, and the music coming from the dance floor was muted.

There was an undeniable sense of romance in the air. We had entered another world, one washed by perfume in addition to the smoke drifting from the long cigarettes these women toyed with. Their perfectly curled hair, bright lips, and rouged cheeks were familiar and alien at the same time. Their intelligent, lively eyes and easy laughter were not so different from the other women I had known, but something set these girls apart. I couldn't say what it was.

Finally, I felt Alice tugging at my wrist. I had never let go of her hand.

"Vera, I think we should go," she said. I knew I couldn't argue with the finality in her voice. Her fear had gotten the better of her.

"What about the men you wanted to talk to?" I asked.

"I was wrong about them…" Alice said. "They aren't the type of boys I would want to marry." Her face was still white. She'd freed her hand from mine, and her knuckles blanched as she clutched her purse against her body. She shivered, her lips quivering as she spoke, and I took pity on her.

"Let go back out front," I said, unwilling to leave Sweethearts entirely. "I want another drink."

Alice looked relieved, so we pressed through the crowd to the steel door. Another drink calmed Alice, and some light chit-chat brought the color back into her face. We said goodnight and parted ways once we finished our beverages. I knew she wouldn't be back. I knew I would never drink anywhere else.

I became a fixture at Sweethearts, and it was there that I began to understand and explore my desires. My initial shock faded during my second and third visits, and by my fourth, I was accepting invitations to dance. I chatted easily with the other women, just as I had at the factory, but always left alone. Flirting with them felt awkward. I was a novice.

My job at the plant ended with the war. With a family as large as mine, every little bit helped, so when Sweethearts advertised a waitressing position, I jumped at the opportunity. I had a clumsy start. A few patrons caught beverages in their laps, but in time I got the hang of it. The more I chatted with the customers, the more comfortable I became. Tips were better if I smiled and flirted, so I got the hang of that, too.

My family noticed the difference in me. I had always been friendly, but now I was more outgoing and talkative. I struck up conversations with neighbors whenever I could. My father kept telling me to quiet down and limit the amount of time I spent with friends. He badgered me about going out and very nearly didn't let me work now that I wasn't contributing to the war effort anymore, but we needed the money. The old Ford was acting up, and my father was afraid we'd have to buy a new car. I used our rusty old truck to my advantage. I pleaded and cajoled, finally convincing my father he could afford a better truck if I helped financially.

Of course, I didn't tell my family where I was really working. I lied, telling them I'd found a night job as a waitress at a 24-hour roadside diner across town. It was far enough away that my family wouldn't come to see me at work, and it explained my odd hours.

I bought an old, light blue diner uniform and white apron from a friend. She was a war widow who had remarried and stopped working. I wore that drab thing to Sweethearts, where I changed into a low-cut black cocktail dress and heels. I was careful about my laundry, occasionally spilling something on the fake uniform's apron just to make it look worn. I took my real dress to the laundromat and washed it in the coin machines.

I was lying to everyone, but as long as I said little of importance, I could keep my stories straight. My odd hours helped. I slept during the day when my family was awake, frequently missing meals and other fraught interactions because I was asleep.

Work was my sanctuary. The outside world became more frightening by the day. I tried to ignore it, but snippets of news drifted over the threshold of Sweethearts and into my ears. The local legislature made it illegal for bars to allow rendezvous between homosexuals. I feared we would be raided or forced to close, but management kept a sharp eye on the vault door. If they didn't know you or the person you were with, you weren't allowed to enter. The front of the establishment, with its mixed-gender clientele, deflected suspicion, and many people who knew the truth were unwilling to admit how they'd learned it. It was a fragile sense of safety, but it was all I had.

Local politics weren't the only thing stacked against me. As time passed, my home life grew more fraught. After my father purchased a new truck, there was no more reason for me to work. It had been three years since the end of the war, and my mother and sisters insisted that I find a husband. Instead, I worked additional shifts so that I would be at the house less and wouldn't have to listen to their constant badgering. I knew that I would not be able to ignore them forever. When one of my younger sisters became engaged, the focus on her wedding took some of the pressure off of me, though there were enough snide comments to keep me wary.

I wasn't the only one on edge. Paranoia bloomed everywhere, but was especially bad at home. The radio in the living room screamed that the *communist* threat was spreading. My parents, raised by immigrants from now-communist countries in Eastern Europe, were terrified. They were afraid they would be seen as un-American because they spoke Hungarian, Croatian, and Polish like their elders.

And our last name sounded foreign: it had too many consonants in it. My father's fear that our family would be fingered because of our origins came naturally to him. Not only did he bear his family's grim history in war-ravaged Europe, he'd learned that banks – and by extension, the government – in America could not be trusted.

As the calendar turned to 1950, Senator McCarthy claimed he'd found communists working in the federal government. That dreadful word spread to include not just political affiliation, but also people like us: the employees and clientele at Sweethearts. Another legislator went so far as to call us sexual perverts, suggesting that we were just as dangerous as *the Reds*. We were supposedly more susceptible to blackmail because of our deviant ways. Fear that we would spill state secrets spread. McCarthy and his followers implemented a "loyalty test," and many failed and lost their jobs. People at Sweethearts feared the hysteria would spread beyond the Capital and reach us here in the Motor City, as private companies began using the same test to eliminate workers deemed disloyal.

Yet it didn't feel real. Even as pastors screamed about moral turpitude and newspapers ran headlines about communist espionage, we heard that a woman in Flint had opened an establishment like Sweethearts. She called it State. We figured that was a reference to the political climate and laughed, glad to hear the news. We vowed to make the trip up to Flint in support of our sister.

I never got the chance. My next shift was a Saturday night, our busiest evening of the week. I looked forward to the weekends. That's when Sweethearts would bring in female impersonators. They were flamboyant and so bold. Their shows had also been illegal for years, but I had long since gotten over my aversion to breaking certain laws. They were just entertainers for heaven's sake, and boy, could they sing. With their platinum blonde wigs and overdone make-up, they gave us the illusion of movie stars in our midst. Their sweet voices drowned out the poisonous cacophony of the national news.

The incident started when I was passing out drinks to a table of men who had come for the show. It was mostly beer, but there were glasses of whiskey as well. The vault was packed, and it was difficult to maneuver around the table to deliver the beverages. I gave them my best smile even though they were demanding, bordering on belligerent. I knew their type. They were the same kind of men that had repulsed Alice. The ringleader was a regular, but his cadre that night was not. I hadn't seen any of them before, and their sallow, drunken faces left little impression until I felt a hand squeeze my behind.

It wasn't the first time a drunken patron had done this, but I was still surprised and stood quickly, almost dropping the glasses.

"Sorry, boys," I said, apologizing without confronting the perpetrator. I leaned over, intent on delivering the last of the beverages when the hand grabbed me again, harder this time. The man gripped my dress and pulled me backward into his lap. His face was inches from mine, his foul breath sickened me as he ran his lips up my neck. I laughed even as I struggled to get away.

"I'm not your type of girl," I said, masking my disgust, "You'll have to excuse me."

I tried to stand, but the pervert grabbed the tops of my thighs and pulled me down harder into his lap. I could feel his erection straining against his trousers.

"Don't tell me you're one of those," he said, whispering in my ear.

"I'm afraid I am," I said. I swallowed against the urge to vomit.

"Maybe you just haven't met the right man." His slurred voice grew louder this time. "I like you, sugar. I could make you like me." One of his hands moved up my side toward my breast.

"I think what you like is whiskey, and you've had enough."

"I'll tell you when I've had enough. Keep 'em coming." He picked up the glass I'd set in front of him and downed the liquor in a single gulp, still holding me in place with his free hand.

Only then did he release me so that I could get him another drink. I scurried away from the table, shaken and afraid to go back, but I needed those tips. I had the bartender water down the man's whiskey and stayed out of reach when I brought the next round. His predatory eyes followed me.

He didn't molest me again, and shortly afterward, the group left the bar. They complained of boredom loudly as they made their way out the vault door. Once they were gone, I was able to relax and chat with the other customers and enjoy the show.

It had been a good night, and the jingle of coins in my purse diminished my disgust as I prepared to leave. The incident earlier was an unfortunate part of the job. I had accepted that long ago, which made it easier to forget the unsavory parts of working at Sweethearts. I was glad my shift was over, though. I walked out the front doors, my sore feet screaming.

I was digging for bus fare when I heard feet shuffling on the pavement in front of a darkened part of the building a few feet away. I looked up and saw a single point of orange light, the tip of a burning cigarette in a man's slack mouth. My co-workers were still inside, finishing their tasks. I was alone.

"Hello, sugar."

I recognized the voice. The man from earlier emerged from the darkness flicking away his cigarette and flashing his teeth at me. His bloodshot eyes glinted red as he came closer. I bolted for the door, but his long strides closed the distance between us in seconds.

"Like I told you inside, I'm gonna *make* you like me."

The stench of stale whiskey and sweat invaded my nostrils. I dropped my purse and turned to run. He grabbed my hair and

RUNNING WILD ANTHOLOGY OF STORIES VOLUME 6

dragged me backward towards the darkened side of the building by my scalp. I clawed at his hands, but his hold was too tight. I couldn't get enough air to scream even if someone could hear me. The pain was overwhelming. I stumbled in my high heels and fell hard on my backside. My weight ripped my hair out of his hands at the cost of a large hank of strands.

I tried to scramble up and away, but he was already on me. He mounted me, shoving my torso down with one hand while scrabbling to raise my skirt with the other. I screamed. I'd never made such a feral sound. It shocked us both, which bought me a split second to claw at his face with my fingernails. He crushed my wrists together, but his grip meant he couldn't undo his pants. I shot a knee upwards, hoping to connect with his crotch. I hit him in the stomach instead, knocking the wind out of him. He released my hands and rocked back, wheezing and gasping. I struggled to shove him off of me, but he was heavy, and I was tiring.

"You'll pay for that!" He hissed at me once he had caught his breath. I could see him winding up, making a fist, and drawing it back. He landed a haymaker on my left eye so powerful that my head flew back, smacking the pavement. Stars exploded behind my eyes, and I had to fight to stay conscious.

He was fumbling with his pants when Sarah, another waitress, walked out of the building, her shoes clicking on the pavement.

"Help," I moaned.

As soon as Sarah realized what was happening, she screamed. Her shrill cry became words, "What are you doing? Get off of her!" She ran at him, swinging her purse like a war hammer. I felt my attacker's weight lift off of me as she charged him.

"I'll call the police!" she screamed, aiming the bag at his head. I knew it was a lie. We couldn't afford to invite any attention that might lead to a raid, but the man didn't know that. He fled, his pants half undone, his shoes slipping on the pavement in his haste.

"Vera! Are you alright?" Sarah was beside me in an instant, helping me sit up. I grabbed my throbbing face, sobbing with relief. She tugged at my wrists, but stopped when she realized I was in too much pain to take my hands away. She held me there on the pavement, rocking me back and forth.

"Let's get you inside." Sarah said when I'd caught my breath. She steadied me as I struggled to my feet. "We need to get some ice on that eye."

The bartender, a former medic in the army, patched me up as best he could. Sarah was afraid to leave me alone, so she rode the bus home with me to ensure I made it. It wasn't the first such attack, though the previous ones had involved female customers. I was the first waitress jumped by a man who wouldn't take no for an answer.

"We'll leave in pairs from now on," Sarah promised as she left me at my doorstep.

No one was awake. Though I wobbled in my heels, I managed to make it up to my bedroom, where I could inspect the damage in my mirror. I was a mess. I had to squint through double vision to see my face. Under my smeared make-up, my eye bloomed a disgusting purple. I curled into a ball in bed and wept until morning.

I heard the household stir shortly after first light. It was Sunday, which meant church. I would be expected to go, and I had no viable excuse. I couldn't let my family see me like this. I pulled the covers up higher around my shoulders, running my hands up the side of my dress as I did. I realized that I hadn't remembered to change back into the waitress uniform. My stomach dropped as I realized I was still wearing the black cocktail dress. Before I had a chance to do anything about it, there was a knock on my door.

"Vera," my mother said, "It's time for church. Are you ready to go?"

"I'm not feeling well." I sounded hoarse from hours of sobbing.

"What's wrong?"

"I think I've got the flu." I coughed, willing her to stay out of the room. "Don't come in here."

"Don't be silly," My mother says, her hand turning the knob, "Let's have a look at you."

She stepped in, and I turned away from her, hunching under the covers to hide the shiner.

"Let's see if you have a fever." She tugged at the covers, but I wouldn't let go. "Stop being ridiculous and let me look at you!"

Her exasperated tone told me not to argue. Reluctantly, I released the covers. Her horrified gasp confirmed my fears.

"Vera! What happened? Who did this to you?"

I begin to cry again. She saw my dress and stepped up the interrogation.

"Where were you last night? We thought you were working."

"I was," I sobbed, "A customer attacked me."

"At the diner?"

"No."

The word hung heavy in the air, Mother's silence demanding answers. I hadn't planned for this contingency. I'd always thought there would be a way out, that I'd find a way to talk around the truth. But this morning, I just didn't have the strength. I told my mother everything, leaving out no detail. Years of lies unraveled beneath her mournful gaze. I stared at my folded hands in shame as I admitted what I was. I told her where I worked and what happened there. I began to sob when I thought of the man grabbing me and forcing me down, crying so hard I could barely speak as I described how he tried to take my innocence, something I had reserved for so long, knowing how she and father felt about such things. When I was finished, I could not look her in the eye.

When she spoke, her voice was hushed.

"I suspected," was all she said.

The tale took so long that it attracted father's attention, and he came to see what was keeping us. He found us, huddled on the bed together, my mascara smeared on the coverlet.

My mother grabbed his arm and pulled him from the room, and I could hear them speaking in low tones just outside the door. I didn't know what she would say to him. I knew how he felt about kikis. Silence punctuated their long conversation as father digested what my mother told him. As I lay prone, I thought back to the night before, and how hard I had fought. I realized that the battle wasn't over and I prepared to defend myself again.

"James, don't!" My mother cried, but father burst into the room anyway.

"You'll quit the bar. You'll quit all of this immediately!" He yelled, his face florid with anger and revulsion. "You'll find a nice man, and you'll settle down like you should have years ago."

"I won't!" I yelled back, surprised by my own fury. I was beaten and broken, but not defeated. My attacker had taken a chunk of my dignity along with my hair. I would not allow my father to take what remained.

"This is your last chance. Phone them and quit."

"I will not." My mother looked on from outside the doorway, her face white as I stared my father down.

"Communist! I will not allow you to endanger this family!" He stormed out, leaving me quivering with rage, but victorious. He had not forced me to agree to leave my position. Surely, my mother would talk sense into him. She followed him out, and I burrowed back under the covers to wait.

Sometime later, my mother came back and sat down on the bed. I could hear my father on the phone, his voice deep and angry, but I ignored it. My mother was silent, stroking the uninjured part of my head until late afternoon when I heard a commotion outside.

"What's that?" I tried to sit up.

"Shhh," she said, patting my hair. "It's nothing."

I heard the front door open, and my father's voice directing someone upstairs. Heavy footsteps told me several people were on the way to my room.

"Mother, who's here?" I pushed her hand away.

"You're sick, and they've come to help you." She said, tears starting down her face. "Don't fight. You'll only make it worse.

Two men in white uniforms burst into the room. My mother jumped away from my bed. One man had a white jacket with straps and long sleeves. The other man held my shoulders while his partner wrestled my limp arms into the garment. They tilted me forward and tightened the straps. I was too shocked to fight.

"I'm sorry. I'm sorry," my mother sobbed, "He had to."

They led me downstairs, past my father, who didn't look at me. Frightened and confused, I struggled to understand what was happening. I hadn't done anything wrong. After all, I had never known a woman's touch.

They hauled me outside, shoved me into the waiting van, and locked the doors.

My Fire On Your Cutting

Anna Idelevich

I want to choke on hopes and not with neck ropes. Breaking vertebrae, constricting arteries, sprays of blood sprayed the memory glass, the rest relieved.

My fire is on your cutting.

The wave climbs over the gate in blue, black anger.

Suck the blood, I'm not afraid, I'm not afraid. I have a plant for the production of leukocytes, it will hurt in the plasma - I'll still dream, I'll fill up more.

Swim into the cage to me.

I am a piece of meat that will stick in your mouth for a long time. We're not underwater, Baby, we're in an elevator high tower. The casinos roll the balls until you drop thrown from above, in the kaleidoscope of the city, they flicker, but we cannot see, we are inside.

It's gray inside.

There is an elevator inside.

A pumped chest will knead on me without a barbell, a stoic shark heart that cannot withstand the walls of an aquarium. You watch the yen fall and rise, day after day, in your universe, coins are devalued. The obscenity of the mind is starving for another leap. Tinted slime smears a palette knife - their pictures tell you nothing.

I show you my world.

Poems reveal time for things that you usually don't pay attention to.

Sometimes you enter me in tight spirals, but I do not notice at the other end - as if you appeared simply and easily or have always been here. The main arteries, the lavatory arteries, quiver the steam.

The valve is a bridge, behind it the heart is already roaring the sun. Caressing, not roaring, just do not hide from the light.

The smoky armor stood long before you were born, and I was born. Not to demolish its walls, but to demolish each other with a stream of tenderness and passion, reviving a rainbow from an anachrome.

Put on your black glasses, now it will be bright down the drain armor, you merge with me.

Black limousine, darker inside than out.

Soft, a foot longer than your tongue if you take all of me, penetrate to the throat. Stuff underfoot, I speak with an accent, but your receptors are taking in a mixture of smoke, love.

This is how the media mogul turns a foreign tape. Gradually understanding every roughness, taking it for a plot. I am already much of you, but inside it is free, the tightness does not press.

It gives.

The Mole Catcher

Peter Roxburgh

It was early doors when I walked into the bar of The Rat and straight into the middle of a feisty conversation. At the far end of the bar, a trembling hand was struggling to preserve the contents of a jug of bitter; at the other, a glass of red swished through the air; and between the two, behind the bar, the landlord, shaking his head.

"So, a mole catcher now, is that it?" said the trembling hand, splashing beer to the floor; a Jack Russell promptly moved in to lap up.

"Green-keeper, actually," replied the glass of red, returning said glass to the bar for replenishment.

"Mole trapping is mole trapping, I'd say." The trembling hand appeared to become more agitated, much to the delight of the Jack Russell. "You know, up in Wales, they say the village idiot's a mole catcher."

Hoping for a pint, I settled on a stool in the middle of the bar. The landlord took a pint glass and rested his hand on the IPA tap.

"You're from that neck of the woods, what do you say?"

"Pour me that pint and I'll tell you what I know."

An empty red and an empty best bitter slid along the bar, and their owners shifted on their high stools in readiness.

Life as a mole catcher for Dai, my great grandfather, wasn't easy

(I told them), that's for sure. He'd work late into the night when everyone else had retired for the evening; it was a lonely occupation. There was the constant ingress of earth; it got everywhere. It didn't matter how much he scrubbed, caked browns and greys lined his fingernails, and the soil sought out the creases and cracks of his hands, hands that were forever numb and swollen through the constant thrusting into the little mounds of the moles' handiwork. And if the nights and the dirt were not enough, there was the pay: a shilling for a mole—5 pence in today's money—that was the going rate. It didn't matter how many of the little blighters he caught, there were never enough to avoid suppers of soup and yesterday's bread.

Indeed, his life as a mole catcher was not one filled with joy and happiness.

If life was so hard, you might ask: why did he follow the path of a mole catcher? It's a good question, and one to which I can tell you there was a common story back then in the mountain villages of North Wales. Dai's parents weren't poor, nor uneducated, nor ignorant. No, these weren't the reasons behind his woes. His father, my great-great-grandfather, farmed eighty acres in the valley floor and, during summer, he let the livestock roam the hundreds of acres that surrounded the family home. He and his wife, who ran the household, had had only three children.

The eldest child, Gruff, could read from the bible before he started school. And he could tell anyone why things were, well, the way they were. He was the smartest, and like many intelligent children, he left the hills and headed to the city where he studied medicine and became a GP in one of the market towns of the Marches. Next, less than a year after the birth of Gruff, Thomas arrived. He proved to be strong and quick thinking, though not possessing the kind of intelligence blessed upon Gruff. But Thomas was an eager student and remained in school until he was eleven, which was a good education back then, when he left to help on the family farm.

Last, as you may have guessed, was Dai. He was unexpected. His brothers said he was a mistake, but his mother said that he was a gift from God. Alas, God chose not to bless Dai in the same way as his brothers. He struggled throughout school. The letters would jump off the page—dyslexic, I guess—and he found it impossible to concentrate, always dreaming of adventures, catching salmon beneath the falls, or lying under the rays of the summer's sun whilst he watched clouds float by. When he left school, there was no medical school for him, no farm to tend, and no one willing to take him on as an apprentice. Eventually, his father pulled out some rusted traps and told him to go out and make a living for himself; he'd had enough of supporting Dai.

Now, you might think that everything thereafter was history, but no: once, Dai almost had it all.

It was April. The snows had cleared from all but the highest peaks, and warm southerlies had pushed the thermometer up into the high teens. It was what you'd call an Indian summer if it had been in the autumn. The nights remained steadfast and frigid, yet Dai worked hard setting as many traps as he could, because April is when moles are actively breeding and escaping their deep-winter tunnels. It was exhausting, bitter work; so, during the day, he would descend from the farm to the valley below. There he would pass his days dreaming, fishing for trout, and sketching the tumbling rocks, jumping goats, and streams that raced from the higher grounds.

One particular day, no different from any other, he was lying on his back with the sun teasing his face, and the gurgling of water filling the air, when his peace was broken.

"Hello," said a voice full of youth and vibrancy.

The syllables seemed to separate and float through his consciousness.

It was as if nature herself was beckoning him, wanting to engage in conversation. He watched as the syllables floated by, and he sank deeper into nature's sunny embrace.

"Hello, I said." This time, there was a certain insistence.

He felt the shadow of someone standing over him. He opened his eyes. It was, he thought, as if God had taken all of nature and wrapped it up in human form. He blinked to confirm that the sun wasn't playing a trick on him. Yet, she was still there, standing above him, hands on hips, looking down at him.

"Have you got nothing to say?"

Words failed him; yet, he knew right then, right there, that he was in love.

He smiled.

She smiled.

He pushed his elbows into the scrubby grass and sat up, wanting to consume her and feel her energy flow inside him.

"It's a beautiful day," she said.

He replied, "I think I love you."

She pierced him with vivid, shamrock eyes, which seemed to absorb his every word. Then she turned, sprang from where she stood, crossing the stream, and set herself down on the bank opposite and looked back at him. She giggled, and the sound filled the air, surrounding him with its music. But before he could get to his feet, she took flight, dancing away towards the folds of the surrounding hills. All that remained was the gushing of the stream and the echoes of her words and laughter.

That night, as Dai set his traps, her words encircled him, and he felt her presence like a fleeting memory, not knowing if she was a mere daydream or if she had said those words to his waking self. So the next day, he revisited the little spot by the stream and waited for her to reappear. As time passed, the rustling of the grass and bubbling of the stream worked their magic, and he drifted into a dream-filled slumber.

"Hello."

He awoke with a start.

"Come swim."

She stepped into the water and floated downstream towards a pool. He followed. They swam. They embraced. He wished he could kiss her and feel her warmth, yet he held back, not daring to sully this bond between them. His feet curled around the pool's cool-pebbly base; he imagined that kiss, its warmth, its connection.

"A penny for your thoughts," she said.

If only! A penny for a thought, not a penny for hours spent on his knees, digging, scraping, trapping. Now, that would be something.

"I was thinking, that's all," he said.

She fixed him with her eyes. "Don't think, *be*." And she flopped onto her back and, with a single stroke, propelled herself to the centre of the pool.

He followed her lead. It was just the two of them, floating, suspended between heaven and earth. Their hands joined, and they watched the clouds build castles in the sky.

"Marry me!" The words tumbled from his mouth without thought or conscious effort on his behalf.

"Marry you?"

"Yes, marry me."

She paused and then replied, "But you're nothing more than a mole catcher. What kind of life is that? For me?"

Her hand let go of his, and she kicked away towards the shore.

"Wait!" He chased her wake, but it was too late; she was gone.

The next day, Dai packed his bags and headed for the station. He would make his way to the city and find his fortune; then she would take his hand in marriage. He bought a third-class ticket for

Chester—a London fare being beyond his means—and hurried through to the platform. As the train pulled to a halt, he slipped into a second-class carriage. Maybe a touch of luxury, he thought, wouldn't be such a terrible start to his new life.

He positioned himself towards the centre of the carriage so that he could spot any approaching ticket inspector and, thus, make his escape to third class. Content with his position, he settled down, allowing himself to sink into his seat's plush cushioning. As he stared out of the window, a cloud of smoke engulfed the platform and hid his previous life, perhaps forever.

The carriage had few occupants. Other than himself, there was a well-dressed couple who looked uncomfortable in their attire—possibly London bound for some special event; a small studious man tucked into a book so that only the top of his balding head was visible; and a young lady who had, perhaps, mistaken the carriage for first class. She was dabbing her eyes with a lace handkerchief, and she let out little moans and sobs as if the weight of the world was on her shoulders. Having surveyed his travel companions, he sank deeper into his seat and watched the grey coastline race by.

The stark walls of Conwy Castle interrupted his panorama, and after passing through Llandudno Junction, which later in the year Northern families would crowd whilst heading for the seaside, they rejoined the coastline. On arriving at Rhyl, a gentleman with cropped grey hair, a monocle, and a walking cane that had a head carved in the shape of an eagle, hurried along the gangway while muttering to himself. He promptly stopped beside Dai, took off his coat—a heavy coat of tweed, which glittered as if threaded with gold—rolled it up, placed it on the window seat, and sat down opposite Dai. To avoid drawing his attention, Dai returned his gaze to the window and watched as mud flats rolled into view.

"They're telling me to do it, you know," the cane-bearing

gentleman said, catching Dai unawares.

Pretending not to hear, Dai stared to the outside with such vigour that his eyes smarted. It would be a poor start to his adventure to engage in conversation with a lunatic who, at a moment's notice, could beat him around the head or, on alighting, follow him and plunge a dagger into his back, leaving him to die alone in one of the meandering back alleys of Chester. Silence seemed to work; that was until the eagle-topped cane banged against the carriage floor and a gloved hand tapped Dai's knee.

"Are you deaf or an idiot, boy?"

Dai turned to face the eyes of a lunatic.

"I'm telling you, they want me to do it and do it soon. What do you say?"

The truth is Dai didn't know what to say. How do you respond when asked such a thing by a madman aboard a speeding train? Of course, his brothers would have known how to respond. Gruff would have diagnosed the man's condition, popped a pill from his medicine bag, and sent the fellow on his way; and Thomas would have flexed his muscles, sending out a warning that he wasn't someone to mess with. Of course, neither having the brains nor the brawn, Dai said nothing and did nothing. He considered his best hope of survival was to sit still, say a prayer, and hope that the lunatic was of the harmless variety.

As they pulled into Chester station, Dai saw it was a hive of activity. There stood suited gentlemen discussing affairs, younger men wearing clothing that he had never seen the like of in his life, and urchin boys darting between the crowds whilst dodging porters and a solitary policeman. It all looked so foreign, so scary, yet so full of possibility. Dai was ready to explore this metropolis and see what awaited him. He turned back to the now emptying carriage and saw that his unwelcome travel companion had already left, leaving his coat behind. Dai's first thought was to leave it where it lay because though he knew he should try to reunite it with its owner, he had no appetite to remake that acquaintance. Yet, as he looked at its quality cloth and golden thread, a desire to take it and make it his own overcame him. Surely, he reckoned, if the lunatic had left the coat, it was not of that great a worth to him, and a good coat like that would take many months of work to purchase. He put a stop to his indecision and took the coat, tucking it under his arm to remove it with stealth.

I shalln't dwell on Dai's first day in the city. Needless to say, it was busy, noisy, and confusing. He had spent the entire afternoon seeking work by calling at the tanneries, breweries, and brickworks, which sat on the edge of the city. Every call ended the same: we've got nothing here for you; you should head back to the hills where you belong. He soon realised that it would take some considerable effort to make something of himself in this place. But, for now, he had more pressing needs: he needed something to eat and some place to sleep. Unfortunately, he'd spent all of his money on the train fare, so he was at a loss as to where to turn next. Not knowing the city, he begrudgingly headed back to the station: the only place he knew.

Though early in the evening, the platforms were full of comings and goings. He looked for a place to sit, somewhere out of the way where he might later sleep. On finding a bench tucked behind a roof support on the farthest platform, he pulled on his newly acquired jacket, sat down, and thought. He drifted back to the little spot by the stream, the sound of water, and the smell of mountain air. Life had been so simple back then; he had to remind himself that back then was, in fact, only yesterday. As he wrestled with his thoughts, someone sat down beside him.

"Oh, I don't know what to do. I truly don't." The voice of a young woman interrupted his musings.

He looked across and saw that it was the girl from the train: the one who had been sobbing into her handkerchief. Like most people, he didn't like to see a young woman distraught, so he knew he had to do something. He searched for words that might bring her comfort. And then, as if from out of nowhere, he could hear saying out loud, "The sun has to set to make space for a new day."

She withdrew the handkerchief from her face and, with reddened eyes, looked at him and asked, "But then what?"

Again, from out of nowhere, words floated from his mouth. "With the dawn of a new day, the troubles of yesterday are mere memories, which have no more significance than the smoke of yesterday's fire."

"I say, you have it." She wiped the tears from her eyes. "I need to forget him and move on."

She turned towards him and, without hesitation, planted a kiss on his cheek and pushed something into his hand.

"Thank you. You're so wise. Thank you, thank you, thank you." And with that, she skipped along the platform and ran up the station steps and out of sight. He opened his hand to reveal a crisp pound note. A pound note, I tell you. To save you the calculation, for it took me some time, 24 shillings made a pound; thus one pound equated to 24 moles. During a most profitable week, he'd be lucky to trap that many moles, and now, with nothing more than a few words, he had earned an entire pound. As you can imagine, he felt elated. Jumping to his feet, he headed directly out of the station, crossed the forecourt, and made his way to the nearest hotel where he dined on roasted beef until it utterly defeated him.

With a pound in his pocket, he had sufficient funds to spend a few days without the worries of hunger or a lack of lodgings, but he knew he would soon have to find employment. That said, he took the opportunity to explore the city and, in a modest way, enjoy himself. He passed three days by walking along the river and watching the barges transporting goods back and forth; sitting in the park, taking in the fresh air and throwing the odd crust to the ducks; and, of course, eating in the various places that lined The Rows. On the fourth day, he turned out his pockets to discover all that remained was a solitary shilling. So, yet again, he had to choose between trawling the industrial areas for work or buying a one-way ticket back home. As he considered the situation, he became despondent, fearing that a further search would yield no employment, so he headed back to the station to sit and consider his options.

As he sat contemplating the hardships that seemed to block his every turn, a middle-aged man, greying around the temples, sat down beside him and let out a deflated sigh.

"What am I to do?" He stared at his shoes as if they held the answer. "If I choose this, I'll have endless opportunities, but if I choose that, I will have security." He started to shake his bowed head. "My, my, what a dilemma."

Then a strange thing happened yet again: words tumbled, without thought or prompt on Dai's part, from his mouth.

"At a crossroads, all directions lead somewhere. Who is to know where they lead?"

The middle-aged man raised his head. "Yes, that's so true. Where do they lead?"

Again without hesitation, Dai said, "Does it matter if one leads to the valley floor with its lush pasture, or the other to the mountain with its endless view? Indeed, both offer a gift, which those who fail to choose can never hope to receive."

"By Jove, you've hit it on the head!" The gentleman rose and turned to face Dai. "You, my man, are a genius."

With that he grasped Dai's hand, and Dai felt the crisp texture of paper brush against his palm. The gentleman patted Dai on the back and without a word he ran off along the platform and bounded up the station steps. Dai, on opening his hand, discovered a five-pound note. Only once had he held such a note, and that was as a child when his father had sold some ewes at market and he had allowed Dai to touch the money, just to know how it felt. Dai folded his reward and slipped it into the security of his jacket's inner pocket.

Twice, while sitting at that bench, Dai had met a stranger and said words that had come from nowhere, and twice they had given him money. Maybe, just maybe, this was his destiny, his means of making a fortune and marrying the woman he loved. Without hesitation, he resolved to pass his days sitting on the bench waiting for strangers in need of his assistance. He thought it was a marvellous plan and, if his calculations were correct, it would not take him many weeks to amass more than enough money to return home a rich man.

As the days became weeks, he offered those that crossed his path words of wisdom and, more often than not, they compensated him with a note or occasionally a handful of change. And though life in the city wasn't cheap, he built up a considerable sum, so much so that the wad of notes stashed within his jacket's pocket pressed heavily against his chest. With this money, he would never need to set a trap again, he could marry his true love, and they would buy a grand house on the coast far away from the windswept mountains and the sombre valleys. His head filled with images of their happy, beautiful life together. Right away he decided to take the next train back to Bangor.

He knew, all too well, the saying *a fool and his money are easily parted*, but he indulged himself one last time by buying a first-class fare. A porter took his bag and carried it on board while Dai installed himself in a voluptuous leather chair. Presently, a steward dressed in a fresh-pressed suit offered him a drink of his choosing; He took a whisky, which arrived in a tumbler that sparkled against the carriage lights. And, as the train pulled from the station, he glanced out at the grey platform where he'd spent so many hours. Finally, he was homeward bound.

The mudflats of the coast passed by without notice, and the train was soon pulling into Llandudno Junction. From his seat, he could see the distant peaks of the Carneddau: dark, grey, and forbearing. He was nearing home and nearing a new, wealthy future with the woman he loved. His anticipation grew. What would she say? What would she do when she saw him as a rich man? His pulse soared, and his breathing became shallower. The driver sounded the engine's whistle, and the train lurched forward towards Conwy. He began to sweat; passion and anticipation were engulfing him. He took off his jacket and placed it on the facing chair, mindful of not letting it out of his sight.

Within minutes, mountains loomed to his left, and Puffin Island appeared to his right, both marking the final miles towards Bangor. He willed the train to go faster, the stoker to pile on more coke, and the driver to open the throttle to its maximum. Minute by minute, mile by mile, the train edged closer. Soon the mountains gave way to the terraces and yards that fringed the city's limits. And those soon yielded to the ramps that marked the platform ends. The train pulled up abruptly, and as the engine's smoke cleared, Dai looked out of the window. There, standing on the platform, just yards away, she— nature herself—stood. He waved. She returned his gesture and smiled. He rushed to alight, to embrace her, to swim in her beauty and light.

He bounded down the steps to the platform and ran open-armed towards her. She mirrored his pose, waiting to engulf him in her essence. The engine whistle sounded, and the metal-on-metal clunk of pistons, cross-leads, and wheels filled the air. He stopped dead.

"My jacket! My money!" The realisation hit him; they must have tumbled to the carriage floor.

His shoulders slumped; he put his head in his hands and closed his eyes. Breathe, he told himself, breathe. Love is greater than money, greater than money, greater than money—the words ran through his head, and then they surged from his mouth. He opened his eyes, and nature herself melted away. Youth was replaced with age; joy with horror; light with darkness; and beauty with grotesqueness. He stood frozen as she said, "You are nothing more than a lowly mole catcher: an idiot boy with foolish dreams."

With that, she was gone, leaving him with nothing more than this simple tale.

The bar was silent except for the pawing of an intoxicated Jack Russell. I slid my now empty glass forward. The landlord, palms against the bar top, leaned in towards me and asked, "Now, tell me again: are mole catchers idiots?"

The Justice of Dust

Wes Choc

Spring 1967, Khe Sanh, Vietnam

Wild whining hums, clinks, clunks, snapping cracks, or booms greeted ears at Khe Sanh, Vietnam. But no one's ears tuned into such dissonant symphonies as, from dawn to dawn, Marines acquiesced to eat, talk, and sleep through ear splitting gun firings. Like strikes in Saturday night bowling alleys, artillery fired every two or five or fifteen minutes at random, so *Charlie* couldn't guess when or where *next* would occur. Such broken-record rhythms were always present amidst a background of tin pans, distant weapon rumblings, explosions, chopper whop-whops, or radio brouhahas. Ear canals were cluttered, but no one remembered anything five minutes later.

Five minutes later gave way to five minutes later in a sequence of five minutes later until the day was over, and I was in my rack beneath the wool blanket. Growing up, a blanket had been a cover. Linguistically, *cover* was Marine lingo for hat. And, yes, fantasizing about being covered with covers could be perceived as nonsense. *Cover* was also an amusing side thought thinking about how balding Marines used covers to cover what they didn't want women to see. But now, covers were blankets. Marines substituted words for lots of things, calling sides of a tent *bulkheads*, or floors *decks* even when on land. While Navy-esque words didn't seem right, we verbalized them to identify being unique, indoctrinated professionals.

Few of us ever *saw* the VC closeup despite their grandfather-clock-like pendulums banging its mortar barrages. Evidence of John-Wayne-type combat wasn't here right now. Instead, Marine forays out and onto two mountainsides (881N and 881S) overlooking Route 9 were routine. These pursuits produced their share of wounded Marines, some slight, some grim. Casualties were handled, then handed from corpsmen to aircraft with speed and skill. Another page in this war book turned.

Sure, war was going on. Marines were hurt, killed. MEDEVACs transported wounded. Witnessing such events pressed us into indoctrinated professionals staying serious as these platoons patrolled. Transports roared in with tons of replenishments, food, water, ammunition, and, of course, more replacement Marines. Helicopters whop-whopped in and out. There was gossip about friends of friends, about injuries, about blood. We did see and touch enough of it, often enough to be respectful as well as afraid. Our toughest roles were played inside nightmares, but we seldom exchanged glances about these things. We tended to look down at our boots instead.

We knew our lines in this unfolding script with responses covering up stress no indoctrinated professional would allow himself to show. We knew buddies who went *out of country* with not-too-life-threatening wounds, and sometimes departed in one of those slick, dark, green-zippered bags. Poignant reminders were everywhere, but we didn't obsess over them either. These were daily corridors everyone walked but hardly ever talked about. Trembling hands and nightmares were ignored.

Food choices and warm beer were predictable, but at least there was warm beer. Cigarettes were cheap and most of us smoked. We never ran out of cigarettes but were always careful not to smoke at night in case glows would attract the sharpshooting skills of snipers. We'd cuff the ember end in our palm when we did smoke. Nicotine was a simple fix, a drug for those five-minute highs we needed. Solitude and boredom were everyday companions. We dealt with them. First Sergeant's "just suck it up" comments were anticipated when he was on stage, so sleeping was a retreat to savor every night, goddam clock pendulums or not!

Suddenly, underneath that blanket, I was conscious - not awake totally, but conscious. Lying face up on my cot, sweaty, ears open, half dreaming, with whims and impulses slithering around in my head, my blanket wrestled with me. Being longer than the cot, my shoulders and hips forever needed repositioning. Tonight, Achilles tendons reminded me to roll over. At least this was canvas, not mud. The heavy blanket added comfort as I felt naked without *some*thing over me. Except as pillows, most guys never used blankets, especially in May. Right now, with a calm mood, cool dreams should have kicked back in. Instead, a heavy sponge-like sensation churned left and right inside my head. Though painless, it felt like kneading bread dough.

Was it morning yet? Letting my bread dough head comfort me in the dark, my forehead senses made it seem like I had a helmet on *even though of course I didn't.* Fingers clutched behind my head, eyelids stayed semi-closed, and numbness between my hands and my raw biscuit brain had a tough time triggering deliberation. Stretching, more awake than my body wanted, I felt drugged.

Although there was no unnecessary illumination at night in Khe Sanh, it was never entirely dark either. Lights crept inside tents creating outrageous images feeding wild dreams and nightmares. Now, on *that night* there was *that moon!* A reflective moon capturing my senses in an awe-struck audience in a surreal theater. As body parts came to, one by one, this voyeur moon challenged me to stay put - even though my groin said a piss was imminent. "Please, not yet!" Muscles contracted through my bladder. Competition between sleep and release became unforgiving. Sleep was *so* very precious.

The moon winked! One second it pinpointed bright light, next it was gone, reappearing in a different spot. In this half-dream state, my brain demurred. It wasn't a flashlight, it was a gigantic fluorescent mosquito, or maybe that loony moon had actually found a way to get *inside* the tent. Mirages wrestled with other night-light sightings, grappling with don't-want-to-get-up- yet postures, stiff spicy-cumin-mixed-with-dirt odors ambushed my nose. Stretching arms up as far as I could, my Achilles tendon was massaged by the ache of that wood and canvas cot. At times when more sleep is needed, instead of counting sheep, maps capture my subconsciousness. The rural village Khe Sanh was a thousand paces east, Laos a couple thousand west, and the DMZ several thousand or two north. Stimulating my brain's map synapses this way, it was easy to envision how we were tucked in the upper left-hand corner of this skinny, tropical country. As strategic as tactical maps geographically suggested, and as much as the *Stars and Stripes* newspaper insinuated, nothing weighty occurred since the 26th Regiment had arrived.

But tonight, there were no maps to ease me back to sleep! The moon was a distraction unwilling to be tracked or traced or prepared for navigation. My arms clutching the back of my neck, these eyes decided it truly *was* the moon, and it *was* moving like moons do. It shifted over the tent with new flashes of light and shadows. My body was being extracted from deep, much needed rest into this moonlight swimming in my forehead. Time to get up! But, for inexplicable reasons, my head wouldn't move. This heavy painless *bulge* of skull lay between my nested palms and a swooshing brain. "Oh please, give me another few minutes!" was whispered as the mind resigned to the inevitable. But that smell? My nose bivouacked on an edge of aromas. Coming to, I glanced sideways toward neighboring cots now lit by the moon. My unliftable head wobbled to one side. Pete's cot, just 18 inches away, was empty. In less than two or three pulse throbs, a dozen things swamped my rubberized head. Hot blood infused my temples as my face chilled dry. There was *not one other person* in any of the other six cots! None at all, just me!

Alone!

Panic shrouded my body with a fast chill. The moon had entered the tent. No. It was moonlight alive and maneuvering; creeping through the flaps of canvas!

Rolling sideways, my head jerked off the cot by elevating my shoulders. Twisting my glasses onto my face, my arms cocked back to prop my body into a half-seated, one-elbow on-the-cot position. Saliva dripped out of my open mouth. In five more heart pounds, muffled stillness swathed my face. Mixed messages stewed behind my wide-open eyes. Despite a sagging head, ears sensed left, then right, in 180-degree jerks.

Alone!

Taking in a gulping breath, inhaling saliva, coughing while trying to listen, I smelled fresh herbal and burnt carbon aromas right smack in front of me. Flowers and fresh gunpowder? My heart hammered panic-pumping blood in another hot flash of chilling hysteria. Gut muscles shivered in disbelief. Free of the blanket, fully dressed, except for my boots, cocking my head upward, afraid to move, yet afraid to stay put, I zeroed in on how the full moon created bizarre shadows inside the tent. My mind raced. No, it lumbered like rocks sliding down a hill seeking shaded, in-the-dark enemies.

Two or three more blood thumps passed before being able to sit all the way up, listening for cues as toes pounded the deck. My femurs were braced by shaking knees. Still brain hazy, steadying myself on a tent pole, senses overlapped. Were those distant voices? After two failed attempts to stand, my upright position survived bursts of jerks. Shuffling the cards in my brain into workable acuity, I remained standing, two size 14s planted on a dirt deck, semi-ready to ante up on this table of unknowns.

Where *was* everybody? "Hullo?" I questioned with a timid whisper. Aligning my body by hugging tent poles for balance, full shadows *inside* the tent seized my focus! Dilated eyes discovered detail even through dirty glass lenses. As my brain de-clotted, vision became alert. Leaning toward the tent flap while holding two tent poles, I threw the flap open and observed an eerie sci-fi landscape in a misty Frankenstein movie scene. It was gelled quiet, moon bright. No guns or explosions, no noise at all. Eyes stared open, now awake; shocked awake...*by the silence!*

A white ocean of floating dust fixated my eyes. As far as I could see in all directions a cloudy wave of pure dust reflected the moonlight with a bright white glow. About waist high, creepy undulations were caught in the play of light and reflection rocking gently, listing with shadows, flowing through the compound, bearing only slight motion. It was a huge sea of supernatural water with glowing ghostly trees sticking out. Above the fluorescent dust layer was clear black sky, a full moon, and radiating stars as witnesses. That spicy smell of gunpowder lingered.

An ocean of dust reflected this rigid judicial moon umpiring new tranquility. No, it wasn't serene at all. It became alien as perceptions swam in slowmotion above this surreal sea of powdered white dust. Calm terror. Coming to had not been easy. Now alert, I stood at attention - an indoctrinated professional- overwhelmed and *alone!*

In the next few seconds, there were distant gagging yells, "Carmen! Carmen, o'year!" But these sounds were muffled as if voices were wrapped in flannel, inside this helmet I was *not* wearing. More sounds. Two high-pitched overlapping voices hollering "Ampin! Ampin!" and "Helmy! Helmy!" and "Inking!" echoed from inside a muffled tunnel. The ocean undulated into disappearing wisps of mist. As my ears recalibrated, "Carmen" translated into "Corpsman! Corpsman! Over here!" I tried standing without holding onto the tent pole with legs further apart to assure stability.

Air moved. There were no airplane sounds, no guns, just underground vibrations and far-off yellow flashes of bright light followed by faint thunderstorm rumbles, and the hissings and the echoes in my mind translated "ampin" into captain, "helmy" into help me, and "inking" to incoming! White surf heaved into fluffy vanishing swishes.

My belly belched as I yelled out a gurgled "h'lo! anybody there?" along with cough and spit. Not knowing what else to do in these three or four more heartbeats, I stepped outside in a swaying gait. Not one other person could be seen as the whiteness streamed through tresses of moving air into nothingness.

"Hey jerk-head, g'down here," came a high-pitched retort fifteen feet away,

"Incoming!"

This was the real thing! I ogled the long black rectangle, First Platoon's foxhole. Diving with an awkward gymnastics maneuver into the trench beside our tent, my torso rolled with a warm thud onto a heap of breathing bodies. A couple feet wide and five feet deep, it compacted fifteen or so Marines garbed with flak jackets, hand grenades, rifles, and sweat. No one talked although there were stifled groans from guys at the bottom upon my grand entrance; it was a bonding experience of indoctrinated professionals.

Coincidentally, there was a rush and swoosh of more incoming that sounded like landing transport jets, followed by crashes of not-too-distant explosions, one after the other steadily growing louder and closer even through my "rubber helmet." VC's mortars were being "walked in" toward us, but reverberations were still distant enough, maybe a hundred yards away, pounding nearer every two or three seconds.

With nothing on my feet but socks, no weapon, no helmet or flak jacket, there was only the back of my olive-drab tee shirt facing that neon moon now frowning near the Laotian horizon, and me at ground level. Distant explosions peaked as the pendulum of our guns then resumed, a solemn banging mixed with sounds of incoming mortars battering the other side of the clock. Then it all stopped suddenly again creating that eerie, silence in my ear canal.

Screams, then high-pitched "help!" screeches shouting "Captain!" and, moaning "over here!" punctuated the air. Clear sounds. After opening my eyes from sleep to looking up at holes in the tent to my now closed eyes with a nose punching down atop two hand grenades on the butt of a Marine's web belt took a few minutes to adjust my senses. Nonetheless this human-soft trench was a refuge. This smelly pile of humanity was comforting security albeit pasted together for common survival.

Minutes passed. Those distant explosions had rapidly approached then stopped. Blanketed voices became frequent, audible, and understandable. Incoming sounds ended and the skies began to lighten. Deliberate but cautious movement out of trenches commenced, one layer at a time with me rolling out sideways first. Exiting was a methodical, nonstop crawl up, out, and above, standing with hunched-down shoulders. Everyone sought updates as dawn-cooling breezes evaporated sweat.

Without a helmet, weapon, or flak jacket, I shivered, exposed and defenseless in this crowd. But I huddled with them confused about what to do. Next steps were discussed by those who did seem to know.

Marines began scurrying around darting toward cries for help. Corpsmen maneuvered their wares like fast-paced basketball players. Officers refereed traffic with hand gestures and subdued commands. Others assisted by moving the injured with speed and care. The rest of us went to our assigned stations amid typical grunts and profanities.

"Wu'happened?" I asked Pete as we re-entered the tattered tent for our boots, for my M-16, flak jacket, and helmet. I straightened my gait. "You okay?"

"Wow! It hit so fast." Pete wiped some blood off his forearm. "Got dinged, but I'm fine!" Both Pete and I booted up and hustled to pre-assigned stations near the perimeter where we gained more news. "You okay?" he asked as he dismissed his wound.

"I guess so. My head's a little out of whack." Trying to hurry helped blood get to my legs, and I bounced along right behind Pete despite my zigzagging gait. The fact that I had slept through that first barrage was now sinking in. How could that have occurred? I shuddered with what-if questions. My thoughts attacked as the episode retreated.

That dust layer I had seen had been stirred up and dissipated quickly. The moon was now kissing the horizon. By the time we got to our post, the sun was creating its own shadows. It was a new day. Repeating guns resumed, officers' commands became animated and forceful. My white ocean was a byproduct from that first wave of mortars exploding and settling during the silence afterwards. That dust ocean had lived for mere minutes that few others ever even saw. The ordnance odor lingered into familiarity.

I was safe.

Grappling with afterthoughts about how everyone scurried to designated dugouts of safety as we all were supposed to do, and how they must have been yelling out loud "incoming, incoming," I struggled with feelings about being left alone undisturbed, about discovering no one noticed my occupied bunk in moments of panic and haste.

No one thought to wake me! The intricacy of being forgotten and waking up alone in a sea of battlefield dust waving over me was etched onto my heart.

It is a tattoo I still carry, but few ever see.

Lost and Found

Matt Hardman

Old wasn't the right word to describe Jusuf Ahmetovic. By the calendar, he was only in his mid-forties, a far cry from being elderly. Weathered was a better description. Jusuf, finishing his morning coffee and contemplating the long-stemmed pot and battered, copper serving tray, on which rested a spoon and a spare lump of white sugar, was like the picnic table where he sat. With every season, he was deteriorating. Haggard. Worn.

He was a tall man, slender and narrow-shouldered. At first glance, he appeared quite ordinary. The face atop his thin neck was slim, creased, and tanned from years of wandering, contemplation, and sorrow. The hair, unruly and unkempt, was fighting a losing battle to retain its original black luxuriance. Gray had seeped in everywhere, including into the stubble that crept up his chin and cheeks, with more than a few white hairs now making their incursion, testing the waters, trying to discover a place for themselves in the man's life. The nose and the ears, both of which were a little too big for the face, were wholly unremarkable, pre-determined in size, shape, and placement by a genetic soup which had simmered for centuries to produce this one human being.

The eyes were different. Set deep in their sockets, underneath a pair of bushy brows that arced away and down in a permanent question, the eyes were dark, a rich walnut color that communicated a mixture of intelligence, courage, and sadness, with an extra helping of the latter. Those eyes bore into the extra lump of sugar, concentrating on it as his mind sketched out a plan for this beautiful October day.

Jusuf decided that, after checking on his flock, he would go to the woods. The decision, made with a solemn resolution that might have seemed out of place to the uninformed or un-initiated, would be perfectly logical to those who knew Jusuf best. He went into the woods almost every single day, having done so for almost twenty years now, searching for fragments of a life long since passed.

Hearing the bleating complaints of a dozen fat sheep, Jusuf lifted his head and looked around at his farm. The briefest hint of a smile graced his lips, a half-sardonic grin that his wife usually described as distasteful. She'd point out the world around them and ask him how he could always be so grim surrounded by a landscape crafted and painted by God himself. Jusuf never answered the question. She wasn't scolding him. It was always a rhetorical question. *Sure,* he'd think as she hugged him and tousled his unruly hair, *God might have painted this place, but man has defiled it.*

The ancient farmhouse, a white-washed combination of stone and rough-hewn wood built by Jusuf's own ancestors, stood nestled in the crook of two ridgelines which pushed east towards Srebrenica, a small town in Bosnia and Herzegovina with a population just under three thousand.

An old mining town that could trace its roots back to the Roman Empire, Srebrenica had been an ancient crossroads for trade; the name of the town itself derived from the local word for silver. Importance as a trading center, especially for precious metals and minerals, had made Srebrenica and the surrounding areas points of contention through the centuries. Possessed in turns by the Serbian,

Bosnian, and Ottoman Empires, Srebrenica and its residents had become used to strife and conflict. Suffering was a way of life, as familiar to the residents as the faces of each family member and the ground they scrounged a living from.

Jusuf noted smoke from a wood-burning fireplace trailing lazily from the home's lone chimney, evidence that his wife, Marija, was up and moving, working at all of the tasks necessary to keep a small farmhouse operating in the twenty-first century. Watching the smoke, he felt pangs of guilt.

I should help her more.

Jusuf watched the smoke drift and swirl, prone to the whims of a slight breeze that brought cool air down into the valley, swishing through the leaves of the forest, and carrying ghostly sounds to his ears.

That sound. The whisper of voices. Ghosts of the past, buried deep in the forest. The voices are why I don't help my wife. Why she's doing so much and I do so little. She never complains. Never. Not once in twenty years. She lets me chase the past and she remains here, feet firmly in the present, doing the work of the farm, keeping us in meat and vegetables, wool, and firewood.

Jusuf smiled at the house, watching the small window in the kitchen where Marija was standing, preparing food for him to take on his daily trek through the forest. He watched her through the window as she finished her preparations. She was still beautiful, her strong face unlined and un-creased, her dark, chestnut hair untouched by grey. Her eyes, the same walnut color as his, always flashed with a fire that Jusuf knew his own eyes lacked. She looked up, caught his gaze, smiled at him.

She's so strong. Stronger than me. She has let go of the past, has confronted the ghosts, has laid the voices to rest. She has found a way to deal with it. It's been more than twenty years and she is here, thriving even, in the land of the living. I'm not. I'm stuck in the land of the dead, chasing voices and memories through the woods in hope of…what? What exactly am I doing? Would they do this for me? Would they? Or would they just move on with life, without even thinking about my voice and my memory?

Jusuf raised his eyes from the small kitchen window to an even smaller one just a couple meters above it. His mind wandered through time, searching for a memory. *The loft.* Jusuf smiled sadly. *My loft. Lejla's loft. Our little reading nook. The day it all started. Twenty-five years this past July.*

*****

A seventeen-year-old Jusuf sat in the dark corner of the loft, just a short ladder-climb above the farmhouse's kitchen. His early morning chores were long since finished, and he was watching his younger sister as she sat among piles of worn books, their pages yellowed and dog-eared. He listened attentively as she talked about the book they were currently reading.

"How could he?" she asked, her question dripping with incredulity. What she'd read, how she'd interpreted it, was clearly unforgivable. More to the point, Jusuf knew the current twist the tale had taken didn't fit with Lejla's romantic notion of propriety. Books, she'd argue, shouldn't end this way. Stories should have happy endings. Gleeful ones.

"What?"

"He's going to let Valentine die! The Count knows she's being poisoned. He knows who is doing it! What is he doing about it? Nothing. He's doing nothing!" Lejla's face, even in the dim light provided by the loft's tiny window, was flushed with anger. And frustration.

Lejla Ahmetovic was roughly the same age as Valentine de

Villefort and was completely despondent about the girl's impending death. Jusuf gazed impassively at his sister.

Of the Ahmetovic children, the two of them were the closest in age and they had been inseparable since Lejla could walk. They did everything together, always with the goal of returning to their little hoard of books. A love of reading was something that the rest of the family did not quite share with the two teenagers. Neither parent could read or write, although both indulged the youngest of their children. The elder Ahmetovic children, Mirza and Demir, could read and write, having been educated briefly, but both considered such things a waste of time, focusing instead on the day-to-day toils of running a small, family farm.

Formal education had always been a difficult prospect for rural Bosnians, even more so since the outbreak of hostilities just three years before. That didn't stop Jusuf and Lejla from becoming voracious readers. They were largely self-taught and their humble library of books had been collected over years of family trips into Srebrenica. The Ahmetovic family traveled regularly to the city's markets to sell or trade the products of their farm, a trip that usually ended with Mehmed Ahmetovic providing a small amount of money which Jusuf immediately used to purchase second and third-hand books.

"Does it matter?" Jusuf inquired. He'd read a little further and was deliberately baiting Lejla.

"*Does it matter?* How can it not matter? What did she ever do to Edmond? She's being poisoned because of what her father did. How is that fair?" Lejla was getting angry.

"Do you really think the Count will let her die?"

"He's not doing anything to stop Madame de Villefort. He knows she's the poisoner. He's just going to let it happen."

"Maybe."

"Maybe?" Her voice got louder. "What about Maximillian? What about him? Edmond loved Monsieur Morrel and he's going to just let Valentine die."

"Probably." Jusuf saw her cheeks flush. She was going to explode.

"How can you say that? If Valentine dies, Maximillian will die too. He'll kill himself. I know it. How can the Count let this happen? Maximillian is going to kill himself and he is almost the only family the Count has left. That's the whole point. What would you do for family? What would you give up? The Count isn't willing to give up his hate to protect what little family he has left."

"Probably." Jusuf could no longer control his face. A smirk escaped briefly and his sister caught the look. She punched him in the chest.

"Why would you do that?"

"Do what?" replied Jusuf, feigning innocence.

"You read ahead. You did. Didn't you? You read ahead and you know what happens next and you...you...you let me think..." She trailed off, crossing her arms and pouting.

"I didn't do that. Dumas did. He wrote the book."

"But you let me think Valentine would die." She threw part of a roll at Jusuf, which he was not agile enough to avoid. He started laughing.

Lejla shoved Jusuf over and stormed off to the ladder, descending into the kitchen of the Ahmetovic home. When Jusuf finally stopped laughing, he descended the ladder, cut through the kitchen, and headed through the door to the yard, unsuccessfully ducking two more doughy missiles as he headed for the picnic table to join his father and brothers for their morning coffee.

*****

Jusuf blinked at the memory and took his last sip of coffee before placing the cup back in its copper holder. Brushing his hands off, he reached through the neck of his sweater - an old, torn one his mother had knitted for him more than two decades ago - and pulled a small notebook from the breast pocket of his shirt. He opened it to the first page and looked at the names written there. *Mama. Tata. Mirza. Demir. Lejla.* Five entries on this page. Mom. Dad. Brothers. Sister.

He began flipping through the rest of the pages. There were other names throughout the book, penciled in in Jusuf's own hand, the precise block lettering of a trained engineer. Names of those who had been found, by him, during his wanderings through the Kamenicko Brdo woods surrounding his home. Whole families of people were listed there, remains of people he had found, bringing them back to the living, helping others to achieve closure that he had yet to experience, but there was a difference in the names. The people listed on pages two to two-hundred and three were names that were written into the book *after* they had been found, their identities confirmed and families notified. After funerals had been held and goodbyes had been uttered.

The names on page one, the names of his own family, had been scribed onto the page the same morning that he had started this search. He had expected to have crossed them off by now, to have found them, to have been able to say goodbye. But they weren't crossed off. Jusuf had not found them. He hadn't buried them. He still had never said goodbye. They weren't here now, and there hadn't been time then. Jusuf forced a smile and lowered his gaze to the worn wooden planks of the table, tracking an ant as it wandered, as drawn to the remaining lump of sugar as he was to the forest.

While he watched, the ant dropped into a series of deep grooves in the wood, scrambling here and there through a collection of straights and swirls carved into the unpainted grain. As Jusuf watched, the ant explored freely for a few minutes before climbing out of the gouges and making a beeline for the last lump of sugar.

Jusuf ran his hand over the carvings. He knew them well. He remembered the day he'd made the deep scratches. He thought again about his search and the ant. He knew he couldn't quit. *They wouldn't quit.* He hoped they would do as he did. He hoped he had mattered enough that he would be searched for. He hoped he would not be forgotten. He touched the carving again.

*****

Still rubbing the spot where one of Lejla's rolls had scored a direct hit, seventeen-year-old Jusuf Ahmetovic clambered awkwardly into his spot at a picnic table just meters from the kitchen window of his family's home outside Srebrenica. He'd grown in the last year, and trying to fold his tall, lanky frame onto the bench seat built by his late grandfather was becoming quite a challenge. An innocent and toothy grin spread across his thin, childish face as he pulled a pocket knife out and began whittling lines and curves into the smooth wood, the scent of freshly cut beech greeting him with the removal of each splinter and shaving. He continued carving and digging into the stiff grain until his father set a hand on his arm. Jusuf pocketed the knife and lifted a cup of early-morning coffee from the pressed copper plate his mother had just delivered. He stirred in two lumps of crystalline-white sugar, leaving the third on the tray, just like his father did. Jusuf did not know why there were always three lumps of sugar waiting on the tray. *Tradition maybe? Maybe it was the way coffee was always served.*

He'd never asked and he'd never tried mixing in all three lumps. Jusuf merely imitated his father, stirring in two lumps of sugar to cut the acidic bitterness of the early-morning coffee.

At the table with him were his father, Mehmed, and his two older brothers, Mirza and Demir, the four of them partaking in a new family ritual; drinking morning coffee while they discussed the violence which had engulfed their homeland. This hadn't always been the tradition. There was a time, not long past, when the four Ahmetovic men simply sat, enjoyed their coffee, and discussed whatever topic seemed of particular import. *Market prices. An ill sheep. A new lamb.* It seemed like a lifetime ago.

Jusuf remembered how his country, just three years earlier, had secured international recognition of their existence as an independent republic. He'd heard his father speak of this, praising the Muslim majority which had made freedom possible.

Now, the conversation in the mornings mainly concerned how the Serbs, the largest minority group in the area, had been against the move, and how they'd mobilized forces within Bosnia and Herzegovina to suppress Bosnian independence. His father and brothers spoke of Radovan Karadzic and Slobodan Milosevic, men whose troops had quickly engaged the Bosnian military and forced the newly founded nation into a bitter war which had been characterized by the indiscriminate shelling of military and civilian targets.

"They're murderers. Allah will deal with them when their time comes." Jusuf's father pronounced with conviction.

"But they're rounding us up. I've heard rumors that people are disappearing. Even worse, that people are being executed by the hundreds. Surely, Allah wouldn't permit that." Mirza was concerned and had, more than once, proposed fleeing the country.

"Where would you have us go, Mirza? We cannot afford to leave. We do not have the money to travel that far, even if we sold the entire flock." Demir replied, ever the realist.

"I don't know where we could go. I don't know how we could pay. I just know that it is dangerous to stay here. The stories have to be true. Each week, the market grows smaller. Each week, there is one less stand. Maybe we only need to get to the nearest army post. I don't know."

"And leave all of our belongings here? What then, Mirza? What then? What happens when we reach the post with nothing but the clothes we wear and a parcel of food? You and I would be able to serve in the army. We would be useful to them. What of Mama and Tata, Jusuf and Lejla? What happens to them? Our parents are too old for such nonsense. Lejla and Jusuf are too young. Are we to expect charity from the army?"

"I don't know Demir. I don't know. I just know that Karadzic and his Srpska men are killing Muslims. Its called genocide. Fifty years ago, it happened to the Jews. Today, it is our turn. We will die if we don't leave. Our lack of money will be irrelevant then. We have to do something."

Jusuf had not spoken. He rarely spoke during these discussions. He just listened to the argument and sipped his coffee, waiting for his father to weigh in on the debate.

"You are both correct. We are in danger here and, yet, we cannot afford to flee. Allah has protected us. He will continue to protect us. We must have faith. We must trust in His Will."

The pronouncement was met with nods. Mirza clearly wasn't happy, but openly defying their father was something that none of the Ahmetovic boys would ever consider. The family would remain in place for now, wary of the danger of doing so. The conversation turned to an amateur dissection of the war itself. They considered the actual fighting, each adult offering his opinion as though the commanding generals themselves were waiting on the analysis. Mirza's dangers, very real ones, were relegated to the subconscious for the time being.

To the left of the house, near where the chimney was belching the fragrant smoke of a well-tended wood fire, the family's small herd of sheep started, bleated loudly, and moved with deceptive quickness to steer well clear of some perceived danger, heading instinctively for their accustomed grazing lands in the hills and woods behind the Ahmetovic home. In a way, the sheep were wiser than the family that tended them. Neither evolution nor Providence had seen fit to supply sheep with weapons. To them had only been given the ability to sense danger and run, an instinct which would have served Jusuf and his family well. Knowing the area as intimately as they knew each other, had the family followed the lead of the frightened livestock, they would have stood a fair chance at survival. But they didn't run. They simply sat, looking around, wondering what had spooked the flock.

Less than a minute after the abrupt and noisy departure of the sheep, the men seated around the table heard the sounds of automatic weapons fire, a cease-less chattering that was both easily identifiable and decidedly foreign. The sound coming from the wooded area to the rear of the house, about where the sheep had disappeared, was accompanied by the high-pitched screeching of a mortally wounded animal, a noise which ceased abruptly following another round of gunfire. The Ahmetovic men began to get up from the table, an icy lead weight forming in the gut of each, fear growing exponentially.

As Jusuf worked to disengage his gangly legs from the table, his eldest brother and father were already off, disappearing around the same side of the house as the sheep with Mirza yelling.

"Demir! Jusuf! In the house. Now!"

Jusuf and his brother broke for the kitchen door, reaching it, and stopping to listen to a pair of new noises. From behind the home, angry, unintelligible yelling reached Jusuf's ears. From down by the single road which crawled up from Srebrenica, the barely audible sound of engines could be heard.

Jusuf and his brother halted, trying to think. The shouting from the rear of the house was louder now, angrier. The sound of approaching trucks was close, only one winding turn on the dirt road away from being visible to the occupants of the ancient farmhouse.

The boys, unused to violence and lacking the instincts of trained soldiers, froze. The engine noises to the west increased while the voices to the east, impeded by the bulk of the home, grew quiet.

Jusuf was shocked into action by a crash inside the house and a pair of screams. *Mama! Lejla!* He reached for the door, heard another crash and more screams. He pushed against the door and realized that something blocked it from opening. He listened to the sounds of a struggle, a fight within the close confines of the home's spartan kitchen. He heard dishes crashing to the floor, an unmistakable cacophony of shattering ceramics. Jusuf pushed harder, felt the door move, felt whatever blocked the door scrape backwards across the wooden floor of the kitchen. He pushed again, setting his nearly two-meter-tall frame against the door, his feet searching the ground for purchase. Another scream from the interior, a barely decipherable insult, was delivered loudly in his mother's voice. Jusuf pushed with everything he had, straining at the door, willing it to open as the sound of more gunfire pierced the air. Another scream, his baby sister this time. More gunshots. Then silence, the only sound still reaching Jusuf's ears now was the low, growling rumble of diesel engines belonging to trucks which were just becoming visible, driving towards the house in swirls of dust.

The trucks approached the Ahmetovic home as Jusuf continued to struggle with the door, halfheartedly believing that his mother and sister would still be alive and well just beyond the barrier. As the futility of what he was doing settled on him, Jusuf turned from the door to face the trucks, watching them travel the last fifty meters and turn into the yard.

Each truck, covered from tires to roof in mud and dust, was painted in the same manner, a flat, splotchy combination of dark and light green paint, interspersed with patches of medium brown. With troops already deploying from the back, the trucks drove through the

Ahmetovic's yard, turning away from Jusuf and his brother before coming to a stop near the picnic table where the morning coffee still sat, not yet cold. Jusuf and his brother, confronted by more than a dozen armed men, held their hands up, palms toward the Srpska soldiers, a supplication for mercy from the men now pointing loaded rifles at them.

Jusuf and his brother were pushed roughly to their knees by four of the soldiers, kept at gunpoint the entire time. Jusuf watched them, noting that most of them were his age. He had heard of this group. The Army of Republika Srpska, it was said, was the force responsible for unheard of atrocities, raping and pillaging their way across Bosnia and Herzegovina to exact vengeance on the civilian Muslim population as recompense for the embarrassing defeats handed to them by the fledgling Bosniak and Croat armies. Mirza had said that they were bullies who had been unable to enforce their will against armed foes and had resorted to attacking the civilian population. And they were here. They had him at gunpoint. They had his brother, Demir, at gunpoint. They had, he suspected, murdered his mother and sister and, probably, his father and eldest brother. Knowing he was going to die; Jusuf began to pray.

The kitchen door behind Jusuf opened and he heard the footsteps of two people behind him. They walked by, heading to the picnic table where a Srpska officer stood drinking Jusuf's own coffee, having thrown the extra lump of sugar in. One of the soldiers, Jusuf saw, was bleeding a good deal from fresh scratches across his face. This one, Jusuf noted, wore a rumpled uniform, his tunic disheveled and ripped from, Jusuf assumed, the struggle within the house. Jusuf stared at the soldier, cataloging the features in his memory, hoping that he might get a chance to tell Allah about this man, a man who attacked and murdered unarmed women. Jusuf noticed a detail about the man's uniform that made his blood boil. His pants were undone, the fly unbuttoned and the belt hanging loose in the loops around the man's waist. Rage filled Jusuf. This man, this monster, had assaulted either his mother or, more likely, his sister. He had attempted to rape one or both of them. Jusuf forgot about begging for Allah to give him justice and began to rise from his knees. He never made it.

A barked command from behind, the angry voice of a guard that Jusuf had not seen or heard, was accompanied by pain as the uniformed man delivered a crushing blow with the butt of his rifle to the back of Jusuf's head.

Jusuf collapsed into the dirt as thousands of tiny points of light exploded into his consciousness. Instinctively curling into a ball, he drew his knees up to his chest and moved his arms to cover his wounded head as two more men piled on top of him, using their full weight to flatten him out and wrench his arms behind his back. One soldier perched on his hips, working to secure his ankles with a length of rope while the other crouched near his head, a single knee pressing forcefully across his neck, driving the right side of his face into the loose dirt and gravel of a footpath. While Jusuf blinked in the dirt, trying to breathe, he felt a searing burn as a third man yanked a rough piece of line tight about both wrists.

*****

Jusuf paused at the entrance to the forest, taking in the smells and sounds and rubbing his wrists. It was a nervous habit he'd been unable to cure. Whenever he felt trapped, Jusuf would rub his wrists. He'd done it in university. He'd done it on the job. Even, briefly and regrettably, he'd done it at his own wedding ceremony. It had started that day in 1995 and had become a subconscious urge he'd never been able to control. He was feeling for the bindings that had changed his life, the bindings that were no longer physically present, but there nonetheless. Jusuf caught himself and dropped his hands to his sides, closed his eyes, and took a deep breath. Then a second. And a third. Finally, Jusuf exhaled and opened his eyes.

Birds chirped merrily away, twittering gaily while they flitted here and there, darting in and out of the forest like the tiny streaks of color and joy that they were. Jusuf smiled. They were preparing for the winter. A few wild rabbits and squirrels were doing the same, bolting quickly from spot to spot, the latter checking on their caches of food and screeching in rage each time a rival came into view. The leaves, a vibrant mixture of scarlet, tangerine, lemon, and brown, were getting sparse, falling from the thin branches to form a mosaic carpet on the forest floor. Sunlight filtered through a sparse canopy that subdivided the brilliant whole into individual rays of clear, cold light that reached down to touch the ground, pillars of pale gold interspersed between the damp, gray, moss-covered trunks of primeval trees.

Jusuf pulled the notebook from his pocket again, did not open it. He simply held it in his hands, entreating Allah to help him find his family, praying once more that this would be the day. His simple prayer complete, he kissed the cover of the small, tattered book, placed it back in his pocket and stepped into the woods.

*****

Young Jusuf had heard the orders, had been able to pick up snippets of conversation as he struggled uselessly in the dirt. They were to be taken into the woods. He was not able to turn his head, still held in place by the knee of a soldier who outweighed him by at least twenty kilograms. He was stuck there, hands behind his back and ankles tied together by a short length of rope. His wriggling and struggling ceased only when he heard one voice, rising above the commotion, direct someone to "put them there." Jusuf calmed himself and, though he thought he already knew, waited to see who "them" would be.

He lay there, looking at a world turned ninety degrees from the norm as two figures were dragged into view, both coughing and struggling and...alive. Tata. Mirza. He could not see their faces, but he could see them move, rebelling against their bonds and coughing in the dirt. They lay there, to his left, upper bodies convulsing as their lungs tried to expel whatever dirt and dust they had inhaled. Jusuf closed his eyes and thanked Allah for keeping them alive.

His eyes snapped open when he heard two more thuds, also to his left. Dust swirled into his open eyes and he tried to blink it away, only able to see a solid mass between himself and his living family. He knew that Demir was on his right, could hear him struggling against his own bonds. Tears formed as Jusuf blinked rapidly, trying to rinse the dirt from his vision.

Slowly, the shape became clear. First, the outline of a body. Then, the clear shape of a head. A few more blinks, and Jusuf found himself staring into the face of Lejla, her eyes unfocused and a tangled mess of hair and blood above her ear. Jusuf wanted to cry, to scream. Instead, he was jerked to his feet, held upright by two men. He looked to his left and right, saw his brothers, eyes flashing and teeth clenched with rage. He found his father's face, saw the old man's jaw set, his face as impassive as the situation allowed. Only Mehmed's eyes betrayed the profound sadness and malevolent anger the patriarch had to be feeling.

*****

Jusuf Ahmetovic had his father's eyes. They were deep soulful eyes, ones that knew every inch of these woods. They'd examined every proud, gray tree, observed every cold, sharp rock. Those eyes had looked upon every small bush and thorny bramble and had memorized the appearance of every clear, bubbling stream. His childhood aside, Jusuf had been walking these woods for eighteen years now, on a self-appointed quest to find his family.

He wore stained blue jeans and an old, yellow button-up shirt, the front left breast pocket of which held his notebook and a short, stubby pencil. Supple leather hiking boots and a thick pair of woolen socks adorned his feet. Over his shirt, he always wore the same sweater, dirty and torn from years of catching on thorny bushes and the slim branches of trees that reached out to grab him as if to say; *No Jusuf, not this way.*

On his back, a small, oiled-leather pack held some food and water for the day's wanderings, stowed there with loving care by his wife, a woman who had grown accustomed to the daily routine of Jusuf's life. His family had died here, as had hers. They had vanished from the face of the earth in these very woods. Jusuf wanted to find them. Needed to. Jusuf knew she knew. Knew she understood. There was a time she'd needed the same closure he still sought.

*****

Jusuf had escaped the atrocities of that day, as had she, and together, they had fled the country. The two of them had met in a refugee camp, taking turns comforting each other before moving on to France, each having accepted an offer from the University of Paris which provided housing and education to college-age refugees. They had fallen in love in Paris, married, and completed their degrees, his in engineering and hers in literature. She had accepted a job teaching other refugees and he had found employment with a railroad company, planning new tracks and switching stations out in the French countryside.

Throughout their time in France, Jusuf's mood had darkened, a heavy sadness settling on his soul. It had not been difficult for his wife to discern the cause. Jusuf had been drowning in guilt, the only survivor of a close-knit and loving family. She had felt it too, though not as much. She had aunts and uncles who had survived the Srebrenica genocides. Jusuf did not. His grandparents had died years before the atrocities of July 1995 and neither of his parents had living siblings. The only family Jusuf had known were those who had lived with him in that farmhouse by the woods. Marija had tried to help him, tried to talk with him, tried to comfort him. Nothing had worked. Even their attempts to start a family had failed. Her body, severely damaged by a horribly inept army doctor's attempts to fix the damage done by multiple rapes, had rejected even the concept of pregnancy.

In April of 2001, Jusuf remembered walking into his Paris flat smiling, the brooding sorrow temporarily absent, and the weight he normally carried somehow eased. Marija had been instantly wary. He'd seen the caution on her face as he unloaded his feelings. We should move home, he had announced. We have to move home. There is something I have to do. He explained, briefly, and she had asked for time to consider the idea. He had acquiesced and she had spent a week contemplating his entreaties. They had discussed the issue further with Jusuf pointing out that he still owned the farm outside of Srebrenica, courtesy of a court ruling after the end of hostilities. She told him that she *did* want to go home. France was nice enough, she thought, but she always felt like an outsider. The French, she'd learned, only truly accepted those who fully adopted a French identity and she held dearly to her past, unwilling to give up what made her…her. One day, after Jusuf had returned home from a job in Normandy, she had said yes. She said it was time to go back. She also told him she knew he needed to.

It had taken a few weeks to set the paperwork in order, but when the time came, Jusuf and Marija had resigned from their jobs in France and traveled back to the old Ahmetovic farm near Srebrenica. Jusuf was surprised on his return. The farmhouse was, barring the evidence of obvious neglect, largely as it had been the day he'd been taken to the woods. Everything was covered in more than an inch of dust, but the belongings, especially in Jusuf and Lejla's reading loft, were oddly untouched. Jusuf was both fascinated and saddened. His home had become a time capsule of memories that were both joyous and horrifying.

Jusuf and Marija had spent the first few weeks restoring the home, cleaning here and painting there, while Jusuf planned out his search. Finally, confident in his strategy, Jusuf purchased an empty notebook and made his first excursion into the forest.

Eighteen years later, Jusuf's grand plan had not come to fruition. For nearly two decades he had ambled through the woods, sifting through the dirt and poking around with his walking stick, looking for the bones which he knew to be here. On his third day, back in 2001, he had found his first fragment, part of a tibia which he had placed into the leather pouch he wore tied to his belt. A few days later, he had uncovered part of a skull and two sections of vertebrae. Those had gone into the pouch as well. For almost twenty years, each bone he found was described in his notebook, and annotated with a pin in a map in the old library at his home. Red pins for finds. Green pins for identification, a process that was accomplished by the students and staff at a nearby university. Each month, Jusuf would hand over his collection and the researchers would work to identify the victims, comparing DNA from the skeletal remains against a list of missing persons from that area.

In only the second month of his venture, Jusuf had recovered some of the remains of his wife's family, a remarkable occurrence that had helped her gain some degree of closure and reinforced the notion that this was a good thing, that he was helping people. This wasn't some selfish endeavor, some pointless, self-centered ploy to get back something only he'd lost. Jusuf Ahmetovic was bringing families back

115

together, helping to heal his tiny nation. Word spread about Jusuf. Reporters and historians descended on Srebrenica, dubbed him "The Bone Collector." Strangers, people from nearly every part of the world, sent notes of support, most praying to whichever God they believed in that Jusuf would find his own family, allowing him the sense of peace he'd afforded to so many others.

To almost everyone who knew of his excursions into the woods, Jusuf was a hero, a man who gave selflessly of his time to help others, to give people their families back. To himself, Jusuf was a failure. Eighteen years and he had not crossed off any one of the first five names on his list. So, he was out here again. Looking for Tata. Looking for Mama. Looking for Mirza, Demir, and, most of all, Lejla.

*****

Jusuf traipsed through the woods, heading for a portion of the forest he'd not visited much, squeezing between narrow gaps in the trees and enjoying the relative quiet of the woods. His walking stick probed the ground in front of him, brushing leaves and surface clutter aside, as he kept a keen eye open for the tell-tale gleam of white bone against the dark, healthy soil.

Jusuf stopped suddenly, crouching. He'd glimpsed a sliver of white under some leaves. He carefully brushed the pile away, heart racing, and peered into the soil. *There.* More lustrous white. His rough hands moved the earth gently, his fingers probed the ground and removed…a stone. A small, brilliant pebble. Not a bone. Jusuf dropped it to the earth and stood, brushing his hands off against his pants. Picking up his walking stick, he moved on, something that was easier physically than it was emotionally, probing the fragrant earth as he went.

*****

A teenaged Jusuf stood, filthy, shoulder to shoulder with what remained of his family, each labored breath filling his nostrils with the perfumed scents of verdant pine and rich earthy soil he knew so well. Two hours ago, they had been drinking coffee while his mother and sister prepared the day's meals, discussing the horrors of war. Now, the horrors of war were here, ten meters away, and his mother and sister were dead, their bodies lying in the back of the truck parked between the trees. Jusuf had been marched here, at gunpoint, with what was left of his family and several hundred others, all ethnic Bosniaks, each ambulatory person bound hand and foot, making it impossible to flee.

Jusuf was numb, his seventeen-year-old body unable to deal with the massive influx of emotions he'd experienced in such a short period. He should have been terrified, knowing that there could only be one reason that these soldiers would march them into a remote portion of the forest, but he wasn't. He should have been angry at the murder of his mother and sister, one a woman who cared for him since birth and the other, his best friend on earth. But he wasn't. His body didn't know how to feel, how to process this much tragedy. It had become overloaded and had simply shut down like a circuit drawing too much power. Jusuf just stood there, next to his family, intellectually knowing what had to come next, but unable to care.

The rows and lines of bound men, women, and children, nearly a thousand human beings in total, stretched far to Jusuf's left and it was from that direction that the Srpska soldiers started. They would collect ten individuals, march them off past the trucks, and then gunfire would be heard. The gunfire was the signal for the next group of soldiers to select ten more prisoners and march them off beyond the trucks, each iteration of the exercise taking roughly five minutes. Jusuf and his family were near the end of the line and had to watch and listen to their own deaths approach over the span of hours.

By three in the afternoon, there were only a few rows of prisoners left, another group having just been led off beyond the trucks. Only four soldiers remained in the immediate area, ordered to keep an eye on things and ensure no one ran off, a task that would have been very nearly impossible given two facts: the soldiers were armed and it was exceptionally difficult to run away from bullets when your stride was restricted by the half-meter length of rope tying one of your ankles to the other.

Jusuf and his family were standing, still numb, mourning the death of friends and family, when one prisoner, about ten meters to their left, attacked the nearest soldier. The prisoner, who had managed to remove the ropes from his wrists and his ankles, was much larger than the soldier he targeted and Jusuf watched as the two struggled for control of a rifle. The struggle, initially unnoticed by the remaining guards, attracted attention when the prisoner's hand and forefinger seized the weapon's grip, depressing the trigger and sending bullets spraying into the prisoners and guards alike. Four prisoners dropped, struck by random bullets, injured but not dead. One guard fell, a single round transiting his chest, tumbling through and destroying the man's heart as the bullet exited the corpse and collided with a tree. The deceased guard's partner, after ducking behind the solid trunk of a felled tree and having no wish to subject himself to the vagaries of random gunfire, pulled two grenades from his chest harness, removed the pins, and threw both over the trunk, exposing only his upper arms, wrists, and hands to danger.

The grenades landed between the Bosniak and Srpska combatants and the remaining group of prisoners, all of whom had begun to move, ducking and scurrying for cover. They went off simultaneously, sending razor-sharp shrapnel flying in all directions. The struggling prisoner and guard were killed instantly, the two of them standing upright less than a meter away from the twin blasts.

More than twenty prisoners went down, Jusuf saw, including both of his brothers. Mirza had caught a piece of shrapnel in the neck and was writhing on the ground, his constricted hands unable to grasp his throat to stop the profuse bleeding. Demir's body was prone and unmoving, a crimson stain spreading across his chest and another growing from his stomach. Jusuf's father, knocked off his feet by the blast and bleeding from his shoulder, was sitting and staring directly at Jusuf. His eyes screamed at Jusuf to run. Jusuf did not move. *Run!* The old man's eyes bellowed at him. Jusuf still did not move, frozen in place by fear.

The guard behind the fallen log lobbed one more grenade, a poorly thrown one which bounced off of a tree and skittered to a stop near Jusuf's father. There, it exploded. Jusuf watched as his father was engulfed in the explosion and felt himself knocked backwards by the blast. He laid there for a second, shell shocked, arms still tied painfully behind his back and legs splayed widely apart.

The first conscious thought that flitted across Jusuf's frantic mind was brief.

Legs splayed.

How?

He looked and felt the burning. The rope which had bound his ankles had been cut and was only hanging off of one leg, the loop around his right ankle had been severed by shrapnel from the last grenade, shrapnel which had sliced part of his ankle open. He could run.

Jusuf would not remember much of the next few hours, only really aware of the first few minutes when he had flipped over in the dirt, drawing his legs underneath him. Pushing off against the soil, he rose slightly and stumbled off into the underbrush in a wobbly crouch like a newborn deer. He had run like that for twenty minutes, crashing headlong into trees and bushes and rampaging through streams, before collapsing, partially hidden, within a collection of boulders. There, he'd maneuvered his arms past his feet and had used his teeth to remove the ropes from his wrists. He'd checked his ankle and, satisfying himself that the wound was nothing more than a deep scratch, he'd removed the length of rope and pulled himself back to his feet. Jusuf had peeked out from behind the boulders, checking every direction, listening, straining to hear the noises which would mean he'd been followed.

Hearing and seeing nothing, Jusuf had taken off again, racing through the forest, putting as much distance between himself and the horrors behind him as he could. Jusuf had spent three days running through the forests east of Srebrenica, eventually coming out near an encampment of Bosnian Army soldiers. He had collapsed within sight of the guards, two of whom approached him with rifles at the ready before calling for help. Jusuf had been carried, unconscious, into a field hospital. A week later, he was placed in a truck to a refugee camp, trundling, bouncing, and rolling to the growling of engines and the smells of diesel exhaust and human filth, through the very same forests through which he'd escaped.

*****

Jusuf had been walking through the woods for hours, searching the ground, eyes tracing over everything, his gnarled old walking stick shuffling ground cover from here to there and back again, without so much as a glimpse of anything white. He stopped and stretched his aching neck. He looked around again, listening to the sounds of the forest. He was tired and his stomach was angry, rumbling and acidic and shrunken with stress and a lack of nourishment since the early morning coffee. *Lunch. I need food.*

Jusuf looked at his watch, a simple timepiece with two silver hands on a white face and a soft, worn leather wristband the color of fresh-brewed coffee. Almost three o'clock. He saw a log, a massive tree felled simply by age, resting on its side, and he headed towards it. Jusuf sat on the trunk and eased his pack from his shoulders. Inside the knapsack, he found three sandwiches, individually wrapped and packed neatly on top of a piece of paper. Jusuf selected a sandwich, set it on his thigh, and pulled the slip of paper from the bag. It was a note, a simple sentiment from his wife, a woman who had put up with him and this quest of his for more than two decades. He looked at the note, looked at his wife's handwriting, read the words in his head.

I love you.

Jusuf Ahmetovic began to cry.

He had not cried in more than twenty years. The last time was on that truck, the one that had taken him to the refugee camp. He had cried the whole trip, everything hitting him at once. The pain, the hunger, the breaks and bruises, and, ultimately, the profound realization that he'd lost everything that mattered. His whole family was gone. His mother and father, his brothers and sister. All gone. His home, gone.

This was different. This was more than twenty years of pent-up sorrow, anger, and frustration released in racking sobs and a flood of tears that he could not stop.

Jusuf cried for all of those who had died in these woods, for all of the people he had known and returned to their families. He cried for the people he'd never known. People he'd never shared a living moment with, and yet, had somehow reunited with their loved ones. He cried for his father, a kind old man who had always been patient with his wife and children, constantly reminding them that family was the most important thing that they shared in this world. He cried for his mother, the woman who sacrificed for him, who raised him while his father had tended to the farm. He cried for his brothers, who had taught him his chores, as patiently as his father had taught them. His brothers, who had also taught him the art of the practical joke, a jovial pastime for an otherwise hard-working family. Most of all, he cried for his sister, his best friend, closest to him in age, with whom he had shared a love of reading. He cried for them all, his whole body shaking uncontrollably.

After more than an hour, Jusuf Ahmetovic stopped sobbing, the flood of emotions nearly at an end. He drew a handkerchief from his pocket. He wiped his eyes and blew his nose, his sinuses stuffy and his head aching from an emotional outlay years in the making.

An odd, unbidden thought formed in his mind as he sat there, looking around at the serene forest. *Maybe I'm not supposed to find them.* The thought was alarming, but he tried to apply an engineer's logic to it, to discover where it had come from, the design behind it.

In the last eighteen years, I've found thousands of bones. Why? To help people?

Is that it?

He didn't think so. There was something different. He thought, hard.

I never meant to find the other people. That was never my purpose. I've always prayed that I would find my family. Why am I so desperate to find the bones of the five people I know are here? Because they were family? No. That wasn't completely it. There was something else. What was different?

He muttered aloud.

"Think Jusuf, think."

An idea formed, slowly at first. A single word. *Burial.* He let the word tumble out past his lips, speaking to the trees around him.

"Burial."

Over the last eighteen years, he had given the families of the victims the ability to carry out the simple Islamic burial rites that their loved ones deserved. Bathing the remains, wrapping them in a shroud, and the utterance of a simple prayer, a salat, before interment, was a simple ritual that he had been denied.

Was it that simple?

It was, he knew. Jusuf knew. In that instant, he knew.

He was jealous. For years he had enabled others to perform this ritual for their loved ones, and he was jealous, wanting the opportunity to restore dignity to his family, to perform that crucial service to his mother, father, brothers and sister. And all that held him up, for all of these years, was the idea that he did not possess something concrete to bury, the bodies were not physically present in his hands, but he knew they were here somewhere and that this place, this forest with its excitable, scurrying little creatures and vibrant foliage, a place that had been washed clean by the very waters of nature itself, was as beautiful a place to be buried as he had ever known.

Jusuf moved slowly and purposefully from the fallen log and stood in the middle of the small clearing. Using a bottle of water and a clean towel pulled from his pack, he washed his hands and face, the dirt and grime of the day falling from the towel and returning to the earth at his feet. He stood there, trembling slightly. surrounded by the ghosts of the past, performing his own private salat for his family. When he was done, his supplication to Allah on behalf of his family complete, he smiled, and his shoulders rose, the burden he'd borne for more than twenty years dissolving in the sparkling rays of sunlight.

Jusuf went back to the log, and began to collect his belongings, knowing that it was getting late and his wife would begin to worry about him. He noticed the wrapped sandwich on the ground and knelt to pick it up, feeling a sharp prick in his knee. Jusuf jerked back instinctively, nearly falling over. Rubbing the sore spot on his knee, Jusuf looked at the ground.

He expected to see a rock or a branch from one of the brambles nearby. Instead, among a small pile of richly colored flora, he saw a sliver of white.

A bone?

Jusuf carefully excavated the fragment with his fingers, brushing off the dirt and mud. It was a bone. He looked at it closely. Possibly a femur, part of someone's upper leg. Jusuf stood, placing the bone in the pouch on his hip and withdrawing the notebook. He penciled in the location and the type of bone he thought he'd found, tucked the notebook back in his breast pocket, and finished packing his belongings. He looked at the area once more, smiling this time, and turned for home.

Jusuf was still smiling when he returned home. He climbed the ladder into the small loft above the kitchen and eased the pack from his shoulders. He unhooked the pouch from his hip and then took the small notebook from his pocket before going about the business of transposing the day's find to the map affixed to one wall. He pulled a red pin from a small, wooden box which sat on top of a battered copy of *The Count of Monte Cristo* and stuck it in the appropriate place on the map to mark the spot he'd annotated in the old notebook. He backed up, looked at the large map, and then headed to the kitchen for dinner.

"Find anything today?" His wife hugged him.

"Just one bone. Maybe a femur."

"Where?" She placed two bowls of soup on the table and took a seat next to him. They always sat on the same side of the table.

Jusuf explained where. She looked at him curiously. "You seem different today. You're smiling."

Jusuf grunted. *How do I explain?*

"I buried my family today."

He watched for her reaction. She was waiting for more. He

explained. He told her about the clearing and his thoughts. He went on for more than a half hour, trying to describe how he'd felt, what he'd thought. She listened intently, watched his face. When he finished talking, she said nothing. She simply leaned in and gave him a kiss.

After they finished eating, Marija pointed at a small wall calendar.

"It's the end of the month, Jusuf. The students will come in the morning to pick up the fragments."

"I know. I'll pack them up after I clean up the kitchen."

She walked to him and wrapped her arms around his midsection. "Go ahead, Jusuf. I'll clean up."

After a prolonged hug, Jusuf climbed back into the loft. He quickly packed up all of his October findings, wrapping each bone carefully in plastic and cotton. He numbered each fragment with a wire and paper tag and included a handwritten sheet of paper that described each bone, where he had found it, what he thought it was. Jusuf then placed all of these items in a plastic shipping box and sealed the lid, placing the box by the door for the representative from the university to find.

Jusuf slept in the next morning, a rare thing. He and his wife had stayed up late discussing literature, much in the way they had in college. Much the way he and Lejla had. When Jusuf finally went out to the picnic table to have his cup of coffee, he noted that the shipping container had already been picked up.

He smiled.

*****

Jusuf Ahmetovic sat at the battered picnic table watching as black smoke, carrying that burnt wood fragrance characterizing winter's frosty arrival and drifting heavily away from the chimney on the left side of the house. Through the small kitchen window, he could see his wife cooking the meals for the coming day. Jusuf looked around the farm, a fresh blanket of clean, sparkling snow covered everything in sight while a lone sheep braved the cold, trotting here and there for no reason other than sheer curiosity. The frigid, crisp air of a winter day bit into his hands and crept inside his coat, causing a small shiver as he raised the coffee to his lips.

A noise caught Jusuf's attention and he turned to find it. There, at the bottom of the hill leading from Srebrenica, a truck lumbered up the curving road, taking the corners slowly and carefully, the rugged outline visible between the trunks and branches of the barren trees. *The students from the university*, thought Jusuf, feeling just a little guilty. He'd taken time away from his search after that day in late October, using the break to recover and reflect. By the time he'd felt ready to resume the searching, a series of early winter snows had blanketed the region. Searching for white bones in a sea of white powder was a nearly impossible task. He knew that and the staff at the college understood. Still, there was an unofficial protocol to this search, an unspoken understanding between the searcher and the scientists, more courtesy than anything. And here it was, the last day in January and he had forgotten to send word that he had not found anything this month. *Those poor students, driving up that road for nothing.*

Well, at least I can offer them some coffee.

The truck made the final turn and lurched into the yard, the young driver trying to maneuver the large vehicle, an old military truck, without stalling the manual transmission. When it stopped, the cab doors opened, and a single man got out, walked straight to Jusuf, and handed over a sheet of paper and a small brown box secured with a piece of twine. Jusuf took the package and folded sheet and looked at the man, wanting to explain that he had found nothing this month.

Something about the man stopped Jusuf from speaking. The man, one of the professors at the school, had a strange look on his face, a half-smile he was trying to hide behind some sort of dignified façade he'd probably learned by performing hundreds of lectures. He nodded toward the sheet of paper in Jusuf's right hand. Jusuf looked down, unfolded the paper, read the printed email.

January 31, 2020

Dr. Hukic,

Please let Mr. Ahmetovic know that we are grateful for his continuing efforts to locate the remains of victims of the Srebrenica genocides of July 1995. His dedication over the past two decades has helped identify more than four-hundred victims and has provided closure to thousands of survivors and their families.

It is also my pleasure to inform Mr. Ahmetovic that the remains shipped to our university on October 31, 2019 contained a bone fragment of particular interest to him. The bone in question was collected on October 30, 2019 and is indeed a femur belonging to a young girl. After extensive DNA testing, our laboratory is able to conclude, with 99.997 percent certainty, that that bone fragment belonged to one Lejla Ahmetovic, aged 15.

I have enclosed the remains in this package. Please see that it is delivered to Mr. Ahmetovic.

Sincerely,

Dr. Amar Marjanovic

Two hours later, after having bathed the bone, Jusuf wrapped the fragment in a small white shroud and buried it in the sunniest part of the yard, saying a brief salat while he did so. When the short, but dignified ceremony was complete, Jusuf Ahmetovic cried for only the third time in twenty-four years.

Gun Love

J. T. Townley

The shots came from inside Shooters. Gun shots, not the usual tequila and oysters. Thomas unzipped his backpack and aimed his Canon, just as the disheveled man stumbled backwards across the sidewalk, .12-gauge smoking. Thomas framed the shot. The man pumped the action, chambering a new shell, then pointed the barrel at Thomas.

Don't shoot! Thomas said.

The man took half a step closer. Hollow cheeks, patchy hair coming off in fistfuls, skin a strange green pallor despite the September sunshine. You work here? he growled.

Only part-time, said Thomas, still rolling.

The man was almost close enough now to jab Thomas in the ribs. A fetid miasma drifted on the hot breeze, road kill and swamp rot and Old Spice. Furry on the tongue.

Service is terrible, he said.

Thomas nodded, trying not to stare at the mud smeared across the man's face, the clods of dirt in his ears, the overlarge, decomposing suit.

Nice gun, said Thomas.

Smith & Wesson, the man said. Or is this my Winchester? Eyesight's completely shot.

Can I have a look? said Thomas.

The man took a step back, eyes wide. From my cold, dead hands! he yawped.

You remind me of someone.

The man's smile looked like a snarl. Call me Charlie, he said, extending a greenish hand.

It felt glacial. And spongy.

Thomas, said Thomas, taking short, shallow breaths.

Charlie clicked on the safety and lowered the barrel, but kept a hawkish watch on the door. What's with the camera?

I'm a documentarian.

A filmmaker?

Of documentaries.

Thomas held his breath and leaned in. He caught a quick peek of the gun's label. Remington, he said.

Ole Bess, said Charlie. How I love this gun! Blow a hole in a man's gut you could drive a truck through.

Sirens wailed down Hollywood Boulevard.

Listen, Charlie, can I give you a lift somewhere? He pointed at a metallic blue Prius. This is me.

Charlie nodded, wiping slime from his nose. Figures, he said.

They were sipping espresso at the kitchen table, or Thomas was, when his roommates came home.

Jezus, what's that smell? said Liz, black bra visible through her *Je suis Charlie* t-shirt.

Patrick covered his mouth and nose. Who died? he said.

You'll never guess, said Thomas.

You can't keep bringing these guys home, said Liz, chewing her lip. I know it's harsh, but that's what shelters are for.

Wait, he's that guy, right? From those old movies? Patrick

puckered his face and pinched an imaginary cigarette from his lip. So many guns around town these days, he said, and so few brains.

Je suis Charlie, said Charlie.

Solidarity! Liz said.

Thomas turned to the man. Do the thing, Charlie.

The what?

Patrick poured steaming water over cinnamon-apple tea bags, then handed a mug to Liz. They held the aromatic beverages just below their noses.

The thing, said Thomas. The *thing*.

Liz pointed at the Remington leaning against the wall and said, Is that a gun?

Why is there a shotgun in our house? Patrick said.

If in the first act you have hung a pistol on the wall, then in the following one it should be fired. Otherwise don't put it there.

We're bending the rules a little today, said Thomas.

Liz set her tea on the table, then took three steps across the tile, reaching for the .12-gauge. Before she'd even touched it, Charlie grabbed the shotgun and held it out before him like a samurai sword.

From my cold, dead hands! he bellowed.

Omigawd, said Liz.

Why didn't you say so? Patrick asked.

Liz shook her head, beaming. Do you know what this means?

That evening over takeout from Sari, Thomas explained everything. The chance encounter outside Shooters. The early footage. The documentary they'd always wanted to make.

Like that *Columbine* whatever, said Patrick.

Only better, Liz said.

That what's-his-name's a liberal commie douche bag, Charlie said. He sat in the papasan chair in the corner, looking dour.

Along with the Nag Champa Liz lit, the fragrant odors of biriyani, tikka masala, and vindaloo went a long way to mask their new friend's heinous funk.

I don't want to make another propaganda film, Thomas mused, forefinger on chin. I want to step out of my politics, look at this issue objectively. After all, guns don't kill people.

People kill people, said Charlie, massaging Ole Bess.

Thomas's roommates fidgeted.

You're kidding, right? said Liz.

What's wrong with a fair and balanced perspective?

Patrick shook his head. You realize that's the Fox News motto?

The gun nuts don't need another voice, Liz insisted.

They've got the NRA, said Patrick, the most powerful special interest group in America.

And we've got their most famous president, Thomas said. Money, connections, one of the biggest private gun collections in the world.

They stared at the man. He stared at his gun. The rice grew cold and clumpy.

Welcome to Bigshot Filmwerks, Thomas said.

Some production company, said Charlie, wheezing with laughter.

They listened to the fan thump incense smoke around the room. What sounded like gunshots echoed in the near distance.

So, said Liz, when do we start shooting?

Thomas grinned. We already have.

It took a couple-three days of arm-twisting, but Charlie eventually gave in. He probably just needed a place to stay. Still, he offered to show Thomas his gun vault. He offered to introduce Thomas to other firearms aficionados, including famous actors, musicians, and politicians. He even offered to bankroll the entire production.

That's amazing, said Patrick.

Any strings? Liz wondered.

Thomas gazed at Charlie, who spent most of his time out on the back deck, cleaning and oiling his .12-gauge.

Not strings exactly, he said. Let's call them *conditions*.

Here we go, said Liz.

Anything we can't live with? asked Patrick.

Thomas struck his pensive pose, watching Charlie reassemble his weapon. It was clear the old man had done it thousands of times before.

Don't worry, guys, he said. I've got this.

They started in earnest the next day. Thomas parked his Prius outside the Los Angeles Gun Club, then followed Charlie inside, film rolling. The picture jounced with each awkward step. The place seemed crowded for the middle of the afternoon.

Long time, no see, said the man behind the counter. Where you been hiding?

Charlie raked dirt off his shoulder like dandruff. New digs, he said.

We were all just sick when we heard.

Appreciate that, Harlon.

Staying long?

Long enough to set this joker straight.

Thomas, said Thomas, still rolling.

Sorry, bud, no cameras.

Thomas turned to Charlie, but kept the camera pointed at Harlon.

We're working on something, Harlon. Could you make an exception? I'd think of it as a personal favor.

He gave Thomas an exaggerated head-to-toe. Anything for you, Charlie. Just keep this greenhorn out of trouble.

Harlon comped them a Beretta PX4 Storm, a hundred rounds of ammo, and a couple of targets. Charlie coached Thomas through the basics, safety and trigger, grip and sight.

Watch that recoil, said Charlie.

Thomas passed Charlie his Canon, showed him on and record, focus, and zoom. They strapped on their ear protectors and shooting glasses. Then Thomas went to town, squeezing off ten quick rounds, only landing one shot, in the top left corner. Otherwise, he hit the wall, other shooters' targets, the ceiling, even punched out a couple lights. Thomas killed another dozen rounds with similar results. Finally, Charlie motioned for him to stop.

How'd I do?

Kid, said Charlie, that's the worst shooting I've ever seen.

They went to the gun club every day for a hundred rounds, usually in the afternoon, though sometimes in the evening, depending on Thomas's shifts at Shooters. It took a week for Thomas to hit his own target, two weeks before he hit it where he was aiming. In another week, Thomas could put multiple shots in the head and heart.

Nice work, Tommygun, said Charlie.

Thomas's face hurt from smiling so big.

On the way back to Bigshot Filmwerks, they stopped at Locked 'n' Loaded, where Charlie bought Thomas a Glock 9 mm, a shoulder holster, and a thousand rounds. The owner, who had a swastika tattooed on his forehead, helped them load the ammo in the back of Thomas's Prius, which was now mysteriously plastered with NRA stickers. As they stood there in the parking lot, particulate matter shimmering in the gray September sunlight, Charlie patted Thomas on the back and said:

Proud of you, kid.

Thomas beamed, strapping on the holster, stowing his Glock.

Now you can defend your family against recidivist scumbags who think the world owes them something.

Patrick and Liz seemed less than thrilled about Thomas's new sidearm. When Charlie was outside cleaning and oiling his shotgun, they sat Thomas down for a production team meeting.

Where's this going? Patrick asked.

Should we be concerned? wondered Liz.

Thomas wiped the goo from his Canon. The footage was shaky and poorly framed, but he didn't let on. It's a small price to pay, he said.

You realize you're carrying a concealed weapon? said Liz.

Without a permit? Patrick said.

Thomas hacked on Nag Champa smoke. Liz kept it burning twenty-four-seven. Charlie was staying in Thomas's room, since they hoped to contain the stench, but it had seeped beneath the door and permeated the house.

Would you two stop all the hand-wringing?

Patrick and Liz faked smiles. Outside, someone screamed, then the *pop pop pop* of semi-automatic gunfire. Thomas went for his Glock.

Shooter! yelled Liz and hit the deck.

Please put the gun away, Patrick said, rigid in his chair.

It's only firecrackers, said Liz from under the table.

Someone's motorcycle.

A car backfiring.

Thomas looked at his friends, laughed, and holstered his weapon. When he glanced through the back window, Charlie was on alert, .12-gauge reassembled, a shell in the chamber. They made eye contact. Charlie gave him a thumbs-up and a wet, ghoulish grin.

The next day, they hopped the Santa Monica freeway, then took Highway 1 to Malibu. Charlie flubbed the security code a couple of times, but soon they were through a service entrance, then down in the basement. The old man spun a dial, right, left, right, then cranked open a steel door three feet thick. The Vault. Charlie showed him around, offered a little history of the collection, pointed out some of his favorites. Thomas had never seen anything like it: hundreds of handguns, hunting rifles, and shotguns, as well as semi-automatic assault rifles and submachine guns, bazookas, and missile launchers, plus heavy-duty .50 caliber machine guns and anti-aircraft weapons. He struggled to take it all in, aiming his Canon everywhere at once. Most of the footage, jumpy and erratic, would prove unusable.

The whole thing made Thomas dizzy, also a little queasy, though maybe that was Charlie's funk in an enclosed space. After all, wasn't it like-minded gun nuts with huge weapons caches who enacted all manner of murderous atrocities, from Columbine to Virginia Tech to Sandy Hook? He tried not to let it get to him. Wasn't the whole point to walk around in the other guy's shoes, or combat boots, for a while? Try to understand that weird paradox of patriotism and libertarian fervor, Second Amendment absolutism and survivalist paranoia? To fall in gun love, if only for ninety minutes?

Before they left, Charlie offered Thomas a memento from the Vault.

AK-47, he said. Most famous assault rifle in the world.

I can't take this, said Thomas.

Forget it, kid. I have six more.

It was Charlie's idea to find a parking garage in Culver City and take the bus. When they stepped to the curb a dozen stops later, theirs were the only pale faces in sight. Thomas hit record and tried to keep his hands steady.

The hood? he said.

Gunshots reverberated through the blue day.

Brace yourself, kid.

He felt the bass thumping in his chest before he ever saw the house. Cracked sidewalks, sagging chain link, yard full of weeds. Men on the porch in baggy pants and backwards baseball caps, all of them enormous and reeking of sweat and cannabis. Pistols similar to Thomas's hung from their waistbands. They nodded at Charlie. No one smiled.

Inside was just as crowded. They checked their firearms at the door, then pushed their way through the marijuana haze to a back room. A man who resembled the others, maybe a little older, a little more bling, sat on a drooping couch smoking a blunt, head bobbing to the rhythm.

Sup, Chuck, he said as they filed in.

Thomas, meet Iceberg.

You look just like that gangsta rapper.

Charlie grimaced, but didn't waste any time giving Iceberg the lowdown.

This get back to the po-po, I bust a cap in yo ass.

It took Thomas a minute to realize the comment was aimed at him. Right, he said, of course, naturally.

Ahight then, shoot.

Thomas aimed his Canon, framed his shot, and asked Iceberg about the Second Amendment, mass murders, and gun control.

You think them shooters waiting in line at the gun sto? Hell, no. All that background check bidness just bullshit. Political half-stepping. Real question is, Why the gov'ment ain't give every man, woman, and chil' a gun *fo free*?

Then Iceberg went on a rambling diatribe about firearms, racism, and the Man's systematic efforts to rid the nation of Blacks. Thomas tried to keep an open mind. Still, he couldn't follow most of it, perhaps only because of the contact high. When, an hour later,

Iceberg finally trailed off, blinking against the smoke and staring out the window, Thomas knew it was time to go.

Y'all take some indo, said Iceberg, holding out a dime bag.

No thanks, said Thomas. I've had plenty already.

Speak for yourself, said Charlie. He palmed the bag of weed and stuffed it in the pocket of his shabby suit jacket.

Then Iceberg pulled a gun from beneath the couch cushion easy as flashing his grill. Thomas was sure he'd made a mistake—refusing the gift, recording the interview, following Charlie foolishly into the heart of South Central. Still, he kept rolling, cool under fire.

What you got there? asked Charlie.

Pistol-grip sawed-off.

.10-gauge?

Yup.

Charlie inspected it. Nice, he said, face aglow.

Fo the kid.

Charlie passed the gun to Thomas, who made sure to get a clear shot of it before he took it with his offhand.

Appreciate it, said Thomas.

Keep it real, my niggas.

They were already pushing through the mob scene when Iceberg said:

Get some rest, Chuck. You ain't look so good.

Back at Bigshot central, Patrick was working on a photo collage, reimagining his ex's head onto the bodies of various animals, both barnyards and exotics. Liz was mixing a kale-pineapple-spinach smoothie. They were blasting old school Guns N' Roses, singing along at the top of their lungs. Soon as Thomas and Charlie walked in, Liz scurried around lighting the Nag Champa. Patrick put the ceiling fans on high and opened the windows. They both plastered on fake smiles until Charlie trudged off to his room, claiming he wasn't feeling well. When he was gone, Patrick said:

What's the deal?

Too much pot.

You're high? Liz shrieked.

Thomas burst out laughing, much longer and giddier than usual. Even he knew he was completely blazed—and he hadn't smoked a thing!

What the hell's going on with you, man? said Patrick.

Did you completely forget about the house rules? asked Liz.

No guns.

No drugs.

I know, I know, Thomas said. Absolutely no country music.

Patrick folded his arms across his chest. Then why'd you come home high?

Carrying an arsenal that would make Rambo proud?

It's a dangerous world out there, said Thomas, pawing at the assault rifle and shotgun. It's a world full of madmen and uncertainty and potential mental losses.

Next thing we know, Liz suggested, you'll start wearing boots—

And Wrangler jeans—

One of those huge Texas-shaped belt buckles.

You'll drink longnecks and do the two-step—

And call everyone *darlin'*.

Okay, okay, I take your point, said Thomas, grinning. But aren't we making a movie?

Documentary, Patrick clarified.

A work of substance and gravitas, explained Liz.

That's right, he said. Exactly!

Though Charlie was looking worse than usual, he woke Thomas early the next day, poking him in the gut with the barrel of Ole Bess.

Rise and shine, kid. We've got a plane to catch.

Bleary-eyed, Thomas hit record as they packed their weapons—Charlie, his shotgun, Thomas, his Glock—according to TSA regulations. Firearms must be unloaded and locked in a hard-sided container and transported as checked baggage only.

Thomas kept rolling as they checked in, too, expecting problems, which would be a boon, adding dramatic tension to whatever story it was he was trying to tell.

The desk agent just smiled and wished them a safe flight.

They went Back East, to places Thomas had never even considered. Charlie knew everyone. They met with mobsters in Boston and white supremacists outside of Pittsburgh. Thomas interviewed a biker gang in rural Ohio and flag-waving Confederates across the Deep South. They even met with a representative of Precision Firepower, an ammunition company, at a swanky steakhouse in Chicago. People seemed grateful for the chance to voice their opinions, even if most everyone was fairly inarticulate, ranting in clichés, platitudes, and expletives. They were all dyed-in-the-wool gun nuts, and proud of it: *When in doubt, shoot it out!*

Thomas just kept his mouth shut and the camera rolling. They sent him away with hardware aplenty: .38 Special and Walther PPK, Luger P08, and MAC-10. Plus, enough ammunition to start his own militia.

After about a week on the road, they went to Austin, where they heard gunshots before they were even off the jet bridge. Thomas steadied his Canon and hit record. Guys in boots and jeans and leather vests were firing across the terminal at men in gray western-cut suits and black felt Stetsons. They blasted shop windows and overhead fluorescents, arrival monitors and blaring TVs, but little else. Still, bullets were zinging and ricocheting every which way. It was the Wild West.

At the rental car counter, Thomas wanted a Prius, but this was Texas, so they settled on a silver Silverado, then drove over to campus. Fall semester was in full swing, students chatting, laughing, flinging Frisbees across grassy knolls. Everyone carried handguns—undergrads, teaching assistants, faculty of every discipline and rank. Thomas spotted pistols in shoulder carriers and low-slung cowboy holsters, in front waistbands and against the smalls of backs. Handguns large and small protruded from messenger bags and backpacks, satchels and briefcases.

Charlie worked Ole Bess's pump action. Thomas chambered a round in his Glock.

They met a man, sixtyish and graying, face cut with deep ravines. He wore an expensive tailored suit and a red tie, and he flashed a steely perma-grin. He and Charlie greeted each other like long-lost brothers. Thomas followed them up the elevator to the observation deck of the campus tower. The man, some sort of politician, bloviated at length about the Tower Sniper, a former Marine who knew his way around firearms. Years ago he brought some impressive firepower up here—Remington 700 ADL and Universal M1 carbine, .12-gauge shotgun and Galesi-Brescia pistol—and gunned down sixteen students, professors, and police, wounding thirty-two more.

Our new campus carry law puts an end to all that, the politician explained.

Thomas captured the synthetic gleam in the man's smile, then panned toward the hollering below. A freshman in a baseball cap was screaming at a balding professor, blue book in one hand, Walther PPK in the other. The prof's colleague aimed a .44 Magnum at the student. The student's buddy aimed an Uzi at the prof's colleague. The prof's colleague's graduate assistant aimed an AK-47 at the student's buddy—and on and on, dominos tumbling, to eight, ten, twenty degrees of separation.

Are you seeing this? said Thomas, still rolling.

For a moment, the yelling stopped. Thomas held his breath.

Then a *pop* like the first Blackcat on New Year's. A scream. More shots, more screams. Bodies everywhere, people running, limping, crawling for their lives. Emergency sirens down the Drag. The tang of cordite on Thomas's tongue. A haze of smoke rising into the air, spoiling his shot.

Happiness is a warm gun.

Now they traipsed across the West, visiting Indians in New Mexico and Arizona and working cowboys in Wyoming. Thomas interviewed survivalists in northern Idaho, who lived on difficult-to-access compounds deep in the mountains and seemed to be awaiting the Apocalypse. Charlie had connections with pimps, hustlers, and casino magnates in Las Vegas, who were all happy to share their two cents about gun rights. They went to smoky VFW halls, where Thomas listened to vets from every conflict since World War II rhapsodize about the significance of personal firearms. And they chatted with hard working folks of every stripe, from accountants to landscapers, cardiologists to bus drivers, who said they only felt safe with a loaded gun or three in the house. Thomas's arsenal continued to swell: .357 Magnum, M16, L42 Enfield sniper rifle.

When they landed at SFO, Charlie almost didn't wake up. Everyone had already disembarked before Thomas brought him around. The flight attendants feigned concern. The pilots forced smiles, holding their breath, and nodding. Thomas holstered his Glock, then found a chair for Charlie near the rental car counter and used the old man's Platinum card for a Prius. The old man was already asleep when Thomas strapped him into the passenger seat.

They hadn't been in the car five minutes when Thomas's phone chirped.

Dude, finally? said Patrick.

Where have you been? wondered Liz.

Why? said Thomas. What's up?

Cops, said Liz.

Something about a shooting at Shooters, Patrick explained.

Right, said Thomas, that.

Why didn't you tell us? Liz whined.

We could be in deep shit, said Patrick.

Harboring a fugitive.

Aiding and abetting.

Took them long enough, Thomas said.

A twenty-something blonde in a Beemer convertible came out of nowhere and cut Thomas off. When he laid on his horn, she flipped him the bird and hit the brakes. He whipped out his Glock and punched several holes in her trunk, then blew out a back tire and sent her fishtailing off the highway. Charlie grunted awake.

Where are you anyway? asked Liz.

San Francisco.

Why in hell are we in San Francisco? yelled Charlie.

Get back to L.A., said Patrick.

And answer your phone, Liz said.

Before Thomas could end the call, Charlie grabbed his phone and threw it out the window. Turn the car around, he insisted. We're headed south, not into this godforsaken fairyland.

They pulled off Highway 1 south of Monterey. The air was sweet with cypress and eucalyptus. A cool breeze brought salt air off the Pacific.

Where are we? Thomas asked.

Never heard of Carmel, kid?

Caramel soy frappuccinos?

RUNNING WILD ANTHOLOGY OF STORIES VOLUME 6

Jezus, you weak-kneed, bedwetting liberal shlubs. Charlie hacked for a while, then spat a wad of greenish gunk out the window. Now keep driving, he said.

A guy almost as old as Charlie met them at the gate and led them around the house onto a deck in the sunshine. Charlie called him Harry. The sound of crashing waves surrounded them, but the ocean was nowhere in sight. A maid brought a pair of whiskey sours, and everybody pretended that Thomas and his Canon didn't exist.

You don't look so good, said Harry.

C'est la vie.

Harry nodded, crinkling his prominent forehead. So what's it like?

Cold and damp, said Charlie. Lonely.

Sounds awful.

And not a gun to be had.

Even worse!

They sipped their whiskeys in comfortable silence, mortality hanging in the air between them like sea spray. They shared a glance, then knocked back the last of their drinks. Thomas thought he heard faint trickling, so he panned and zoomed: amber liquid pooling on the tiles beneath Charlie's chair.

Come on, said Harry. Let's go shoot something.

For forty-five minutes, they blasted away at anything that moved, mainly birds. Not that they hit much. The Canon was propped in the crotch of a cypress, but Thomas couldn't vouch for the framing. At least he'd get the audio: steady pistol pops, screeching seagulls, the odd *Hell, yeah!*

Harry had his chef barbecue the birds. When they'd eaten, he walked Thomas and Charlie to the gate.

Keep up the good work, old buddy, said Harry. Then a Smith &

Wesson .44 Magnum with an eight inch barrel materialized in his hand, perhaps from a shoulder holster Thomas hadn't noticed. Harry opened the loaded cylinder, gave it a spin, then snapped it back in place with a practiced flick of the wrist. He let the pistol fall forward, holding it by the trigger guard, and thrust it through the open window of the Prius.

Don't look a gift horse in the mouth, kid.

Thomas took the heavy revolver. Are you sure?

Go ahead, said Harry. Make my day.

Check-in at SFO took a while, given the sheer number of firearms, not to mention Charlie's worsening state. By now, except for a small patch above his left ear, he was entirely bald. His greenish pallor was punctuated with occasional black splotches, including on his cheeks and forehead. The stench hadn't improved, either, so Thomas doused him with Tommy for Men they bought in Duty Free.

As they taxied, Thomas asked, What the hell's in Anchorage?

Outside of Anchorage, Charlie clarified. North and East.

Okay?

Friend of mine.

Long way to go.

Charlie scoffed. I thought you were a *documentarian*?

Annoying finger quotes.

I'm just saying, said Thomas. You don't look so good.

Charlie hacked, offering a limp, dismissive wave.

The flight was bumpy on takeoff and landing, with plenty of rollercoaster turbulence in between. After a jerky shuttle ride, Charlie paid the driver, finger gunk sticking to the bills, while Thomas puked in the shrubbery.

Charlie beat the knocker. A Bull Mastiff gave a guttural woof. Thomas aimed his Canon and framed the shot. A minute later, a fifty-something woman with auburn hair and rimless glasses swung the door wide, Colt .45 revolver in each hand.

Charlie!

Back from the capital, I see.

How'd Juneau?

Sally served them a Molson. Every citizen's inalienable right to bear arms is enshrined in the Constitution, she insisted. What more's there to say?

Ten minutes later, they were aboard a private helicopter *womp-womping* over a meadow in a virgin forest, gazing at a herd of elk through high-powered Bushnell scopes mounted to loaded BAR .30-06 rifles. The copilot was filming. Charlie took the first shot and missed.

You're falling to pieces, old man! Sally goaded.

It was true. Charlie was looking worse for the wear, though at least all the air flow up there kept the rotten funk at bay. He fumbled to reload, then took another shot and missed again. Though he looked like he was made of candle wax, when he fired the third time, he hit his mark.

Now you're talking! said Sally.

The herd scattered, leaping and darting in every direction. Still, Sally leaned out of the chopper, led her target, and downed the next elk not two minutes later.

Now it was Thomas's turn.

Let's go, candy ass! Sally yelled.

Take the goddamn shot! said Charlie.

Thomas aimed and inhaled, closed his eyes and pulled the trigger. The rifle's recoil nearly knocked him out of the helicopter. His right shoulder and arm went numb. But Thomas ground his teeth, working the bolt action to chamber another shell, then took a bead and, without thinking, pulled the trigger. A smallish elk went down.

Attaboy! said Sally.

Charlie clapped him on the back. Nice shot!

They landed in the meadow, and Thomas watched through his Canon as Sally field dressed the elk. Charlie lay down on a mossy log and fell asleep.

You wanna know why I'm a staunch supporter of gun rights? said Sally.

Thomas was having a hard time keeping the camera steady, what with all the gore. She was elbow-deep in entrails, blood smeared across her cheeks and forehead. A stench worse than Charlie hung in the crisp autumn blue.

Well, kid, here's your answer.

Back in L.A., Thomas loaded the Prius with elk venison and the .30-06 Sally had given him, plus the rest of the firearms he'd acquired. The trunk was packed. Charlie lay down in the backseat. He was looking worse and worse, if that was possible, greenish and hunched and wheezing, though he probably just needed some rest. Anyway, Thomas didn't let it get him down. He couldn't wait to show Patrick and Liz the footage.

But they both seemed edgy.

Cops have been back, said Patrick.

Twice, Liz clarified.

They want to talk to you.

And Charlie.

He's in no condition for that.

What's wrong with him? said Liz.

Is he okay? Patrick asked.

Well, no. He's—you know.

They nodded, swallowing what they couldn't admit.

The next morning, Thomas awoke to a yelp, then a scream. He rolled off the couch to find Liz pointing at a mound of goo in the hallway that used to pass for Charlie's left arm. His right leg was in the bathroom. They followed the slime trail to the closed door of Thomas's bedroom.

Charlie? said Thomas, knocking.

What's going on? Patrick asked.

Careful where you step, said Liz.

He knocked again, then pushed into the room. A wall of green funk. They covered their noses and surveyed the scene. It wasn't pretty. Charlie's left foot was under the desk, still shod in Florsheim wingtips. His right arm was on the windowsill, and his head was wedged in the corner next to the dresser, upside down and covered in cobwebs. They found the rest of him in bed, leaking through the sheets. Liz flung open the window. Patrick pulled the door shut, stuffing wet towels into the crack.

Thomas went to the hardware store for rubber gloves and industrial aprons, respirator masks and heavy-duty garbage bags. Also, a trio of matching shovels.

They dug a hole in the backyard. It took all night. Thomas set his Canon up on a tripod, though the lighting was bad. After daybreak espressos, they scooped what was left of Charlie into trash bags and put them in the hole. Ole Bess went in, too. Patrick and Liz raked the dirt back in, while Thomas, voice trembling, mumbled:

From my cold, dead hands.

A crime scene company scrubbed the floors, then hauled off the mattress. Thomas repainted his room, bought a futon, aired the place out for days and days. Liz redoubled her Nag Champa efforts, burning it around the clock in every room. Patrick roasted coffee beans in the living room. Thomas brewed IPA in the kitchen. Nothing seemed to help, so they stuffed earplugs in their nostrils and started postproduction.

The material was amazing. Patrick and Liz were blown away. Had Thomas *really* witnessed those shootouts? Had he *really* hunted elk from a helicopter? The audio could be exceptional, especially when guns were being fired, which happened a lot, but sometimes it was difficult to hear the interviews because of the mumbling and static and ambient noise. Nor were the images flawless: jouncy and out of focus, badly framed and poorly lit.

Good stuff, said Patrick.

Nice work, said Liz.

Thomas knew what they meant: *Not much to work with.*

Still, they labored on *Gun Love* whenever they had free time—and all Thomas had was time, since he'd been fired from Shooters for no-showing three consecutive shifts. He watched every hour of footage, then watched it again. In fact, he spent most of his waking hours in front of his laptop, pulling out his hair. He couldn't see the story for the guns.

Police detectives dropped by on half a dozen occasions, early in the morning, late at night, whenever the mood caught them. Thomas played it cool, though his cache of illegal weapons was hidden in the hall closet. As it turned out, no one had been killed in the Shooters shooting, not even injured. Thomas and his friends politely refused the cops' repeated requests to search the premises. L.A.'s Finest never produced a warrant.

Weeks passed. Thomas obsessed. The house eventually aired out.

The idea hit him after a dreamless sleep. Thomas awoke on his futon, drenched in a pool of radioactive sunlight, Santa Anas rattling the window panes. He bolted down to Locked 'n' Loaded, where he procured cargo pants and t-shirts, balaclavas and combat boots, all in Special Ops black. They had Patrick's and Liz's sizes, too. He acquired a pair of high-powered Bushnell scopes, one for the Enfield, the other for the .30-06, and three bullet-proof vests. He bought ammo for every weapon in his arsenal. Everything went on Charlie's Platinum card.

Thomas donned his new duds, then interrupted Liz's yoga and Patrick's meditation. Put these on, he said. We leave in ten.

Why? said Patrick.

Where? said Liz.

Big shoot in University Park.

Thomas attached the scopes and loaded his weapons. He placed the rifles and shotgun in a duffel, and put the duffel in the trunk of his Prius. He made sure his Canon was charged and remembered the tripod. When everything was ready, Thomas handed Liz the .38 Special and Patrick the .44 Magnum. He had his Glock, plus the Luger and MAC-10.

It took forty-five minutes to drive ten miles. They blasted Guns N' Roses the whole way.

Thomas found a spot for the Prius in Exposition Park. They pulled on their balaclavas despite the suffocating heat and double-checked their handguns. Thomas passed Patrick the duffel, then pointed the Canon and yelled:

Rolling!

They skulked across the street to campus. People were used to film shoots, even guerrilla documentary crews, so no one gave them a second glance. In less than five minutes, they were up the clock tower and out on the observation deck, a hundred and forty feet up. Patrick blocked the door with a trash barrel. Liz set up the tripod and attached the Canon. Thomas unzipped the duffel. He handed Patrick the AK-47 and passed the .10-gauge to Liz.

Why are we doing this? she asked.

What are we even doing? Patrick wondered.

Thomas checked the M16 and .30-06, then positioned the

Enfield, and sprawled out on the concrete. He had no training, but he'd seen lots of sniper movies.

Am I in the frame? he asked.

Thomas? Patrick said.

How's the lighting?

Thomas! hissed Liz.

He worked the Enfield's bolt action and chambered a shell. We're making a movie, right? he said.

Documentary, Patrick offered.

Liz tried to smile. A work of substance and gravitas, she said.

The least we can do is finish it, said Thomas, squinting through the scope. He panned and sighted, panned and sighted. Class had just let out, and potential targets were everywhere.

What would Charlie do? Patrick wondered, massaging the AK.

Liz studied the Canon's viewfinder, double-checking the framing and lighting. Then she worked the sawed-off's pump action and said, *Je suis Charlie.*

Thomas's cheeks burned. His fingers and toes tingled. For Charlie! he called, framing his shot.

For Charlie! they responded.

Thomas checked the safety and found the trigger. He squinted and aimed and inhaled, the sweet scent of bougainvillea wafting on the hot September breeze. Then, camera rolling, he exhaled and squeezed.

Mystic

Jonathan Maberry

—1—

I see dead people.

Make a joke. Go ahead, people do.

Fuck 'em.

I see dead people.

Not all of them. My life would be too crowded. Just some. The ones who need to be seen.

The ones who need me to see them.

—2—

The diner's name is Delta of Venus.

Most people think that's a pun of some kind, or a reference to Mississippi. It's not. The owner's name's not Venus. One of her girlfriend's was. It's like that.

I had my spot. Corner of the counter, close to the coffee. Out of the line of foot traffic to the john. Quiet most of the time. I dig the quiet. Kind of need it. My head is noisy enough.

It was a Thursday night, deep into a slow week. The kind of week Friday won't make better and Saturday won't salvage. Me on my stool, last sip of my fourth or fifth cup of coffee, half a plate of meatloaf going cold. Reading *The Waste Land* and wondering what kind of hell Eliot was in when he wrote it. World War I was over and he wrote poetry like the world was all for shit. Like he'd peeled back the curtain, and the great and powerful Oz was a sorry little pedophile and Dorothy was going to have a bad night. Depressing as fuck.

The coffee was good. The day blew.

Eve, the evening waitress, was topping off ketchup bottles and not wasting either of our time on small talk. Not on a Thursday like this. These kinds of days don't bring out the chattiness in anyone who's paying attention. Outside, there was a sad, slow rain and most of the people who came in smelled like wet dogs.

Then *she* came in.

I saw the door open. Saw it in the shiny metal of the big coffee urn. Saw her come in. Watched her stand there for a moment, not sure of what she was doing. Saw her look around. Saw nobody else look back.

Saw her spot me. And *know* me. And chew her lip for a moment before coming my way.

Little thing, no bigger than half a minute. Sixteen, maybe seventeen. Slim as a promise. Pretty as a daffodil.

Lost and scared.

Looking for me.

People like her find me. I never ask how they heard of me. In my line of work, the referral process is complicated. I get most of my standard clients from asshole law firms like Scarebaby and Twitch. Yeah, J. Heron Scarebaby and Iver Twitch. Real names. Some people are that fucking unlucky, and that dim that they won't use a different name for business. Or, maybe it's a matter of rats finding the right sewer. Not sure, don't care. They hire me for scut-work. Skip traces, missing persons. Stuff like that. Pays the light bill, buys me coffee.

They hadn't sent her, though. She found me a whole other way.

I signaled Eve and tapped the rim of my coffee cup with the band of my wedding ring. Still wore the ring after all this time. Married to the memory, I suppose. Eve topped me off.

"Gimme a sec," I said.

She looked around to see what was what. Looked scared when she did it, which is fair enough. People are like that around me. Then she found something intensely interesting to do at the far end of the counter. Didn't look my way again.

There were five other people in the Delta. Two were regulars: a night watchman on the way to his midnight shift, and Lefty Wright, who was always topping off his Diet Coke with liberal shots of Early Times. Neither of them would give a cold, wet shit if a velociraptor walked in and ordered the blue-plate special.

The other three were a gaggle of hipsters who must have gone looking for one of those no-name clubs, or the kind of dance party that's only ever advertised by obscure Internet posts. Probably got bad directions and brought iffy decision-making capabilities with them because they lingered here in this part of town long enough to order pancakes at a place like this. That, or they were hipster wannabes who thought the Delta was retro cool. It's not. And pretty soon they were going to let common sense trump their peer pressure and then they'd fade away.

That left me and the girl.

I didn't turn, but I patted the red Naugahyde stool next to me. Maybe it was the color that drew her eye. I'm pretty sure it's the only color people like her can see. That's what one of them told me. Just red, white, black, and a lot of shades of gray.

That's fucked up.

The girl hesitated a moment longer, then she seemed to come to a decision and came over. Didn't make a sound.

She stopped and stood there, watching me as I watched her in the steel mirror of the coffeemaker.

"It's your dime, sweetheart," I said.

She didn't say anything.

I picked up the Tabasco sauce and shook it over the meatloaf. Used enough of it to kill the taste. The specials sign over the kitchen window doesn't say what kind of meat is in it, and I'm not brave enough to ask. I'm reasonably sure that whatever it was ran on four legs. Beyond that, I wouldn't give Vegas odds on it being a cow or a pig.

"You want to sit down?" I asked.

Still nothing, so I turned and saw why.

Her face was as pale as milk. She wore too much makeup and clearly didn't know how to put it on. Little girl style—too much of everything, none of the subtlety that comes with experience. Glitter tube top and spandex micro mini. Expensive shoes. Clothes couldn't have been hers. Maybe an older sister, maybe a friend who was more of a party girl. They looked embarrassing on her. Sad.

She had one hoop earring in her right ear. The left earlobe was torn. No earring. No other jewelry that I could see. No purse, no phone, no rings. That one earring damn near broke my heart.

"You know how this works?" I asked.

Nothing. Or, maybe a little bit of a nod.

"It's a one-way ticket, so you'd better be sure, kid."

She lifted her hand to touch her throat. Long, pale throat. Like a ballet dancer. She was a pretty kid, but she would have been beautiful as a woman.

Would have been.

Her fingers brushed at a dark line that ran from just under her left ear and went all the way around to her right. She tried to say something. Couldn't. The line opened like a mouth and it said something obscene. Not in words. What flowed from between the lips of that mouth was wet and in the only color she could see.

She wanted to show me. She wanted me to see. She needed me to understand.

I saw. And I understood.

—3—

Later, after she faded away and left me to my coffee and mystery meat, I stared at the floor where she stood. There was no mark, no drops of blood. Nothing. Eve came back and gave me my check. I tossed a ten down on a six-dollar tab and shambled out into the night. Behind me I heard Eve call goodbye.

"Night, Monk."

I blew her a kiss like I always do. Eve's a good gal. Nice. Minds her own business. Keeps counsel with her own shit. Two kids at home and she works double shifts most nights. One of those quiet heroes who do their best to not let their kids be like them. I liked her.

It was fifteen minutes past being able to go home and get a quiet night's sleep. The rain had stopped, so I walked for a while, letting the night show me where to go. The girl hadn't been able to tell me, but that doesn't matter. I'd seen her, smelled the blood. Knew the scent.

Walked.

And walked.

Found myself midway up a back street, halfway between I Don't Know and Nobody Cares. Only a few cars by the curbs, but they were stripped hulks. Dead as the girl. Most of the houses were boarded up. Most of the boards had been pried loose by junkies or thieves looking to strip out anything they could. Copper pipes, wires, whatever. Couple of the houses had been torn down, but the rubble hadn't been hauled off.

What the hell had that little girl been doing on a street like this? Fuck me.

I had a pocket flashlight on my keychain and used it to help me find the spot.

It was there. A dark smudge on the sidewalk. Even from ten feet away I knew it was what I was looking for. There were footprints all over the place, pressed into the dirt, overlapping. Car tire tracks, too. The rain had wiped most of it away, smeared a lot of the rest, but it was there to be read. If I looked hard enough I'd probably find the flapping ends of yellow crime scene tape, 'cause they never clean that stuff up. Not completely, and not in a neighborhood like this. Whole fucking area's a crime scene. Still in progress, too, for the most part.

Doesn't matter. That's me bitching.

I knelt by the smudge. That was what mattered.

It was dried. Red turns to brown as the cells thicken and die. Smell goes away, too. At first, it's the stink of freshly sheared copper, then it's sweet, then it's gone. Mostly gone. I can always find a trace. A whiff.

And it was hers. Same scent. If I was a poet like Eliot maybe I'd call it the perfume of innocence. Something corny like that. I'm not, so I don't. It's just blood. Even the rain couldn't wash it away.

I squatted there for a few minutes, listening to water drip from the old buildings. Letting the smells sink in deep enough so I could pin them to the walls of my head.

Back in the day, before I went off to play soldier, before I ditched that shit and went bumming along the pilgrim road trying to rewire my brain, smells never used to mean much. That changed. First time I didn't die when an IED blew my friends to rags, I began to pay attention. Death smells different than life. Pain has its own smell.

So does murder.

I stopped being able to not pay attention, if you can dig that. I lost the knack for turning away and not seeing.

There was a monk in Nepal who told me I had a gift. A crazy lady down in a shack near a fish camp in bayou country told me I had a curse. They were talking about the same thing. They're both right, I suppose.

A priest in a shitty church in Nicaragua told me I had a calling. I told him that maybe it was more like a mission. He thought about it and told me I was probably right. We were drinking in the chapel. That's all that was left of the church. They don't call them Hellfire missiles for nothing.

The girl had come to me. Couldn't say what she wanted because of what they'd done to her. Didn't matter. She'd said enough.

I dug my kit out of my jacket pocket, unzipped it. Uncapped a little glass vial, took the cork off the scalpel and spent two minutes scraping as much of the blood as I could get into the vial. Then I removed the bottle of holy water, filled the dropper, and added seven drops. Always seven, no more, no less. That's the way it works, and I don't need to fuck with it. Then I put everything away, zipped up the case and stood. My knees creaked. I'm looking at forty close enough to read the fine print. My knees are older than that.

Spent another forty minutes poking around, but I knew I wasn't going to find anything the cops hadn't. They're pretty good. Lots of experience with crime scenes around here. They even catch the bad guys sometimes.

Not this time, though, or the girl wouldn't have come to me.

It's all about the justice.

The vial was the only thing that didn't go back into the case. That was in my pants pocket. It weighed nothing, but it was fifty fucking pounds heavy. It made me drag my feet all the way to the tattoo parlor.

—4—

Patty Cakes has a little skin art place just south of Boundary Street, right between a glam bar called Pornstash and a deli called Open All Night, which, to my knowledge, has never been open. Someone nailed a Bible to the front door, so take that any way you want.

The tattoo joint was open all night. Never during the day, as far as I know. It wasn't that kind of place. I saw Patty in there, stick thin with a purple Mohawk and granny glasses, hunched over the arm of a biker who looked like Jerry Garcia. Yeah, I know, Jerry's been dead for years. This guy looked like Jerry would look now. His name was Elmo something. I didn't care enough to remember the rest.

"Hey, Monk," said Patty, when she heard the little bell over the door.

"Hey, Mr. Addison," said Elmo. He was always a polite s.o.b.

"Hey," I said, and hooked a stool with my foot, dragged it over so I could watch Patty work. She was half-Filipino Chinese, with interesting scars on her face. Lot of backstory to her. I know most of it, but almost nobody else does. She knows a lot about me, too. We don't sleep together, but we've stayed up drinking more nights than I can count. She's one of my people, the little circle of folks I actually trust. We met the year I came back, and she spotted something in me from the jump. Bought me my first meal at the Delta.

She was working on green tints for a tat of climbing roses that ran from right thumb to left. Dozens of roses, hundreds of leaves.

"Nice," I said.

Elmo grinned like a kid on Christmas. "She's nearly done."

I nodded. Elmo was an ink junkie. He'd be back. Not just to elaborate on the tattoo, but because it was Patty sinking the ink. People come from all over just for her. I do. Like me, she has her gifts. Or maybe it's that she has her mission, too. But that's her story, and this isn't that.

Patty sat back and studied her work. "Okay, Elmo, that's it for now. Let it set. Go home and take care of it, okay?"

"Okay."

"Give Steve a kiss for me."

"Sure." He got up, stood in front of the floor-length mirror for a minute, grinning at the work. His eyes were a little glazed. He walked out wearing only a beater and jeans, his leather jacket forgotten on a chair. I knew he'd be back for it tomorrow. They always come back to Patty Cakes.

She got up and locked the door, flipped the sign to CLOSED and turned out the front lights. I stripped off my coat and shirt, caught sight of myself in the mirror. An unenamored lady once told me I look like a shaved ape. Fair enough. I'm bigger than most people, wider than most, deeper than most. A lot of me is covered in ink. None of it's really pretty. Not like those roses. It's all faces. Dozens of them. Small, about the size of a half-dollar. Very detailed. Photo real, almost. Men and women. Kids. All ages and races. Faces.

"Let me have it," she said, holding out a hand. I hadn't even told her why I was there. She knew me, though. Knew my moods. So I dug the vial out of my pocket and handed it to her. She took it, held it up to the light, sighed, nodded. "Gimme a sec. Have a beer."

I found two bottles of Fat Pauly's, a craft lager from Iligan City in the Philippines, cracked them open, set one down on her work table, lowered myself into her chair and sipped the other. Good beer. Ice cold. I watched her work.

She removed the rubber stopper from the vial and used a sterile syringe to suck up every last drop, then she injected the mixture into a jar of ink. It didn't matter that the ink was black. All of my tats are black. The white is my skin. Any color that shows up is from scars that still had some pink in them, but that would fade away after a while.

I drank my beer as Patty worked. Her eyes were open, but I knew that she wasn't seeing anything in that room. Her pupils were pinpoints and there was sweat on her forehead and upper lip. She began chanting something in Tagalog that I couldn't follow. Not one of my languages. When she was done mixing, she stopped chanting and cut me a look.

"You want the strap?"

"No," I said.

She held out a thick piece of leather. "Take the strap."

"No."

"Why do we go through this every time?"

"I don't need it," I told her.

"*I* do. Goddamn it, Monk, I can't work with you screaming in my ear. Take the fucking strap."

I sighed. "Okay. Give me the fucking strap."

She slapped it into my palm, and I put it between my teeth. She got out a clean needle and set the bottle of ink close at hand. She didn't ask me what I wanted her to draw. She knew.

I didn't start screaming right away. Not until she began putting the features on the little girl's face.

We were both glad I had the fucking strap.

—5—

It took her an hour to get it right, and I could feel when it was right. We both could.

I spat the strap onto my lap and sat there, gasping, out of breath, fucked up. I could see the pity in Patty's eyes. She was crying a little, like she always does. The light in the room had changed. Become brighter, and the edges of everything were so sharp I could cut myself on their reality. All the colors bled away. Except for red, white, black and all those shades of gray. That's what I saw. It's all I'd see until I was done with what I had to do.

Sometimes it was like that for days. Other times it was fast. Depends on how good a look the girl got, and what I'd be able to tell from that look.

Patty helped me up, grunting with the effort. I was two-fifty and change. None of it blubber. A lot of it was scar tissue. The room did an Irish céilí dance around me, and my brain kept trying to flip the circuit breakers off.

"If you're going to throw up, use the bathroom."

"Not this time," I managed to wheeze, then I grabbed my stuff, clumsied my way into my shirt and jacket, and stumbled out into the night, mumbling something to her that was supposed to be thanks, but might have been fuck you.

Patty wouldn't take offense. She understood.

Like I said, one of *my* people.

The night was hung wrong. The buildings leaned like drunks and the moon hid a guilty smile behind torn streamers of cloud. It took me half an hour to find my way back to where the girl was killed. My eyes weren't seeing where my feet were walking, and sometimes I crashed into things, tripped over lines in the pavement, tried to walk down an alley that wasn't there. It's like that for a bit, but it settles down.

Once I was on that street, it settled down a lot.

I stood by the step where I'd found her blood.

This is where it gets difficult for me. Victims don't usually know enough to really help, not even when I can see what they saw when they died. Like I was doing now. Half the time they didn't see it coming. A drive-by, or a hazy image of a tire iron. The feel of hands grabbing them from behind.

It was kind of like that with the girl.

Olivia.

I realized I knew her name now.

Olivia Searcy.

Fifteen. Even younger than I thought, but I was right about the clothes. They were her sister's. Shoes and push-up bra, too. She wanted to look older. No, she wanted to *be* older. But that was as old as she'd ever get.

I knew why she was there, and it was a bad episode of a teen romance flick. She was a sophomore in high school, he was a senior. Good looking, smart, from a family with some bucks. Good grades. A real find, and maybe in time he'd grow up and be a good man. But he was eighteen and all he wanted was pussy, and a lot of guys know that young pussy is often dumb pussy, which makes it easy pussy. So they come onto them, making them feel cool, feel special, feel loved. And they get some ass, maybe pop a cherry, and move on the instant the girl gets clingy. Fifteen-year-olds always get clingy, but there are always more of them. The boy, Drake, hadn't yet plundered Olivia. It was part of the plan for tonight.

They went to a party at some other guy's house a long way from here, in a part of town where stuff like this isn't supposed to happen, which is a stupid thought because stuff like this happens everywhere. The party was fun and it was loud. They got high. Got smashed. He got grabby and she freaked. Maybe a moment of clarity, maybe she saw the satyr's face behind the nice boy mask. Whatever. She bolted and ran.

She didn't know if Drake tried to find her because she tried real hard not to be found.

She *was* found, though.

Just not by Drake.

For a little bit there I thought I was going to have to break some parents' hearts by fucking up their pretty boy son, but that wasn't in tonight's playbook. Drake hadn't done anything worse than be a high school dickhead. He got her drunk, but he hadn't forced her, hadn't slipped her a roofie. And, who knows, maybe if he'd found her in time he'd have become Galahad and fought for her honor. Might have saved her life.

Probably would have died with her.

Or, maybe the killer would have opted out and gone looking for someone else. A lot of serial killers and opportunistic killers are like that. They're not Hannibal Lecter. They're not tough, smart and dangerous. Most of them are cowards. They feel totally disempowered by whatever's happened to them—abusive parents, bad genes, who the fuck cares? They hurt and terrify and mutilate and kill because it makes them feel powerful, but it's a lie. It's no more real than feeling powerful by wearing a Batman costume at Halloween. You may look the part, but you're a long way from saving Gotham City.

All of that flooded through my brain while I stood there and looked at the street through the eyes of a dead girl. Seeing it the way Olivia saw it right as hands grabbed her from behind. Right as someone pulled her back against his body so she could feel his size, his strength, the hard press of his cock against her back. Right as he destroyed her. Right as the cold edge of the knife was pressed into the soft flesh under her left ear.

I felt all of that. Everything. Her nerve endings were mine. Her pain exploded through me. The desperate flutter of her heart changed the rhythm of mine into a panic, like the beating of a hummingbird's wings against a closed window. I felt her break inside as he ruined her. I heard the prayers she prayed, and they echoed in my head like they'd echoed in hers. She hadn't been able to scream them aloud because first there was a hand over her mouth, and then there was the knife against her throat and those threats in her ear.

And when he was done, I felt the burn.

That line, like someone moving an acetylene torch along a bead of lead. Moving from under my left ear to under my right.

I felt her die because I died, too. Olivia drowned in her own blood.

Then there was a strange time, an oddly quiet time, because I was with her when she was dead, too. When he wrapped her in a plastic tarp and put her in the trunk. It was so weird because while he did that, he was almost gentle. As if afraid of hurting her.

Fucking psychopath.

While the car drove from where she'd died to where he'd dumped her, Olivia slipped into that special part of the universe where the dead see each other. Certain kinds of dead. The dead who were part of a family. Victims of the same knife.

His people.

Olivia discovered that she was not the only one. Not the first, not the tenth.

She wasn't sure how many because he moved around so much. *Had* moved around. Not so much anymore. Not since he moved to this town. The victims she met were the ones who'd died here.

Twenty-six of them.

The youngest was eight.

I met those victims, too, because I was inside the memory. Like I'd actually been there. That's how it worked. I talked to them, and most of them already knew who and what I was. The first time I'd encountered that it shocked the shit out of me. But now I understood. Not to say I'm used to it, because I'd have to be a special kind of fucked up to be used to something like that. No, it was more like I knew how to deal. How to use it.

Some of them had died just like Olivia. An attack from behind. Everything from behind. No chance of an identification. He varied it a little. One of those nearly patternless killers that the FBI have no idea how to profile. A knife across the throat, an icepick between the right ribs, a garrote made from a guitar string, a broken neck.

Most were like that.

Most. Not all.

There was one who fought. She'd had a little judo and some taekwondo. Not enough, but enough to make him work for it. It was one of the early ones, after he'd moved here. The one that made him want to never bring them home again. She'd gotten out and he'd chased her into the front yard and caught her before she could wake the neighbors. Single homes, lots of yard on all sides. Cul-de-sac. When he caught up to her, she spun around and tried to make a fight of it.

I saw every second of it.

The yard. The house.

Him.

I saw him.

I saw him block her punch, and then a big fist floated toward her face and she was gone. He was a big guy and he knew how to hit. The punch broke the girl's neck, which made it easier on her, if easy is a word that even applies.

I stood there and watched all of it play out inside my head. No idea how long I was there. Time doesn't matter much when I'm in that space. I was there for every second of every minute of every attack. Beginning to end. All the way to when he dumped them, or buried them, or dropped them off a bridge.

Stack it all up and it was days.

Days.

Shotgunned into my head.

I wish I'd had the leather strap. Instead, I had to bite down on nothing, clamp my jaws, ball my fists, clench my gut and eat the fucking pain.

It wouldn't save any of those girls. Not one. And maybe it wouldn't matter that I felt it all but didn't have to live it. Or die from it. I know that.

I couldn't help a single one of them. I couldn't help Olivia.

But as my skin screamed from the phantom touches and the blades and everything else, I swore that I'd help the next girl.

Goddamn son of a bitch, I'd help the next girl.

Because, you see, I saw the house.

I saw the number beside the door.

I saw the tags on the car parked in the drive.

And I saw the motherfucker's face.

I went and sat down on the step next to the blood. Waited. I knew she'd be there eventually. It was how it worked.

Still surprised me when I looked up and there she was. Pale, thin, young, her face as bright as a candle. Eyes filled with forever.

"You can still opt out," I told her. "I can turn this over to the cops. Let them handle it."

She said nothing, but she gave me a look. We both knew that this guy was too careful. There would be no evidence of any kind. He'd been doing this for years and he knew his tradecraft. No semen, no hairs, nothing left for them to trace. The knife was gone where no one would ever find it. And he wasn't a souvenir collector. The smarter ones aren't. They could turn his house inside out and the only things they'd find would be jack and shit.

Even if they watched him, he'd turn it off for a while. For long enough. Police can't afford to run surveillance for very long. They'd lose interest, even if they thought the guy was good for Olivia's murder.

I sighed. Actually, I wanted to cry. What she was asking was big and ugly and it was going to hurt both of us.

She stood there with a necklace of bright red and those bottomless eyes.

She didn't say a word. She didn't have to.

The price was the price. She was willing to pay it because she was a decent kid who would probably have grown up to be someone of note. Someone with power. Someone who cared. Those eyes told me that this wasn't about her.

It was all about the next girl.

And the one after that.

And the one after that.

I buried my face in my hands and wept.

—6—

It took me two days to run it all down. The girl misremembered the license number, so that killed half a day.

Then I put the pieces together. Bang, bang, bang.

Once that happens, everything moves quickly.

I ran the guy through the databases we PIs use, and after an hour I knew everything about him. I had his school records and his service record—one tour in Afghanistan, one in Iraq. Made me hate him even more. He was divorced, no kids. Parents dead, his only living relative was a brother in Des Moines. I figured there were bodies buried in Des Moines, too, but I'd never know about them. He owned three Jack in the Box franchise stores and had half-interest in a fourth. Drove a hybrid, recycled, and had solar panels on his house. I almost found that funny.

I was in his Netflix and Hulu accounts, his bank account, and everything else he had. If there was a pattern there, or a clue as to what he was, it wasn't there. He was very smart and very careful.

No cops were ever going to catch him.

I parked my car on the route he took to work and waited until I saw him drive past on his way home. Gave him an hour while I watched the sun go down. Twilight dragged some clouds across the sky, and the news guy said it was going to rain again. Fine. Rain was good. It was loud and it chased people off the streets.

Lightning forked the sky and thunder was right behind it. Big, booming. The rains started as a deluge. No pussy light drizzle first. One second nothing, then it was raining alley cats and junkyard dogs.

I got out of my car and opened an umbrella. I really don't give a shit about getting wet, but umbrellas block line-of-sight. They make you invisible. I walked through the rain to his yard, went in through the gate, up along the flagstone path, and knocked on the door.

Had to knock twice.

He had half a confused smile on his face when he opened the door, the way people do when they aren't expecting anyone. Especially during a storm.

Big guy, an inch taller than me, maybe only ten pounds lighter. His debit card record says that he keeps his gym membership up to date. I knew from my research that he'd boxed in college. Wrestled, too. And he had Army training.

Whatever.

I said, "Mr. Gardner?"

"What do you want?"

I hit him.

Real fucking hard.

A two-knuckle punch to the face, right beside the nose. Cracks the infraorbital foramen. Mashes the sinus. Feels a lot like getting shot in the face, except you don't die.

He went back and down, falling inside his house, and I swarmed in after him, letting the umbrella go. The wind whipped it away and took it somewhere. Maybe Oz for all I know. I never saw it again.

Gardner fell hard, but he fell the right way, like he knew what he was doing. Twisting to take the fall on his palms, letting his arm muscles soak up the shock. His head had to be ringing like Quasimodo's bells, but he wasn't going out easy.

He kicked at me as I came for him. Tricky bastard. A good kick, too, flat of the heel going for the front of my knee. If he'd connected, I'd have gone down with a busted leg, and he'd have had all the time in the world to do whatever he wanted.

If he'd connected.

I was born at night, but it wasn't last night. I bent my knee into the kick and bent over to punch the side of his foot. I knew some tricks, too.

In the movies there's a brawl. A long fight with all sorts of fancy moves, deadly holds, exciting escapes, a real gladiatorial match.

That's the movies.

In the real world, fights are, to paraphrase Hobbs, nasty, brutal and short.

He had that one kick, that one chance. I didn't give him a second one. I gave him nothing.

I took everything.

When I was done, I was covered in blood, my chest heaving, staring at what was left of him there in the living room. I'd closed the door. The curtains were closed over drawn shades. The TV was on. Some kind of CSI show with the volume cranked up. Outside the storm was shaking the world.

He wasn't dead.

Mostly, but not entirely.

That would come a little later.

He wasn't going anywhere, though. That would have been structurally impossible.

I went into the kitchen and found a basting brush. Slapped it back and forth over his face to get it wet, then I wrote on the wall. It took a while. I made sure he was watching. I wrote the names of every girl he had killed.

Every one that I'd met there in the darkness of Olivia's hell.

Gardner was whimpering. Crying. Begging.

When I was done I unzipped my pants, pulled out my dick and pissed on him.

He was sobbing now. Maybe he was that broken or that scared. Maybe it was his last play, trying to hold a match to the candle of my compassion.

Maybe.

But he was praying in the wrong church.

While I worked, I kept praying that Olivia wouldn't show up to see this. Most of them do. None of them should. I didn't want her here.

I looked around for her.

She didn't come.

It helped a little, but not a lot. I knew I'd see her again.

Gardner managed to force one word out. It took a lot of effort because I'd ruined him.

"P-please…" he said.

He wanted me to end it. By then, I think that's what he wanted.

I smiled.

"Fuck you," I said.

The storm was raging, and I stood there for nearly an hour. Watching Gardner suffer. Watching him die.

Judge me if you want. If so, feel free to go fuck yourself.

When I left, I stole one of his umbrellas.

I'd worn gloves and a ski mask. Everything I had on was disposable. It all got burned. I'm smart about that shit, too.

—7—

That night I got drunk. Because it's the only reasonable thing to do.

Me and Patty, Lefty Wright, and a couple of the others. Ten of us huddled around a couple of tables in a black-as-pockets corner of *Pornstash*. Me and my people. No one had to ask what happened. Patty knew, some of the others maybe. Mostly not. But they all knew something had happened. We were those kinds of people, and this was that kind of town.

We drank and told lies, and if the laughter sounded fake at times and forced at others, then so what?

—8—

It was nearly dawn when I stumbled up the stairs, showered for the third time that day, and fell into bed.

I said some prayers to a God I knew was there but was pretty sure was insane. Or indifferent. Or both.

My windows are painted black because I sleep during the day. Mostly, anyway. I had a playlist running. John Lee Hooker and Son House. Old blues like that. Some Tom Waits and Leonard Cohen in there, too. Grumpy, cynical stuff. Broken hearts and spent shell casings and bars on the wrong side of the tracks. Like that.

Stuff I can sleep to.

When I can sleep.

Mostly, I can't sleep.

My room's always too crowded.

They are always there. It's usually when I'm alone that I see them. Pale faces standing in silence. Or screaming. Some of them scream.

I wear long sleeve shirts to bed because they scream the loudest when they see their own faces. It's like that. It's how it all works.

When I'm at the edge of sleep, leaning over that big black drop, I can feel the faces on my skin move. I can feel their mouths open to scream, too. Sometimes the sheet gets soaked with tears that aren't mine.

But which are mine now.

Olivia was there for the first time that night.

Standing in the corner, pale as a candle, looking far too young to be out this late. Thank god she wasn't one of the screamers. She was a silent one. She with her red necklace that went from ear to ear.

My name is Gerald Addison. Most people call me Monk.

I drink too much and I hardly ever sleep.

And I do what I do.

Killing Slugs with Salt

Asya Marie

You just pour it. Yes, like that. A little more. More.

"I'll be right back," the girl's dad said, kissing her cheek. "My friend, Mr. Harvey, will watch you, so stay put, kiddo."

By then, the girl had gotten used to that routine. She was in 4th grade. Her mom and dad had started arguing. Her dad had gotten his own apartment and spent half of his time there and the other half at home. Sometimes, when she spent time with her dad, he'd need to go somewhere. He'd be gone for an hour or two, leave her with a coworker at his office, with a friend at the shopping mall, with a nanny at his apartment.

"Don't tell mommy about this, okay, kiddo? It'll just make her mad, then we'll all be unhappy. You know Daddy gets really busy with work sometimes, and Mommy doesn't like that."

That day, her dad left her at a park with Mr. Harvey, his business friend. Her dad waved goodbye, got inside the car, and left. She watched the car as it passed by, watched it become smaller and smaller, blurring then disappearing around a corner.

They were sitting side by side on a rusted metal bench speckled with bird feces and dried pieces of gum. There was a play area in front of them, surrounded by the shore of the lake, a forested area, and a small neighborhood. The sun was out, but it was cold and windy.

The girl wore a tank top under a thin cardigan, a ruffle chiffon skirt with flowers on it, sheer shimmer tights that she had begged her mom to buy. She didn't expect to be there when she had gotten dressed that morning. She was freezing.

Mr. Harvey leaned back, scanned the girl up and down, then shook his head, clicked his tongue. "Look at you! It's freezing out here and you're barely wearing anything! I've got a sweater in my bag, want it?"

Before she had said anything, he already started unzipping his bag.

"Thank you," the girl said.

He set a brown sweater vest on her lap and straightened it out, meticulously tucking it in at the sides. His hands touched against her legs. They were incredibly warm. "There we go."

Go on. Pour it. They need a lot. Don't be a baby.

The girl had only seen Mr. Harvey a few times before that, when her dad had taken her to his office to file some papers, or to speak with a client, or for some other thing that had to be done. She'd wait in an empty conference room, color, flip through a book, or just look around making up games in her head that she could play alone. Mr. Harvey would sometimes pass by, smile and wave, ask her how she was doing in school. But that day at the park was her first time seeing him so up close.

Mr. Harvey had a beard that ran along the sides of his face and around his mouth, light grey at the tips, almost white. He always dressed similarly whenever she saw him, with a grey or black suit and a colorful, patterned tie. That day it was navy with tiny yellow ducks all over. Beneath his narrow, rectangular frames were murky blue eyes with layers of wrinkles at the outer corners. He smelled like cigarette smoke and soap.

"You're what now, huh? Twelve? Fourteen?" Mr. Harvey asked the girl.

"I'm only nine, almost ten," she said, looking out at the park toys, swinging her legs back and forth in the air.

"Oh, that's right. I remember when you were only a toddler, couldn't barely say more than a few words. Shouldn't you be in school then?"

"It's a half day," she told him.

"Oh, I see," Mr. Harvey said, then, after a pause, continued, "You have a boyfriend at school, yes? You're dressed very nicely for someone."

"No, I don't," she said, blushing. Her ears began pulsing with heat. Her mom had asked her the same thing a few times before because she knew it bugged her, made her turn red.

"No boyfriend, huh? Well, I didn't know girls your age dressed this way for nothing." He reached into his bag, lit a cigarette. "That skirt really is something."

It just so happened that there weren't many people out around the park that day. Occasionally, a runner would jog past or a car would drive up, park, and a kid would jump out, go down the slide a few times before a parent would call from the car saying it was time for them to go. Before the girl noticed, it was only her and Mr. Harvey.

"When is my dad coming back?" the girl asked. She wanted to go home. It was cold. She didn't like the smell of his cigarettes. She had homework to do.

"Well, your dad is a busy man, yes, very busy," Mr. Harvey said, laughing. The mucus in his throat cracked and popped, startling a few birds that were roaming around in the grass nearby. "Why not just enjoy the sunshine and the park for a while? I'm in no rush, don't worry."

It was cold and windy and she didn't want to ruin her new tights and get in trouble with her mom, but her dad probably wouldn't be back for a while. She was especially excited to go on the swings. She hadn't been on a swing in a long time. But just as she tried to get up—she'd go on the swings first, the one with the red seat not the blue—she felt a sudden warm pressure against her leg making it difficult to move.

In a single, quick gesture, Mr. Harvey had scooted over next to her and slid his hand underneath his sweater still covering the girl's lap.

"Just stay still, dear. Just trying to keep you warm. Don't move."

Ew! Gross! Look at them squirm! Sad, nasty little things.

When her dad came back, the girl ran up to him before he had barely gotten out of the car and gave him a hug. He returned with his suit jacket off and she could feel his body warmth through his dress shirt. He smelled sweet.

"Did you miss me that much, kiddo? Sorry I took so long this time."

When they had driven down the street, around a few corners, so that the park was out of sight, the girl told her dad that she didn't want Mr. Harvey to watch her anymore.

He asked why.

What are you crying for? Grow up, would you?

"*Hello?* Tell me. Why not?"

* * *

"Look, Ma! Look! There are three of them together. Are they a family?"

Her mom looked over at the three slugs gathered on a part of the porch that was still wet from when they had watered the plants. They were sitting out front, eating watermelon, enjoying the evening breeze. It was summertime and the house was too hot. The girl's dad was in his office on the phone, working, despite the sweltering humidity inside. It was back when he didn't have a second place yet, and her mom and dad weren't fighting as often, back when they spent more time together, the three of them. The girl was maybe five or six.

"Go get the salt," her mom said.

The girl ran into the house and came out holding a glass mason jar of salt. "What's it gonna do to them, Ma? They like it? Eat it?"

"Hush up and pour it on them," her mom snapped.

They crouched down, hovered over them. The girl poured a little salt. Her mom nudged her shoulder: *keep pouring.*

The slugs squirmed wildly, coiling up, uncoiling, and coiling up again, struggling, slowing, stopping, contracting into tiny clumps of grey and brown sitting in sticky puddles of gunk. Her mom laughed a little laugh.

"And there you have it! Poor little bastards never had a chance."

Henry, Kabir, and That Little Book

David Fitzpatrick

It wasn't the fluid groove of the sentences, or any finesse on the author's part—frankly, the tiny book featured far from perfect prose. But the simple, *aw-shucks* style struck a chord with Henry, made him smile, and feel lifted, or at the very least, eased. The story worked because it didn't pretend to be anything other than unabashedly sentimental.

Take that line: "Every love story is beautiful, but ours is my favorite." Henry's wife, Sarah, had presented the gift to him on his fifty-third birthday, and that sentence was also half dribbled in dark chocolate across his celebratory cake that night. The couple gathered with his extended family at a Turkish restaurant near the Ninth Square neighborhood of New Haven.

It was early March, always a difficult time for him, and although no family member mentioned it that evening, they weren't surprised to later hear Henry was admitted to Yale Psychiatric, a spot he'd avoided for eleven years. Henry felt crumpled and ashamed to be back—the ward had morphed into a 50+ Geriatric Unit since he'd been away.

He tried to stay even keeled by reading a book of poems by Mary Oliver, "Blue Horses," which contains the following epigraph by 15th century mystic, Kabir:

"If you don't break ropes while you're alive, do you think ghosts will do it after?"

Henry obsessed over the line—so much so that he imagined Kabir would be a colleague, a good friend even, if he were around today. For the record, though, he figured what the mystic *actually* meant about breaking ropes was that Henry should separate from his conscious mind for now, and use a new moisturizer on his face.

Forget Clinique, Noxzema, or Neutrogena—instead use hearty splashes of low cost, homegrown urine added with a sign of the cross to Henry's forehead, lips, chin, and cheeks. Henry committed this act at home, and in the hospital numerous times, and it both titillated and shamed him, a secret between him, the mystic, and a willowy, visiting shrink from Prague.

Kabir even appeared before Henry in the hospital on the first two nights, hovering on the ceiling in a white robe, sandals, and a saffron polo, holding a flashing neon purple sign reading: "Let your ropes dissolve, my friend, and pursue everything."

Barbo, Henry's roommate at the hospital, was an eighty-five-year-old stocky Italian Brit who got enraged at one psychiatric nurse in particular, a six-foot-five Gambian gentleman with a shaved head named Scotty. As soon as Barbo spotted Scotty anywhere on the unit, wild shrieking began.

Henry snuck back into his room to hide from the noise—he also told the staff he wouldn't write about his experience at the hospital as he'd done numerous times before. He believed it would be detrimental to separate himself as a narrator, figured he would stay involved, turn down urges to put pencil to paper, and concentrate on his own recovery.

Immerse yourself in the healing, Henry told himself, trying to cram the mantra into his head like it was a sponge. *Don't observe life from the periphery any longer.*

But his thoughts stole away to an old writing mentor, a deceased eighth-grade teacher who told Henry that a healthy back and forth in prose—like a good volley in tennis—is essential to making tales more palatable. The teacher recommended using juxtaposition, and liberal doses of the unusual and ordinary to offer balance.

"One additionally has a duty to lift readers," he informed Henry. "Give them hints of redemption, along with illumination, and make the tale universal, if at all possible."

Henry tried to appreciate the decency of the other patients as he listened to one cherubic green-and-blue-haired African-American gentleman in an iridescent housecoat and Garfield slippers beautifully croon Ave Maria in the cafeteria, before a nurse told him to *knock it the hell off*. Which somehow made Henry recall his retired minister Mom sending a keepsake to a famous psychiatric clinic in the Midwest while Henry was stationed there in the mid-nineties. It was a refrigerator magnet of a lone white church steeple in a forest with a quote from Isaiah, 9:2:

"The people who walked in darkness have seen a great light."

How Henry had wept over that gift, sobbed like a little boy. Back on the unit in New Haven, Henry joined others in the Day Room with its squishy yet impenetrable furniture that had a coating like algae, which glowed green under the harsh lights. *Judge Judy* was dispensing her truth to a group of seven patients from an enormous TV propped high on the wall, which was protected from shattering with a Plexi-glass cover.

"Judge Judy rakes in the dough," Ben explained, a fifty-three-year-old depressive who overdosed after finding his daughter dead from a self-inflicted gunshot wound.

"What do you think Judge Judy's secret is?" Henry asked him.

"Judy insults well," Ben said. "Belittles folks terrifically."

"Right," Henry said. "Anything else?"

"Her rapier wit slays all," Ben went on, scowling. "Plus, her loyal viewers are like conversational cannibals—they dig discomfort, verbal takedowns, and shame."

In group later that week, Ben wept about what he discovered in his basement ninety days ago - his daughter sprawled by her drum set, blood pooling around her head.

"My wry, sweet, and favorite percussionist in all the world," Ben whispered. "Do you understand how rare it is for a female teen to shoot herself with a shotgun?"

The doctor from Prague shook her head.

"Does anyone get how rare that is?" Ben asked, looking around at us. "Can someone answer me now, *please?*"

"Others in the group don't know how to respond," the doctor said. "Which doesn't take away from how sorry we all are for what has befallen you, Ben."

"Yes," each of us said, coughing, blushing. "Of course, yeah, so terribly sorry for your heinous loss at this tragic and hellish time, Ben."

Over Henry's hospitalization, the green-and-blue-haired performer in Garfield slippers sang more outlawed, though tender renditions of Ave Maria as Henry made steady progress reading an article in a writing magazine called, "Magic and the Intellect." The gist was that every narrative has such possibility, numerous magical avenues, though Henry knew he could be way off with that summation—his inner gyroscope had been failing him as of late.

After four days on the unit, Henry started back in with journal writing—a comely recreational therapist on the unit had suggested it to him. Henry's wife, Sarah, brought in that colorful birthday book on love, "Primitives" by Kathy Phillips, something she found in the discount bin at a chain bookstore for seventy-five cents. Henry studied it each morning like it was scripture—it was a basic way to keep life and love within, a meditation, and it acted like a type of superhero shield for him.

That said, Henry also couldn't stop seeing himself licking walls, floors, windows, and toilet seats. It's like the love book was blessed and rested on one shoulder, while on the other sat negative, sinister copies of Henry's acts, his many sins. Good versus Bad, Angel versus Devil, Redeemed versus Cursed. The caustic pictures flew up into Henry's face one after the next like a swarm of hornets.

Once Henry knelt to lick the commode at his home in Middletown a month ago, things unraveled—whacked out voices ricocheted inside of him, boundaries dissolving, psychic dominoes tumbling. But Henry combated the images by thinking of the diminutive book, so brightly colored, teeming with a kind of schlocky, pithy wisdom. Henry's brain had Sarah offering the voice-overs.

"You are the blue in my sky," she read. "You are the mac to my cheese."

While at the Psych ER, Henry sprawled naked on the cold concrete floor before the steel toilet, mind swirling, offering his tongue and body up for forgiveness, or something more sacred. Or was it only an oblong face he spotted in a horror film as a graduate student while tripping in a Belfast theatre with his soused great-uncle? Back and forth Henry's mind raced—left, right, up, down, real, dream, nightmare, paradise, inferno, peace, and wild, hoary violence.

Sarah read from the book, her voice so distinct:

"You are the water to my ocean."

Roommate Barbo was unchanging his whole stay—forever at the nurses' station, shouting so profanely at Scotty that the TV was turned off, and Henry and other patients retreated to their rooms, covering their ears, using ear plugs staff offered as a "relaxation tool."

"Don't talk to me as if I'm some juvenile, Scotty," Barbo said. "Where has your respect for elders gone?"

Butch Cassidy and the Sundance Kid, was the feature at movie night, and when it ended, many geriatrics spoke of how sorely missed Paul Newman was in Hollywood, and how younger stars should be more like him and donate substantial portions of their earnings to charities. There was even an octogenarian lady weeping in the next room, sobbing over the whole thing.

"Oh, that film icon, Paul," she cried. "What an eternal heartbreaker."

"Newman was a pussy," Barbo roared at her from the Day Room before nurses finally gave him an injection, and then he was out of the picture for the next three days. By 10 p.m., the graveyard shift arrived and dimmed the lights, and the TV was switched off, and most patients disappeared into their thick, medicated slumbers.

Two weeks later, Henry scrawled in his journal that Kabir would want him to live a more self-respecting existence and enjoy his life. Henry thought strictly of sweet, singular Sarah and her colorful book. One page displayed a dove soaring in a near perfect cerulean blue sky, an olive branch in her beak.

"With love, there are always miracles."

Days later, Henry finds himself outside on an early morning, carrying his duffle of clothes in one hand, holding Sarah's left hand tight with the other. The sunshine feels strong, healing on Henry's cheeks—his once chapped lips are healthier, slightly moist. Henry leaves the ruinous mess of his past on the ward.

The couple head home, exiting the raw city with its noise, poverty, potholes, and tipsy undergrads stumbling into traffic, defiantly lip-synching Lou Reed tunes into their adoring mobiles. Sarah and Henry accelerate up the I-91 ramp, away from the Yalies and other urban terrors, both imagined and otherwise, and head to the middle of the state.

Henry lowers the passenger side window of their car after a while and feels the blast of wind, as three wide women in leather jackets zoom past on their Harley Davidson's, their helmet-less hair blowing wildly, and their black, bug-eyed, wrap-around sunglasses make them look potent, brash.

He's hoping for an epiphany, or clarity, or something grace-filled that he can't seem to attain. *Stay true*, Henry tells himself. *Don't quit, deep breaths, keep the faith, never give up, and carry on as best you can.*

He tries to figure out which club the bikers hail from, but his vision is unreliable. He studies the women's cracked and worn brown jackets, the designs of something like a dragon, cobra, or even a tiger sewn onto their backs, but it's futile. Images blur.

He removes his glasses and studies Sarah, who offers her hand and squeezes his. Henry weeps, thinking of what doctors of every stripe have told him, thirty-something years of counseling, explanations, and clinical tips on nervous breakdowns, anxiety, paranoia, schizoaffective disorder, and self harm, and how disappointing, insufficient, and silly it seems.

Henry ponders ECT, blood, hypnosis, scars, sutures, and tons of medications that have coursed through his body—all the latest treatments, plus the 145 pounds of fat he gained, lost, gained, lost, and gained all back again. So at that precise point in time, Henry feels not reborn in the slightest, but enraged, branded, re-classified, a bloated pharmaceutical experiment of the worst...

"Don't go that route, honey," Sarah says, looking at him, reading his thoughts. "Today we got another chance. You and me got another shot at this, okay?"

So, for dear, bright Sarah, Henry packs away the toxicity and the arguments against life: Swan diving off the Arrigoni Bridge in town; embracing the razor blade genre; and giving in to the beast and its miseries.

Henry recalls their honeymoon in Colorado decades ago, Sarah up front in a bulbous, ten-people, whitewater raft, her purple life-preserver, flushed face, and blonde hair soaked by the enraged, churning rapids of Snake River. Her sinewy neck tendons stand out like some newly unwrapped string instrument, aching to be strummed and played.

Henry holds on for dear life in the rear, watching his new wife with hunger and awe, working up his courage to free one hand so he can snap a photo of Sarah in action, the brightest, most pulsing constellation in the firmament by far.

Back in the car, Henry closes his eyes as the duo approach their home, feeling Sarah's grip on his palm, and the sun on his skin, and he tries to feel it spread through his whole body, one solar and emotive balm. All Henry sees is a colored page torn from the corny, ridiculous book, a green and blue planet Earth whirling as Sarah's voice resonates:

"Life brings us to unexpected places, but love brings us home."

Shark Tooth

Anastasia Jill

Elodie's mother claimed she never went to medical school because they didn't admit women *in her day*. *In her day*, women knew their place among the men, without credit, or property, or sense of self. Everything about her was sacrosanct; a woman built on an empire of predecessors, other women who were complacent as jaw-locked prey.

Elodie, conversely, became a predator, like the Megalodon shark; the largest and strongest living on this side of the Econlockhatchee. She wore blue jeans and trench coats, carried a book with her at all times, collected worms, refused to cook food or wash her hands before eating. Her mother scolded her daily, "You'll have to learn to do these things in order to serve your husband."

But thirteen years on Earth had taught Elodie many things - much more than mother could ever hope to learn. Sure, Mother taught her the difference between the forks and how to burp under a napkin. Library books taught her about prehistoric animals like the Megalodon shark, whose fangs could grow up to seven inches in length. But it wasn't until she met quiet Dipsi Paz that she learned about herself and what she wanted. The two became fast friends over science field trips, held hands behind the reefs of trees tucked in the back of their parochial school. Elodie learned what she wanted from life; she wanted a wife, she wanted science, she wanted anything but her mother's feminine strife.

One Saturday morning in June, Elodie's mother was preparing for a shift in the maternity ward where she would bring other young women into their "full potentials" as mothers. Elodie sat at the kitchen counter with a bowl of cereal. She picked at the sugared flakes, fingers turning menacing circles in the milk.

"For God's sake." Her mother's voice was a sliver of noise. "Don't use your fingers. Would you like a spoon?"

"No, I would not."

The two continued their morning in silence save for Elodie, gnashing her cereal to mush. When the food was gone and the dishes were put away, her mother asked, "What are your plans for today?"

"I'm going to the science center."

"With whom?"

"Dipsi."

"Oh. I suppose that's alright."

Elodie wasn't asking permission. Had she asked, her mother would have politely declined. Her mother didn't like Dipsi, or rather, Dipsi's mother, who was everything she both detested and envied; a Yale medical school graduate, a proud single mother, an exemplary woman of the 90s who was doing it all on her own. Most of all, Ms. Paz supported everything Dipsi did, from dating girls to cutting her hair short to capturing wild animals with her bare hands. Elodie wanted nothing but the same from her mother.

As always, she asked her mother, "Do you want to come with us?"

The woman shook her head and mused, "In my day, girls didn't spend their time in places like that."

Elodie countered, "In your day, girls wore petticoats and wiped themselves with leaves."

"You're thinking of *Little House on the Prairie*." She cleansed her hands on a dishtowel. "Science was for the men."

"Mom, you're a midwife. That's a science."

"It's a job."

"Aren't those the same thing?"

Elodie's mother let out a deep sigh, thirteen years of endless questions expelling their answer in one dismissive breath. "Just be careful today, alright? There is no accounting for girls who run around with other girls, wearing dungarees and sneakers, getting dirty...think how you will look to the boys. How will you get dates?"

Elodie jumped up from the counter, ending this conversation before it started. It was all redundant to her at this point, especially since she hit puberty, was gaining curves, which brought on the endless conversation about boys. Elodie's mother had to have known, but lived in denial. There were no boys, except boy sharks.

"Whatever, mom. I'll be home before dinner, alright?"

"Elodie," her mother said as she scooped her feet into dirty sneakers. "Why don't you go upstairs and put on a skirt, maybe brush your hair and put on a little mascara."

Elodie hated make-up. Some girls liked it, but it wasn't for her. And her hair was often set aside in an elastic - what was the point in brushing it out? And she reminded her mother, "We're going to the science center. A skirt would be impractical, not to mention, ugly."

Her mother's smile faltered for a moment, but she recovered, and said, "In my day, girls wore skirts and dresses whenever they left the house."

"I know."

"And brushed their beautiful long hair."

"I hate my hair long."

"Glossed their lips like foam does the end of a wave." Her mother put her hands on her hips in an un-ladylike fashion, only managing to appear slightly stern. "Well, I suppose all little girls go through that ugly stage."

She tried not to let that sting too much, but her mother might as well have ripped proverbial fins off with her fangs.

Elodie double-knotted her laces before standing to face her mother - quite a feat, being a few inches shorter - but eventually the woman gave in, turning away with a reminder, "Don't be home too late. I'm making a casserole for supper."

The walk to Dipsi's house took a half hour, but Elodie wasn't about to ask her mother for a ride. Not now, not ever. She crossed streets and hustled down sidewalks, kicking along pinecones and little stones, shaped like broken teeth. The Paz house appeared at the end of a suburban street, standing out with its indigo, buyant blue door bidding all a welcome.

Elodie didn't knock. This was her second home. When she walked in, she found Mrs. Paz on the couch sandwiched between some pillows and the family dog, Aqua, so named for his raven blue fur.

"Where's Dipsi?" Elodie asked.

Mrs. Paz briefly looked up from the television. "In her room. Can't find her shoes. You know how she is." This was not meant as a dig as it was said with a teasing smile. Elodie envied that.

She walked the short distance from living room to hallway. The door was open, and Dipsi's back met Elodie's view, arched like a great white leaping out of the water. Her slender form gave way to bones, lined like scales beneath crystal clear skin. Elodie did this often - standing back and admiring the form that was her girlfriend - and couldn't help but wonder how her mother could dislike such a majestic creature.

Dipsi quickly found her shoes under a pile of clothes, but still didn't notice Elodie as she walked up to the plastic cage containing her pet rats. Four fat and furry bodies fought for the affectionate hand, afraid there wasn't enough love to go around.

"Rats are lucky," Elodie said aloud, unable to restrain herself.

Dipsi replied quickly, "Not really. They only live a year or two."

"True, but they don't have mothers who hate them."

"Sometimes their mothers eat them."

Elodie leaned on the doorframe. "My mother wouldn't do that. It might get blood on her dress. Manslaughter isn't very lady-like, don't ya know."

Dipsi withdrew her willowy hands from the rat's domicile. "This conversation got dark awfully fast. Are you alright?"

Elodie supposed she wasn't. She was hardly ever okay. She didn't want to concern Dipsi with all of that. Instead, she painted the dainty girl's cheek with a kiss, which made her blush. "Come on," Elodie said. "Let's go to the science center."

Ms. Paz drove them. Elodie could hardly contain her excitement. This weekend they were hosting an exhibition on prehistoric animals, including a megalodon skeleton. The whole adventure had been Dipsi's idea, knowing Elodie and her interests so well.

In the backseat of the car, Elodie pressed her mouth to Dipsi's ear. Her words were humid, moist confessions to her girlfriend's ear. "My mother doesn't like this, you know. She thinks the sharks are weird."

Dipsi shrugged. "Why don't you give her a chance?"

"I don't want to."

"Then who cares what your mom thinks?"

The thought washed over Elodie, a baptism, an emancipation. Yeah, who *cared* what her mom thought. She was her own person, a conqueror at thirteen. It wasn't her fault Mother made no move to modernize, to understand her one and only daughter.

Upon arrival at the museum, Ms. Paz paid their admission, staying by the two while simultaneously giving them their space. Elodie held Dipsi's hand with pride. For once, other people didn't stare. They likely thought them to be friends, or were transfixed by the relics of million year old minerals. There were other exhibits - ones Dipsi was sure to like - but the first stop was the megalodon, the sixty foot skeleton situated behind schools of fish bones. Once the tailfin became visible, Elodie yanked on Dipsi's hand.

"Come on!" she said. "I see the shark from here!" And not a moment of Elodie's life could have prepared her for coming face to face with the remains of her most revered predator.

Before this moment, sixty feet was a number, a calculation. Standing at the exhibit, she could see the shark had no true measure. Long ossian pipes stood like dowel rods holding the creature's body together. Spikes jutted from the rib cage, a firework of cartilage and bone all leading to gargantuan teeth. Just below the shark read a little sign: *Do Not Feed The Megalodon!*

"This is incredible," Elodie said. "The biggest shark in human history, and we're standing right here."

"It's weird to think if it was alive, it would kill us," Dipsi noted.

"There are worse things in the world than a shark."

Though Dipsi tried - much more than most - she was unable to look past her fear factor to appreciate the shark.

"You know," Elodie said. "Sharks aren't all that bad. They don't kill people on purpose. It's just because they're blind." *Like my mother*, Elodie thought. *Blind to so many things.*

Dipsi shuddered a little bit. "They still give me the creeps."

Elodie was no longer listening, nor was she holding her girlfriend's hand. She stood as close to the shark as was permissible, her body reaching over the metal bar. The megalodon's jaw was agape, humble teeth leading to a maw in supplication. Elodie wanted to sit in that jaw, press her ear to the hollow of its mandible like it were a shell and listen to sounds of prehistoric waves. She would understand its hallowed stories. Elodie knew what it was to be misunderstood.

Dipsi came up behind her, taking Elodie's hand back into her own, a warmth welcomed by the girl so in awe of the animal.

"The megalodon could still exist," Elodie mused. "There's so much of the ocean we can explore if we were given the chance."

Ms. Paz - who had kept a thoughtful distance while Elodie met her version of Jesus - eventually caught up to the pair, another figure of a woman in tow. When Elodie turned to see it was her mother, the sight jarred her at first - like the modern humans walking in the body of a million year old shark. The shock of seeing her mother in the presence of Ms. Paz, Dipsi, and all of this progressive, new-age science shook her reality for a second.

"I invited her." Dipsi let out a laugh. "Actually, she invited herself."

Elodie's mother spoke. "I called as soon as you left the house."

Elodie's knuckles whitened. "So, what, you followed us here?"

"No, not at all!" Mother dipped into her pocketbook for a tissue. "What started as a harmless check-in turned into an invite." She sighed and placed a hand on her daughter's shoulder. "I wanted to see what you were doing. I don't understand you, Elodie. I never have." The final words came as a whisper, a prayer in the presence of the megalodon, the guardian watching Elodie from its bony display.

The woman was uncomfortable, but not willing to make a scene at the Dipsi and Elodie, their innocence, their intimacy, their queerness on display in such a public space.

"Come on," Dipsi said. "She's not here to fight. Just give her a chance."

"She's going to hate this."

"I thought you didn't care what she thought."

With a quick kiss on Elodie's cheek, Dipsi fled with her own mother to another exhibit. After, it was just Elodie and her mother, in silent submission to the shark's presence.

"I can see why you're so taken with this strange creature," mother said. "It's fascinating to look at, if nothing else."

Elodie placed her palms inside her pockets, but said nothing.

"The teeth," her mother said. "They're the size of soda bottles!"

"Both of our bodies could fit inside its jaw."

"Would it kill us?"

"Of course Mother, that's what sharks do."

Her mother pondered this for a moment. "I recall you saying something about their poor vision? Perhaps it would kill us, but it would not be intentional." She looked at her daughter. "It's not the shark's intent to cause little humans such harm."

Elodie couldn't look directly at her mother. The concern was too foreign. Instead, she watched them both through the looking glass of the shark's shiny mouth, where they were both distorted figures, indiscernible from one another. The illusion didn't last. Mother drew her back to the present with an arm around her back, a motherly squeeze to her foreign baby.

"I do envy you," Mother said. "You'll go on to be happy, study what you like."

"You could still have that life, you know."

Mother took hold of her shoulder, a silent reconing. "In my day, I was never brave enough to even try and correct my mother."

Elodie's heart felt as big as a tooth in her throat as she choked on Panthalassa waves of breath hitching over her tonsils. She pressed her ear to her mother's shoulder, listening to the sounds of the old-fashioned woman. She didn't sound like a shark, nor did Elodie understand the rhythm of her blood's flow. But in that moment, in the shark's presence, her mother was a medicine - a feminine mystique bound by relativity.

Hand cupped like the shark's jaw, Elodie's mother took tender hold of her hair, curling the ends until it sat short on her shoulders.

The weight of those locks fell from the back to the front. Elodie asked her mother for a cut - maybe even a bob.

Her mother sighed with a placative smile. "I suppose we will see."

The Science Project

Nikolas Thornton

It was a crisp early October morning. A brilliant orange sunrise emblazoned the distant eastern sky. Like the bugle call before the running of the Kentucky Derby, it was a foretelling of the wondrous event to come. A gentle southern breeze tossed Mike's hair as he waited patiently at the corner bus stop. He was smiling. Not like those who just smile all the time for no reason, Mike was smiling due to a sense of great personal accomplishment. He had worked hard, late into many nights, to earn that smile. The world was about to discover that Mike alone had stretched the very fabric of mankind's current envelope of scientific knowledge. He heard the familiar engine sound of the school bus down the street. Today was a very special day. In addition to his regular overstuffed backpack load of unnecessarily thick, heavy school books, dog-eared notebooks, finished homework, nearing-completion term papers, pencils, pens, and snacks, on this morning Mike cradled a secret treasure in his arms. The treasure was hidden under a light blue blanket. The treasure grew heavier by the second as Mike waited for the school bus to arrive. Finally, with a loud hiss the school bus stopped at Mike's bus stop. The bus's bi-fold doors slowly unfolded, welcoming Mike inside. Mike carefully contorted his body to fit what he carried and himself up the narrow stairway inside the bus. Unable to see, Mike carefully searched for each step with his foot before proceeding up the stairs. Mike smiled at the bus driver who wished him a cheerful "Good morning, Mike" as he passed.

"Is that it?" beamed Robin as Mike walked past her down the center aisle of the school bus.

Mike carried his secret treasure under a light blue cotton blanket further down the bus's center aisle. "It is" replied Mike with a sly grin as he slid into the bench seat behind Robin.

Mike held the blanket-covered object on his lap for safe keeping. Robin's freshly curling-ironed brown hair framed her face adorably as she popped her head up over the top of the seat. She kneeled backwards on her seat to face Mike.

"Does it work?" gushed Robin, still beaming.

"Of course it works" replied Mike "Well, it better work if I'm going to win the contest."

"I couldn't think of anything to make for the science fair so you might just win this year" smiled Robin.

"I think I've got a real shot with this" said Mike, confidently nodding his head towards the hidden object on his lap.

"Can I see it?" asked Robin eagerly.

"No, no, no" replied Mike "Showing you now would ruin the surprise."

"Well then, tell me what it does" said Robin a little dejectedly with a frown.

"No, no, no" replied Mike "That too would ruin the surprise."

"Best friends get certain things, you know. Like rights and privileges that others don't get, you know?" said Robin, her face starting to twist into a deeper frown.

"Okay, but just a peek" said Mike.

Robin reached out her right arm cautiously towards the nearest edge of the blue blanket.

"Will it bite?" asked Robin with a giggle in her voice as her delicate fingers gingerly grasped a corner of the blanket.

"Maybe" answered Mike with a laugh.

Robin carefully lifted the corner of the blanket slowly until she could see what was hiding beneath it. Robin gasped slightly as her eyes slowly looked away from the hidden object up into Mike's eyes then quickly back to the hidden treasure.

"You did it!" whispered Robin in a church voice tone of reverence. Her beautiful blue eyes were open wider than Mike had ever seen them before.

"You're going to win, buddy. You've got this," whispered Robin, her jaw hanging slightly agog as her eyes went from Mike's eyes back to the thing under the blanket, then back to Mike's eyes.

Mike smiled feeling even more confident now that he really had a shot at winning first prize at the science fair at his school this year.

"This was going to be a good year" Mike thought to himself as Robin slowly lowered the blanket's edge while winking at him.

The school bus slowly made its way up the school's main driveway. Mike waited until all the other kids exited the bus before getting off. Robin waited patiently on the bus with Mike. Once the swarm of kids had passed it was safe to take his project off the bus. All the students piled into the school building through the rack of glass doors at the school's front.

The school auditorium was decorated with rocket ships, swirling atoms, and several other things that were intended to make the space seem more science-like than normal this morning. There were tables set up all around the edge of the room to display the kids' science projects. Mike picked an empty table nearest the stage to set up his project. Robin rushed up behind him and put her head on his right shoulder.

"Good choice professor!" announced Robin as she hugged Mike

from behind "Right up front where all the best projects should be!"
she said with a smile. "Now set her down gently" said Robin as she
rushed around in front of Mike to help him maneuver his project
cautiously onto the table top. Robin guided him in like a landing
signal officer on an aircraft carrier.

"There!" said Mike as he slowly moved his hands away from his
project now safely resting on the table top, still covered by the blue
blanket.

"Well?" said Robin shrugging her shoulders. "Aren't you going to
unveil her?" She pointed at the blue blanket inquisitively.

"No" answered Mike "I won't do that until the judges are
standing right in front of the table. I want one of those dramatic *ta
dah* moments, you know."

"You are officially a goofball" said Robin as she hugged Mike
around the neck giving him a kiss on the cheek "but I love you
anyway. I'm going to be late for first period!"

Robin turned and ran towards the open doors of the auditorium
to the hallway beyond, her adorable brown curls bouncing all the
way. Mike watched Robin until she rounded the bend to head off
down the hallway. The auditorium was now empty. Mike took the
blanket off his secret project. He carefully lifted it up to his head. The
device made a clicking noise. A few moments later, Mike reluctantly
turned to walk away from his science project and headed off to his
first period class.

The science fair was to be held right after lunch. The morning
dragged by at a snail's pace. Finally the lunch bell rang. Then, in the
cafeteria, Mike sat at the long folding lunch table staring down at his
lunch tray. His lunch tray had a grayish hamburger on a slightly stale
bun, a pyramid of golden tater tots, a small stack of somewhat freezer
burnt carrot sticks, and a slice of apple pie on a small circular thick
white ceramic plate. Mike had barely touched any of it when he felt

a bump against his left side as Robin slid in next to him sliding her own tray next to his.

"Those tater tots aren't going to eat themselves, you know," said Robin, smiling at Mike.

"I'm just nervous, I guess. I'm not really very hungry" answered Mike.

"What the heck is that?" asked Robin excitedly pointing to the right side of the lunchroom.

Mike turned quickly to look, but saw nothing. When he turned back he saw that Robin now looked like a chipmunk with her cheeks both puffed out. "All you had to do was ask, you know. I would have given them to you" said Mike as looked down at what remained of his allotment of school cafeteria tater tots.

Robin slowly titled her head from side to side. She looked inquisitively confused and bewildered like a dog when they hear another dog barking on TV. She acted as if she had no idea what he was talking about as she chewed as unnoticeably as possible.

After a quick swallow, Robin said "You have nothing at all to be nervous about buddy. You've got this in the bag bucko" Robin smiled reassuringly.

"I hope you're right," said Mike as he picked up his gray-meat, cafeteria hamburger.

"I almost forgot" said Robin as she flattened her right hand out. Her knuckles turned completely white, her face twisted into a grimace as her nose wrinkled like a bunny. Her hand slowly worked its way down towards the bottom of her pants front pocket. "There! Got it!" exclaimed Robin as she slowly worked her hand out of her pants pocket.

"How do you breathe in those things?" asked Mike looking down as Robin's hand, still whitened from lack of blood flow, popped out of her pants pocket.

"I don't" answered Robin as she took a deep breath "but I look good, right?"

Mike looked down towards the ground awkwardly, but offered no reply.

"Look at that! Huh? Pretty amazing, right?" said Robin as she opened her hand up revealing a quarter in the palm of her right hand.

"Look at what? The quarter?" asked Mike, confused.

"It's not just a quarter, you goon" answered Robin shaking her head side to side.

"It's not just a quarter?" replied Mike "It sure looks a lot like a quarter."

"I know" gushed Robin excitedly "That's the beauty of it! It's a coin with a secret. A big secret! Want to know what the secret is? Hmm, do you?

"Yes, I want to know what the plain, ordinary looking quarter's secret is please" laughed Mike "Will you tell me its secret please?"

Robin looked around to make sure nobody could hear what she was about to say. When she thought the coast was clear, she told Mike the quarter's secret.

"Well, because you are my best friend, and best friends are allowed certain extra privileges, as we discussed earlier, yes, yes I will tell you. It has a magic spell on it," said Robin with a goofy smile, lifting and lowering her right eyebrow repeatedly for dramatic punctuation.

"It does?" whispered Mike.

"It does!" whispered back Robin looking around to make sure they still weren't being eavesdropped on. "You see laddie, the world's smartest leprechaun hid his gold coins in plain sight by putting a magic spell on all of his gold coins to make them look like regular coins. Smart, right?" Robin nodded knowingly at Mike, then winked at him. "Pretty cool, right? It has magical properties too. It's a wish coin" Robin placed her index finger against Mike's lips. "No telling. It's our secret. Pinky swear?"

Robin extended her pinky up for Mike to shake. Mike wrapped his pinky around hers.

"Yes, I pinky swear, but um, if he's the smartest leprechaun ever, how do you have one of his magic coins? Hmm?" asked Mike tilting his chin down.

"I won it!" announced Robin proudly.

"You did, did you?" replied Mike.

"Yep, I sure did" answered Robin smiling proudly, lifting her chin slightly with her lower lip jutted out slightly with pride.

"How did you win a magic coin from the world's smartest leprechaun?" asked Mike.

"Well, I bet the leprechaun that I could hold my breath longer than he could hold his breath. I'm really good at holding my breath, you know" said Robin as she gave Mike a light tap on his left shoulder with her right fist.

"Show me," said Mike.

"Sure!" said Robin who then took an exaggerated long deep inhale of air then pursed her lips tight together with her cheeks puffed out filled with air rather than tater tots this time. Robin's brow was deeply furloughed as her face went through a myriad of expressions as she continued to hold her breath longer and longer.

"You better breathe soon or you'll die," said Mike as Robin's facial expressions became more and more exaggerated and her skin tone started to change into an unhealthy color.

Finally, Robin let out a loud exhale as her chest and cheeks deflated simultaneously.

"Pretty impressive," confirmed Mike as the color returned to Robin's cheeks. "That leprechaun didn't stand a chance against you."

"I know, right?" smiled Robin "Here it's yours." She handed her magic golden leprechaun coin disguised as a normal quarter to Mike.

"I can't," said Mike as he tried to hand the quarter back to Robin "It's magic. It's yours. You won it."

"Falling on deaf ears here, pal. It's yours now, buddy" said Robin as she refused to take the coin back. "It might just be the thing that helps you win the contest today. Not that you need the extra help, but there you go."

Robin returned her concentration back to the food remaining on her lunch tray. Her right hand had almost returned to normal color. She slowly turned her head towards Mike after taking a big bite of her hamburger. Mike turned to look back at her.

Robin slowly raised both her hands. She made magic fingers at Mike while whispering, "Magic."

"And I'm the goofball" whispered Mike, shaking his head.

Robin then smiled that smile of hers that Mike secretly loved so much. His heart melted. Mike slid Robin's magic quarter down into the front right pocket of his much looser pants.

The auditorium was bustling with activity as Mike and Robin entered. Students had all gathered in the center of the auditorium. Those who had brought in science projects to enter into the contest huddled around the edges of the room at their respective tables. Mike and Robin worked their way through the crowd to their table. There, just as he had left it, sat Mike's science project still safely hidden under the blue cotton blanket.

A bugle sounded. All the students swung around to look towards the stage where the long red velvet curtains slowly parted. The curtains revealed three adults dressed in long black gowns with tall, pointy, black sparkly wizard caps on their heads. Dense black veils completely covered their faces. The veils had small narrow slots cut into them so they could see. These were the judges for today's contest. Everybody knew that they were three of the school science teachers, but their costumes made it more dramatic. Applause broke out from the crowd. The judges slowly bowed in appreciation. One judge almost lost his cap when he bowed but he caught it just in time. The judges turned to their right. They walked seriously in a single file line across the stage, then slowly descended the stage stairs opposite Mike and Robin's table.

"We'll be last." Mike turned and whispered to Robin.

"You should always save the best for last" Robin whispered back to Mike "Like when you are eating a great dinner. You always save a bite of your favorite food for last so that flavor stays with you the longest."

"I do that too!" whispered Mike.

"Great minds, buddy" whispered back Robin with a smile, "Great minds."

The judges made their way around the edge of the auditorium. Each contestant demonstrated their entries. Mike craned his neck trying to see what the other students had made. There were a lot of volcanoes, some potato clocks, a solar powered hamster wheel, and a backpack that doubled as a stool. As Mike evaluated each of the other entries none of them seemed that great to him. Robin nuzzled up close to Mike as the judges grew ever closer to their table.

"Come on! Tell me what it does," said Robin pointing to Mike's blanket-covered entry as her hands tickled his ribs.

"You're going to have to unveil it and tell the judges anyway. I'll be right here, you know? I'm going to hear what you tell them. Don't best friends deserve a little privilege, ahead of everybody else's information? Hmm? I told you the secret of the magic coin, did I not?" said Robin, smiling a goofy smile while tilting her head back and forth again like a dog hearing another dog's bark coming from the TV.

"Yeah, okay" answered Mike. He leaned over to whisper what the device does into Robin's ear.

"No way!" exclaimed Robin in a whispered shout as she put her hands on her hips. "Did you try it?" asked Robin.

"Yep, I did," answered Mike.

"What did it say?" asked Robin.

"Well, ummm, it said, it said that I'm not going to win today" Mike replied just as the judges appeared at his table.

"Well, what do we have here!" boomed one of the judges as they stood in a semicircle around Mike's table.

"It looks like a lumpy blue blanket," laughed one of the judges.

"I don't think we've ever had a lumpy blue blanket entry before!" laughed another of the judges.

"It is a nice blanket," laughed one of the judges "Baby blue too!"

"It's, it's under the blanket," stammered Mike nervously.

"Oh, okay," laughed a judge. "Can we see what you have *under* the blanket?"

"Sure," replied Mike as he cautiously lifted the blue blanket and handed it to Robin.

There, on the presentation table, sat a 70's era green metallic flake, adult-sized motorcycle helmet. It had a weave of spaghetti-twisted electrical wires and small LED Christmas lights festooning it's top. On the helmet's front was attached a full face visor which was painted completely black.

"I see. Okay," said one of the judges "Is it a more padded, lighted helmet that makes motorcycle riding at night safer?"

"No, sir," replied Mike.

"Then what problem does your invention solve?" asked another judge.

"None, sir, I mean it doesn't really solve problems at all," answered Mike nervously.

"Then what does it do?" asked another of the judges.

"It's more like a communication device," replied Mike "A prognosticator of sorts."

"Like a phone you put on your head?" asked a judge "Don't they already have those ear things that act like phones?"

"Yes, sir, they do already have those types of phones, but my invention isn't like those" answered Mike.

"Then what exactly does your invention do?" asked one of the judges.

Clearing his throat, Mike answered, "When you put my invention on it tells you something you weren't supposed to know."

"It does that, does it?" laughed one of the judges, then they all laughed together "That's amazing!"

"What did it tell you when you put it on?" asked a judge.

Mike sheepishly looked at Robin from the corner of his eye then back at the judges "Um, it told me that I wasn't going to win this contest."

Robin let out a disappointed sigh.

"It's not over yet, son" reassured one of the judges. "Let me give this invention of yours a whirl"

One judge removed his cap and veil. It was Mr. Dermit, the 8th grade science teacher, just as they had all suspected. Mr. Dermit placed the helmet down over his head.

"What do I do now?" asked Mr. Dermit, now wearing the helmet.

"You just close the visor until it clicks closed, sir. That turns it on," answered Mike.

The judge slowly lowered the blackened out visor until it clicked in place. The lights on the top of the helmet started flashing and a slight whirring noise emanated from inside the helmet device. The judge had been laughing dismissively as he closed the visor, but then he went completely silent. The other judges removed their caps and veils revealing themselves to be Mrs. Paisley, and Mr. Fred, other science teachers from the school. Mr. Dermit stood in complete silence still wearing the helmet on his head as the lights continued to flash and the whirring sound grew quieter.

"Dan? Dan? You okay?" asked Mrs. Paisley as she started to get concerned.

Mr. Fred reached over and slowly lifted the blackened visor of the helmet. It revealed that Mr. Dermit's face had gone completely pale. His eyes were wide open. His face was expressionless. Mr. Dermit just stood there motionless. He had a vacant, thousand-yard stare in his dilated, non-blinking eyes. Mr. Fred cautiously lifted the helmet off Mr. Dermit's head.

"Dan? What happened? Did the helmet actually tell you something?" asked Mr. Fred nervously.

Mr. Dermit spoke not a word, but nodded his head slightly up and down.

"It did?" asked Mrs. Paisley "What did it tell you? Was it something you weren't supposed to know?"

Again, Mr. Dermit nodded his head slowly up and down. Mr. Dermit turned and walked away slowly.

"I've got to try this!" said Mrs. Paisley excitedly as she took the helmet from Mr. Fred.

She placed the helmet on her head. Mrs. Paisley then slowly closed the blackened visor until it clicked shut. The lights started flashing on top of the helmet as the whirring sound grew louder. Robin looked at Mike with a quizzical look.

"What did it tell him?" Robin whispered to Mike.

"I don't know" answered Mike "I think it tells everybody something different, I guess. It's their own secret that they aren't supposed to know," replied Mike shrugging his shoulders.

A few moments later Mr. Fred lifted the visor covering Mrs. Paisley's face. He gently lifted the helmet off her head. Mrs. Paisley had the same blank, pale, vacant-eyed expression as Mr. Dermit had had. Slowly, Mrs. Dermit walked away. The final judge, Mr. Fred, then placed the helmet on his head. He closed the blackened visor until it clicked. The lights on the top of the helmet lit up as the whirring sound buzzed. A few moments later, Mike lifted the blackened visor to find Mr. Fred with the same thousand-yard stare and pale face as the other judges had had after receiving their message. Mike slowly lifted the helmet off Mr. Fred's head. Mr. Fred then slowly walked away in a somewhat catatonic state.

"Holy crap!" said Robin as she watched the last judge walk away. Robin clutched Mike's blue blanket tightly against her chest "You've really got something there buddy!"

Robin looked from the helmet back to the zombie-like teacher slowly walking towards the stage, then back to Mike's invention.

"Would you like to try it?" Mike asked Robin.

"Yes! No! I mean I would, but I'm afraid" confessed Robin "Maybe we aren't supposed to know certain things for a reason, you know? Did you see their faces? They were like zombies, dude! I would, but no, I'm not going to try it, not now anyway."

Mike nodded in agreement with her decision "I understand more than you know."

"I wonder what it told them? It told you you wouldn't win the contest right, which stinks, and I hope it's wrong, but that isn't earth shattering news. It's just bad news. There's always next year's contest to try again, right? Whatever the helmet told them shook them to their very core. Holy crap!" said Robin bouncing giddily from foot to foot.

Ted appeared in the auditorium's doorway. He waved to Robin. Robin waved back excitedly. Ted ran across the room. He picked Robin up in his arms and spun her around. The two kissed as Ted slowly lowered Robin back down to her feet.

"Sorry I'm late, babe." Ted said with a smile to Robin.

"You're always late" Robin laughed.

The two held hands as they turned towards Mike.

"So what happened, dude? Did you win?" Ted asked Mike.

"They haven't announced the winners yet" Mike solemnly replied.

Mike secretly clutched the magic quarter in his pocket tightly as he whispered to himself "Please be wrong. Please be wrong."

Just then the three judges appeared on the stage behind a wooden podium with a microphone attached to it. The judges were still visibly shaken as they each stepped up to the podium individually to announce the name of the winners. They announced the third place winner of the contest. The crowd cheered. They announced the second place winner. The crowd cheered. Finally, they announced the first place winner. The crowd cheered the loudest. None of the names announced as the winners were Mike's. Each of the winners walked up onto the stage and were presented their trophies.

"That blows, dude" said Ted to Mike as the last winner was announced.

Mike nodded slightly.

"We'll get them next year. You wait and see" Robin said supportively as she patted Mike softly on his shoulder.

Robin then jumped onto Ted's back as Ted turned to leave the auditorium. Robin handed the blanket back to Mike. Ted then started galloping across the auditorium floor. Robin was straddling his back, riding piggyback towards the exit. Robin giggled in delight as they went. Just before Ted and Robin disappeared through the exit doors, Robin turned and waved back to Mike.

"Well, anyway," Robin called back to Mike across the auditorium, "the helmet was right, right? You nailed it!"

Mike waved back, but it was a sad, dejected wave as Ted and Robin disappeared out into the hallway beyond the auditorium, laughing all the way. Mike listened as Robin's laughter grew distant."Yes, yes it was right," Mike whispered solemnly to himself.

Mike slowly picked up the helmet and tucked in under his right arm. He tossed the blue blanket over his left shoulder, and started walking slowly towards the exit door. Just as Mike was passing a line of trash cans next to the auditorium's exit doors, someone placed a hand on his shoulder from behind. Mike turned to see Mrs. Paisley standing there. The color had almost completely returned to her face, but she still appeared somewhat stunned by her experience with the helmet. Mrs. Paisley smiled at Mike.

"You know," Mrs. Paisley softly said, "Your invention was easily the most impressive one here today, but we just couldn't give it first prize, or any prize for that matter, it was just too, well, you know, dangerous, before it's time. You understand, don't you?"

"I do," replied Mike. "I do understand."

"Did you try the device yourself?" asked Mrs. Paisley.

"I did," answered Mike.

"May I ask what the helmet told you?" asked Mrs. Paisley cautiously.

Mike paused for a moment. He cleared his throat. "The helmet told me that the love of my life would never love me back the same way I love her" confessed Mike.

Mike looked down at the ground. He had finally spoken the truth of what the helmet had told him.

Mrs. Paisley gave Mike a hug. "That's very sad, Michael. I'm so sorry." Mrs. Paisley patted Mike on the shoulder. "But, Michael," she continued, "that's the same thing it told me and the other judges. Love is a very fickle thing. The ones we love don't always love us back. The ones we love the most always never love us back as strongly. In romance, someone is always chasing. Someone is always being chased."

Mike nodded in agreement. He took the helmet from under his right arm. He dropped the helmet into one of the trash cans. The helmet hit the bottom of the can with a loud thump. Mike slowly walked towards the exit doors. He had his hand down deep in his pants pocket tightly grasping Robin's magic coin. Mike smiled slightly as a passing breeze lifted Robin's perfume from his blue cotton blanket still over his left shoulder.

Never lose hope. Don't ever let anyone, or anything, crush your dreams. As long as you have hope, anything is impossible. Your wildest dream may come true one day. Mike still carries that magic quarter in his pocket to this day.

How to Act

Aimee LaBrie

First, accept that you are only better than average, talent-wise. As far as looks go, you have understudy potential, but not star power. Your mother warns that you shouldn't get your hopes up too high, what with your orthodontia issues. Your father says your mother is just jealous. Your real role in life will be to serve as a captive audience member for their arguments.

(Use it! Use it for scene study class!)

Your mom, a former actress turned secretary for Bloomer's Plumbing Company, isn't one of those people who believes she could have made it if she had only spent more time in New York. Hell, no! She did live in Manhattan for ten years, scuttling from one audition to another. The closest she came was as a model for Maidenform bras. Photos of her torso hung on department store bra tags across the country for years and years. "Those were some of the best years of my life," she likes to say, after a few gin and tonics. "And then I met your father and had you." She scans the living room, looking for something to reveal character. She catches your eye. "And those were some great years too," she adds with a fifty-watt smile.

You will never give up like your mother did. You will also be nicer, have a more stylish haircut, hire a house cleaner. You will not slam the dishwasher, kick it, and go, "This goddamn piece of shit is the best he could do?"

The "he" is your father, a sad and quiet man with hunched shoulders who likes mystery novels and thinks you are the greatest thing that ever happened. You will later discover that his bar for excellent is pretty low.

You are followed around by an invisible little audience, not a chummy one. They scrutinize every move: *well, that wasn't very believable, was it?* You are always trying to impress them, your cagey onlookers, judging your every move, even when you are merely sitting in a hot car in the parking lot of Piggly Wiggly waiting for your mother to finish talking to the boy who takes away the carts: *The girl sits in the car, sweating. She squints, narrowing her eyes, wondering if her mother knows she's throwing herself at the bag boy.* Even when you are alone, you have to remind yourself to act natural. The audience cheers when you execute a perfect last line aimed at your mother before exiting stage left into the bathroom. They scowl when you flub your lines at dinner, causing your father to drink more. They are particularly raucous at night when you're trying to fall asleep. They sit in their cushioned theater seats, rocking back and forth to replay your performance for the day—oh, look at how she embarrassed herself by attempting to talk to the gym teacher to get out of kickball. How hilarious was that??

Remind yourself that it just takes practice. Practice acting normal, as if everything were okay, and eventually, people will believe you. *Believe in you!*

After you choose theater as a college minor, develop terrible crushes on the actors; or rather on the characters they play (like the psychopath in *The Zoo Story*). These boys are wounded, vulnerable. They tend to wear James Cagney-type hats and women's cardigans.

The one who stops you cold is Michael Chick—seriously, he is the best actor in the whole program—when you're near him, even in close proximity, the same building, the same class room, the same party—your body feels altered, as if you have landed on a different planet and don't know how to breathe. You're weightless, like nothing. You've lost all sense of your own wonderfulness. All those years of tap lessons and vocal instruction, all of the training in becoming someone else, and you are rendered only your worst self in his aura. Scarecrow awkward, clumsy, tongue too thick for banter.

George Judy, your scene study acting teacher, also does not believe your grief in Anne Frank's monologue. "You're faking it,"' he says, arms crossed. Most days, he is a nice man with a calming voice—a grizzly bear with an Abraham Lincoln beard and tousled, thinning hair. Once, years ago, he had the minor lead in a major long-running Broadway show.

He's right. You are faking it all the time—in class, on stage, in bed with your high school boyfriend whose face you used to daydream about and who now, when he visits, makes you feel slightly ill, as if you've swallowed curdled milk. You imagine how sad it will be to break up with him. You feel nothing.

You conjure up the saddest images you can—those starving kids in the Sally Struthers UNICEF commercials, or the commercial that shows pit bulls left in cages with patches of their fur missing, or that time your grandma almost died from high blood pressure but didn't. Remember: she will die, one day. This thought helps you squeeze out one or two tears and George Judy applauds. The praise goes straight to your brain like a cold bite of an ice cream sandwich, making you dizzy.

Later, your friend Wallis Payne (voice major) asks you how you managed to cry on cue. You tell her you thought about your grandma dying. She stares back at you, head cocked. "Why didn't you just think about how Anne Frank's entire family was, like, doomed and being sent to a concentration camp?"

It didn't even occur to you to consider connecting to what was actually happening in the scene.

In your two years as a theater major, you will practice scenes that include: a woman terrorized by a rapist (*Extremities*), a spouse whose husband murders her (*Othello*), a Southern belle driven mad by rejection (*A Streetcar Named Desire*), and a daughter who will shoot herself in the last scene (*'Night Mother*).

In stagecraft, practice falling again and again, in a convincing way without twisting your ankle, bonking your head, getting a black eye. Learning to fall is easy, you just have to not think about it, you have to let go of the fear of pain, and go down with grace, with a sudden thud. You practice this again and again in your living room while your roommates watch a marathon of *Law and Order, Special Victims Unit*.

For the spring Mainstage productions, they post the cast lists on the theater bulletin board. Students crowd around in packs, one wave after another. You search for your name, anywhere, on anything. You don't see it. Around you, girls and boys are screaming and jumping up and down, trilling songs.

Tad, a guy next to you who is wearing a turban for seemingly no reason, says, "Hey, congratulations."

You say, "What?"

He says, "Nice job."

You look again at the list, scanning more slowly this time. You check the cast list again, and realize you've been looking for your mom's name, not your own—she is Donna Martelli. You have a role in *Cat on a Hot Tin Roof*. Not the lead—you're the bitchy neighbor lady. You feel a spike of joy, followed almost immediately by doubt.

Nice try, but you are a minor character.

Then, the counterargument, *It's mainstage! That's a big deal, honey.*

Realize in that moment that these voices are your parents, and they will stay with you, arguing over your value, for the rest of your life.

As a consolation, you are Maggie's understudy. If this were a movie, you would find a way to poison Kiera Reilly so you could be Maggie on opening night. Michael Chick plays Brick, the wounded gay husband who is in love with his best friend, Skip.

During one rehearsal and one rehearsal only, you rehearse as Maggie with Michael Chick play. You fan at the sweat under your armpits. You seem to be speaking in a slightly British accent, god knows why. It's Tennessee Williams, for Christ's sake. But you don't have to act, not a bit. You are Maggie—you have her longing for something. Not for something—for *someone*. For Brick. For him.

After rehearsal, you imagine the director going, "I made a huge mistake! We must switch roles!"

He does not say that. Life is not like the movies. Plays are not even like the movies.

But he does say, "I knew I could count on you. You're a good watcher."

Only once does Michael Chick approach you, after a long rehearsal that ends with drinks at the director's house. You stand rooted in the corner, stuck by a sticky table filled with bottles of alcohol and red plastic cups. You will need several of those drinks before the dusty worm of your tongue can form sentences and what would those sentences even be? *How was your acting class today? Do you believe in God? Where are you from? What were you like as a kid?* The more you drink, the odder your questions will be, so it's a delicate balance of intoxication—too much and you will sound blurry and unhinged—too little, and your voice stalls.

He comes over to you. "I like your broach." His finger hovers near your throat.

Your hand flies to the pin. You have forgotten what you're wearing—can't think how it happens to be on your body. "Thank you. I stole if off my grandmother's corpse," you say, trying to joke around.

He smiles and frowns at the same time. He's in advanced acting class. He has learned to convey complicated, mixed emotions in a single handsome glance. And then he leaves. He always seems to be leaving.

Opening night for *Cat on a Hot Tin Roof.* You are on stage with Brick for a total of one, five minute scene. You have twenty-two lines.

You know your dad is in the audience. Your mom is unable to attend. You cannot look out to find him, but you feel a wave of love for him, knowing he is there.

Curtain falls. You all embrace, a sweaty group hug where everyone gets pancake makeup on each other. *Great job! We did it!* All but Michael Chick, who has left behind only a smudged handkerchief with his left-over make up on it.

Your dad, who has temporarily moved out of the house, shows up at the cast party. He presents you with a dozen wilted daisies. "Honey, you were the only one I could watch," he says. When he hugs you, he seems smaller than you remember.

Your theater friends squeal and exclaim over your dad. One of the boys sits in his lap, draped across his shoulders like a stole, "Darling, your father is a doll!!" Your father's face is lit up like a flame, but he doesn't move away.

Watching your dad, you decide that you don't have the stamina for that type of ongoing performance, the constant parade of big expressions made so that the people in the back row can see them. Something is wrong with you, because you cannot toss your head, you cannot laugh a laugh from the bottom of your belly, you cannot grow suddenly still and distant-eyed and spill out a line of

Shakespearean dialogue: "Parting is such sweet sorrow/That I should like to stay again 'til it be morrow."

Later in the party, you and your dad both watch Michael Chick walk in, wearing a butterscotch suede jacket.

"He was phenomenal," your dad whispers.

"I know."

"Is he straight?"

You say, "I have no clue." If your dad tries to talk to Michael Chick, you will combust on the spot. Your dad, weaving slightly, makes his way over to him. You close your eyes, you cannot watch.

A few seconds later, a hand touches your arm. It's him. Michael Chick. "Hey," he says. "Your dad says he's not okay to drive you home. I can give you a lift."

You nod. You now know what true love is.

Michael Chick has brought along a bottle of red wine with a hand-drawn goat on the label. You sit on the front porch of your rented house, drinking the wine as fast as possible, worrying about the color of your teeth.

He tells you a long, involved story about a book he's reading that describes some guys driving motorcycles across the country.

"I read that," you say. Your teeth clink on the glass as you take another long sip.

"What?"

"I read that one. The motorcycle maintenance book." You go on to wonder why it is that guys think that's such a great book or how they think it's so subversive to fight the system by riding a motorcycle. Like, if you want to make a difference, how about going to India to save some starving kids? You realize that your real self is starting to poke its head out, like a groundhog. You dig your fingers into your thighs, trying to squash that voice.

He doesn't seem to care, because he's standing now, pulling you up next to him as if the two of you might waltz.

When Michael Chick kisses you, it is exactly like a scene from a love story. Moonlight scatters across the blank sidewalk. He pulls your hair away from your face and leans toward you. Up close, his pupils are huge black circles. He smells like suede and wood smoke. His jacket is as soft as a deer. His kiss is not a disappointment, and when he pulls away, he says, "I've wanted to do that for a long time," which rings familiar, like a line from a play.

You stumble inside the house, relieved your roommates are away for the weekend, and take him to your twin bed, scattering the stuffed animals. He lays down next to you, and says, "Why have you been so hard to catch?"

This makes no sense. Of all of the people in all of the world, he is the one you most wanted to notice you. You say nothing. You lie in the dark, heart sputtering with fear. You don't know how to move, but he does, and you follow his lead. He is, after all, a leading man.

And when it's over and he sighs asleep next to you, you can't figure out why you feel a sudden sadness, a shooting pain located in the center of your palm. Why are you suddenly thinking about your grandma when there is no one there to see you cry? Even as you feel real tears sliding down into your hair, another part of you is telling yourself to remember this.

Remember this feeling in case you ever need to use it to play a scene of grief.

The next morning, his fingers fluttering through his curls, his eyes on the peeling white ceiling, he says, "I don't know who I'm going to be today."

You pull the sheet up. "I don't know what you mean. Like, you might be a fireman? A farmer?" He continues to stare, like a man who is used to being observed. You say your favorite line from the play: "Why don't you ask if he makes *me* happy in bed?" He looks at you now, just one emotion on his face now—confusion.

He doesn't know who you are. You stare back. You don't know him either. Maybe what you liked about him wasn't him at all—it was Dionysus and Hamlet and Brick.

And he smokes a little pot from a bong he made of toilet paper roll. You have nothing to say to one another. He doesn't kiss you good-bye. He gets on his moped and he leaves.

Curtain falls.

You watch him go, standing in your underwear and bra on the front porch.

The truth is, you're not good enough. You might make it if you can envision the next ten years in New York, juggling poverty, waitressing, auditioning, and receiving rejection after rejection after rejection after rejection after rejection. Well, all life has rejection, but not that particular form of rejection where you're told exactly what's wrong with you by a blur of faceless men sitting in a darkened theater after you audition with a piece from *The Vagina Monologues*. You'd like to skip that whole part and be discovered, like Judy Garland at a malt shop.

There are no malt shops where you live, only gas stations and consignment shops and places that promise happy hour for undergraduates.

Plot twist: you discover you are more like your dad than your mom.

Switch your major to English. You call your dad to tell him. He says, "You're an amazing actress, but you also have a sharp mind. You'll be brilliant." When he asks you if you would like to speak to your mother, realize that you can say no. Say no.

In English classes, you will analyze the misogyny of Tennessee Williams instead of embodying it. Discover a whole new genre of longing—Daisy Buchanan, Jane Eyre, Hester Prynne—like you and your dad, aren't we all just waiting for the right guy to show up? Or the wrong guy to leave?

English majors drink black coffee and talk about books. They do not break into songs from *Music Man* in the middle of a Victorian poetry seminar. They lean forward, and earnestly (and quietly) discuss the Western Canon. They are incredibly boring and have their own form of auditioning by using words like "deconstructive narrative" and "neocolonial narcissism." But you already know how to fake it, nod at the right time, pretend to understand.

Though you don't know it then, the theater experience has prepared you for certain future life events, such as presenting a PowerPoint at a board meeting.

"You don't even seem to get nervous," Rhonda, a temp-to-permanent hire from the Business Office, will say.

"Thanks," you will answer with a shrug, playing modesty.

The Edge of Things

Charissa Roberson

The sky is the color of used bathwater. Out on the harbor, a stiff wind whips the water into waves, which in turn send the boats bobbing up and down against their mooring lines, their hulls nudging over and over into the rubber bumpers that protect them from the docks. Overhead, seagulls bob up and down like little boats of their own, riding the currents of the air.

I cast an uneasy glance at the sky as I spoon down my oatmeal. The trip to school will be a rough one today. Even when the waves roll with the smooth, easy rhythm of the jazz we sometimes catch on the radio, I still get seasick. After my first day of school on the mainland, my mother gave me tablets for the nausea. By now, letting the chalky white pill dissolve on my tongue is as much a part of my morning routine as waking up. However, with how choppy the water is today, even that won't keep my stomach completely settled on the half-hour ferry ride.

But the school won't let me and the other island kids off the hook just because the weather is questionable. Once, when a winter gale raised the water in the harbor past the level of the docks, we all had to write make-up essays for missing group presentations.

"Take care," my mother says as she hands me a metal lunchbox. She says the same thing every morning, like a general sending his men into the field. Goodbyes are different here on the island—a little more solemn, a little sharper. Maybe because we know that the sea can never truly be trusted, despite all the generations who have made homes on its back.

I tug my cap down to my eyebrows. "Hugs," I tell my mother while my arms remain at my sides. She's never liked physical touch, even from me. My father hasn't told me why, but after twelve years I've learned to only show affection in words.

Now, her eyes crinkle slightly around the edges. "Go," she says, with a motion of her hand.

As I step out the door, the wind meets me like an overeager comrade rushing in for a hug. It is cool, but not cold, with the warm, damp undercurrent that means a storm. I hope it'll stay away until tonight. Above my head, the ribbons tied to our door flutter and snap. Every house has them—ours are pink, blue, and mint green. Someone, long ago, probably as a joke, said they keep the storms from sweeping the houses away. No one really believes it, but no one takes the ribbons down either.

I trot toward the harbor with my thumbs hooked in my back-pack straps. The road turns back on itself as it winds down the sloping hillside where our town rests. There are only a few scattered houses, packed into the earth like mossy stones; then the little chapel with its growing graveyard; and the one tavern we have on the island, where all the workers gather when the day is done. Sometimes there's a bit of music, but mostly the workers just sit in friendly silence, sipping their drinks and listening to the sounds of the sea. Above and behind, the island climbs toward thick peaks of stone, covered in grass and fog; only on the brightest of days can we see the tip, and then only for a moment.

Today, the grey gloom has darkened the morning even more than usual, making six-thirty seem like five. The earliest fishermen will already be back and packing their catch into salt and ice. Every morning, the ferry that comes to pick us up for school also picks up the produce we have gathered from the sea. They deliver it to restaurants eager to display "fresh caught daily" on their chalkboard signs. Later, when it drops us back off, the ferry will bring the supplies we have requested—toothpaste, coffee, appliances—packed into crates filled with straw.

Sometimes I think of us like the mussels that cling to the rocks by the waterline. We hang on at the edge of things, letting the waves wash over us, and when someone tries to budge us, we stick harder. Sometimes I think the mainlanders think of us like mussels too. They don't pay us much attention, until they decide they fancy seafood.

My classmates are waiting down at the docks. There are nine of us in total—the other children are either too young for school or too old to be bothered—but I'm only close to two of them. Jamie, as usual, is balancing on top of the wooden posts along the dock. She has her scrawny arms spread out to either side, nose wrinkled in concentration, as the salt breeze whips her skirt around her knees and tugs her sandy-auburn hair from its straggly braid. Behind her, Tommy is struggling just to stand with both feet on a post. He looks even paler and thinner than usual; his eyes stare out of his face like round marbles. Most of us kids on the island are thin—Jamie's mom says it's a combination of breathing fresh air and eating fresh food and spending most of our time outdoors.

With a yelp, Tommy arches his body back and forth to try to stay balanced. He tips a little too far forward and jumps for the ground. Jamie laughs as she leaps nimbly from post to post, too confident in the placement of her feet to even wobble. To me, her laugh sounds like the cries of the seagulls—wild, free, and as much a part of this place as the mountains above us.

"Cade!" Jamie balances on one foot and waves to me.

I join her and Tommy on the edge of the dock, where we sit and swing our feet over the water. The ferry is moored at the docks, but the crates of fish, mussels, and crabs are still being loaded. Beyond the mouth of the harbor, I can see the stiff peaks of the waves tossing at the mouth of the harbor, like the peaks in the egg-white when my mother makes meringue. Nearby, the other children huddle in their own groups, playing hopscotch or hunting for fish in the shallows. The oldest ones stand in a circle and talk, their arms folded, too grown-up now for something like playing. We laugh at them and toss broken bits of shells into the harbor to see how far they can go. Jamie's, as usual, go the farthest.

"D'you think we'll learn anything today?" Jamie asks as she cocks her arm back for another toss. Tommy and I wait to respond until the shell has sailed out over the water and plunked down between the ripples.

"Indubitably," Tommy tells us. He's always using big words. Once, he read through an entire dictionary for fun. If it was anyone else, I would've gotten annoyed and called him an egghead, but it's just the way Tommy is. Besides, sometimes I wonder if it's possible for Jamie and me to get smarter just by hanging out with him. We could use all the help we can get for our exams next term.

"You, Cade? Think we'll learn anything today?"

"Doubtful," I tell Jamie. It sounds close to what Tommy said, but he gives me a funny look that suggests it means something different. I shrug it off. "Doubtful" is what I meant. I've spent six years in school now, and I still don't see the point to it all. The adults say it will help us get into good schools, get good jobs, and get off the island. I feel funny when they say that, like they want us gone. I don't think that's what they mean, but I still resist school like a jacket when my mother says it's too cold outside.

The clang of the ferry gong signals boarding.

We join the other students climbing up the ramp, and then Jamie, Tommy, and I instantly break away and make for the rail. We secure the best spot on the boat—just to the right of the prow, as far up as we can go. From here, we can see all the waves as they approach. It helps to have warning, so we can brace our knees and squint our eyes against the sting of the spray. For me, it helps keep my stomach a little calmer.

But it's also just the greatest feeling in the world. When the prow of the boat leaps over the wave, and for a moment there's nothing but wood and wind beneath our feet—the weightless, rushing thrill—then the *slam* back down into the water, the swoop in our stomachs, the splash of freezing spray that makes us gasp and laugh all at once. It makes the seasickness worth it.

The clouds thin as the ferry leaves the harbor, and I feel my worry about a coming storm lift a little. The waves settle, like a ruffled tomcat laying back its coat. I'm grateful. I like oatmeal, but I didn't want to see it again today.

It takes about half an hour to cross the sea to the mainland—twenty-six minutes with the wind at our backs and the current in our favor, and maybe thirty-four minutes coming the other direction. Jamie, Tommy, and I spend the whole crossing at the prow. As the ferry rises and falls over the waves, I try to use the trick my father taught me. He said to focus on the line where the sky touches the water, where everything is still. The waves and the boat will always be moving, but that line will stay steady—look there, and your stomach will remember.

My father knows countless tricks. He used to be a sailor, out on the open sea, not just in the semi-sheltered waters of our island like the fishermen. He has sailed on three-masted vessels, cargo ships, schooners, lobster barges, and every other kind of boat I know. He has seen more miles of wild waters and countries than even the oldest folks on the mainland have visited. Once, his old shipmate came to visit us on the island. He stayed for dinner and brought us deep-sea fish from his boat, the kind that's so fresh you can eat it raw. He told me my father had a vagabond spirit. On all the ships they had sailed together, my father had always traveled farther than anyone else on the crew, and he could tie and tell you the name of every knot known to sailors.

I asked Tommy later, what vagabond meant. He said it's someone who doesn't like to stay in one place—they're always moving. That doesn't sound like Father. He doesn't go out to open sea anymore. Instead, he works on the mainland, fixing appliances. He takes his little, one-sail sloop across the waves every morning, just after the fishermen head out, and he always comes back before dusk. Often, he'll sit out on the docks, just looking toward the ocean. Like he's missing it. I think I know why he stays though. Mother needs him.

The ferry slows and pulls into the harbor, just off the mainland. Our school is up the road, not far from the water. We can see the red-tiled roof from where we stand on the deck.

"I don't want to go inside," Jamie says suddenly.

"Why not?" I ask her. I'm always curious to know what she's thinking. It's always something a little bit strange, different from the way anyone else thinks. She sees the world like someone doing a backbend, all upside down with a fascinating slant.

"I love the stormy days," Jamie murmurs. She stares out to sea, turning to face in the opposite direction of where the ferry is headed. The loose hairs from her braid curl around her freckled cheeks like wisps of smoke. Reflected in her eyes, grey-green like the waves, I can see the dark shadow of the clouds gathered overhead.

It sends a chill across my skin. Sometimes Jamie frightens me.

I've never liked the storms; I will never tell her, but when the wind lashes against our house I often hide under my covers and clutch my pillow tight. I want to go to my parents' room and cling to my mother's chest, but that has never been an option. So I squeeze my eyes shut and imagine the storm like a twisted, angry beast hovering over our little island, searching for us with its rain-streaming eyes and growling when we cannot be found.

But Jamie loves the storms. Once she climbed out the window of her room and stayed out in one all night. Her mother asked me the next day why Jamie's dress was soaked through and she was shivering. But I never told. It might make me wicked, I'm not sure, but I'm more afraid of disobeying Jamie than a grown-up.

"I'm ready to go inside," Tommy says. He shivers, rubbing his hands up and down his thin arms. The ferry bumps to a halt against the docks, and we all touch the rail to steady ourselves.

"I guess we don't really have a choice," I tell Jamie with a shrug. I'm glad Tommy said something. I'm glad I get to be the one who sounds like I don't care one way or the other.

Jamie gives a faint sigh and turns away from the open sea. She might want to stay out here all day, but I'm relieved to be forced indoors. The clouds lightened during the ferry ride, but now they're starting to gather again. If I'm lucky, the storm will spend itself early in the day before the ferry has to take us home. Being caught in a storm out on the water is ten times more frightening than hearing it battering on a roof.

Up the road, at the schoolhouse, the mainland children are already gathering outside. They chatter together while we island kids stand apart, a little awkwardly. This is our school, same as theirs, but we never quite feel like we belong. We're stepping on foreign ground, and all of us know it.

As Jamie, Tommy, and I wait for the bell, a trio of girls bounces past us with their arms interlocked. They wear matching floral-patterned skirts, and white blouses with lace collars, and big, bright ribbons tying back their curls. Jamie watches them go, twisting the end of her braid. She's still wearing her plain, blue dress, spotted with little stars stitched in white thread, that her mother purchased for her from a catalog four years ago. The fabric is worn and faded now, stretched so that it fits easily around every angle of her scrawny frame.

Jamie pretends she doesn't care about things like that, like clothes and fashion and what she looks like. But I remember once, about a year ago now, when she stole one of the ribbons that was hanging above her family's door. She kept it in her pocket until we were on the ferry, and then she tied her hair back with it and spent the whole school day striding around with the ribbon bouncing proudly behind her. Later that week, when a storm hit the island, one of the sides of her family's henhouse collapsed under a falling tree limb. A pullet was crushed, and Jamie cried for three days because she thought it was her fault for stealing the ribbon from off the door.

We don't really believe that superstition, but then things happen, and we wonder. Jamie never wore ribbons again.

While Jamie watches the girls, I spot a group of mainland boys my age near the schoolhouse wall, standing with their heads together. I crane my neck to see what they're looking at, and then I tug Tommy towards me. He has glasses, because his mother actually takes him to regular appointments at the eye doctor.

"What're they looking at?" I whisper in his ear.

Tommy adjusts his glasses and squints a bit. "The new *Star Trek* comic," he whispers back, his voice squeaking a little with excitement. "It must have come out last weekend."

"Can you see the title?" I say, bouncing on my toes. On the island, we don't get the new comics until several weeks after the mainland does. The grown-ups don't think comics about space voyaging scientists and adventurers are as important as we do. They'd rather order coffee and newspapers and other things we kids don't use anyway.

Tommy squints once more. "Nah," he says, turning back. "Too far away."

"Think they'd let us borrow it?" I size the boys up from across the schoolyard. A few of them are taller than me, but they have the slightly-too-long haircuts and hand-me-down clothes that make me think they might be willing to share with us.

The oldest boy will be the problem. He's dressed in slacks and a collared shirt, with dress shoes that look like they're polished. His hair is slicked back with water or product, or both, so it looks like the wet, oily back of a sea otter. That's the kind of boy who barely sees kids like me and Tommy at all. Unfortunately for us, it looks like he's the one who brought the comic. I can see him taking something from the other boys, before he passes the comic to the first pair of waiting hands on his left—he's taking coins, in exchange for the chance to look through the bold, color-inked pages for a few minutes.

"We'll get it eventually," Tommy says, shrugging. "I'll ask my mom if she can pick up a copy for us when she goes into town next week."

I could never have Tommy's patience. Last month, I remember me and Tommy reading the final frames of the comic book, shoulder to shoulder on the floor of his bedroom, our noses nearly pressed to the pages. There had been a hint, right at the end, that perhaps not everything was as it seemed. That hint had been nagging at me ever since.

Tommy loves *Star Trek* because of the science. I don't know why I like it so much. It's something about the idea of setting off into unknown territory, going where no man has gone before. The comics remind me of my father's adventures, when he occasionally decides to tell me about his time at sea. Sometimes, when I'm riding in the back of his sloop, I like to imagine I'm Captain Kirk, sitting in the captain's chair of the *Enterprise* and telling my crew to take us out—to space, the final frontier.

"Don't you think they should ship comics out to us too?" I ask Jamie, just as the bell starts to ring.

She shrugs. Even as we walk toward the schoolhouse, she's still looking back, over her shoulder, at the choppy sea. The clouds are gathering over the water, dark and heavy with rain. It makes me uneasy to see the weather getting worse. Before the schoolhouse door closes behind us, Jamie takes one last breath of the cool, salty air, like swimmers do before they dive underwater.

We cover math first: multiplication and division, which we work through doing calculations on the blackboard, each of us taking a turn to tackle a problem with a stick of chalk. Tommy, as usual, solves the hardest problem on the board. He's probably the smartest one in school, definitely on the island. Math is followed by English, where we have to read poetry selections standing at our desks. I'm okay at both subjects, but I can never get the hang of poetry. After my reading, the teacher "takes a moment" to address the entire class and point out that "everyone in general" needs to work on not rushing through the lines without taking a breath. Just because there is no punctuation doesn't mean there are no pauses. Which makes no sense to me, since we learned last week that a period is a full pause and a comma is about half. If there's no period and no comma, shouldn't that mean there's no pause?

When it's Jamie's turn, she stands up at her desk with her knees bent backwards a little bit. She must've memorized her poem over the weekend, because she recites the entire thing word-for-word, with all the right pauses. Her voice is as loud and full as her laugh. It reaches every corner of the room, and everyone listens without even fidgeting. I think that maybe poetry isn't as stupid as I thought. It sounds so much less stupid coming out of Jamie's mouth.

I sometimes wonder if Jamie will become an actress. I think she'd be wonderful, with her big, mysterious eyes, and the way she can speak in front of a crowd. But at the same time, I can't picture her anywhere except on the rocky hillsides of the island, with the salt breeze in her hair and her laughter dancing with the gulls.

Our teacher has been talking, recently, about what we'll become when we grow up and leave school. She tells us that our exams next term will show us where our strengths are and help us get into better high schools. Today, right before lunch, she passes out sheets with different careers listed on them, next to small, smiling cartoons of policemen, or lawyers, or teachers, or plumbers. She says that next week, we'll have presentations where we talk about our parents and what they do for a living. I wonder how I'll present my parents. My dad, who used to be a vagabond on the open sea and travelled from continent to continent, who now fixes appliances for people with more money than us. My mother, who spends more and more time inside, except when she walks down by the docks to collect our daily rations and sometimes comes back empty-handed.

Tommy looks at his sheet with a funny wrinkle between his eyes. Jamie has already put hers away in her school bag.

"Thinking about being a policeman?" I ask him. I'm a little concerned by the creases on his brow. I usually only see them on my father.

Tommy gives a start and folds the paper up. "A teacher, actually," he says shyly.

I look at him as if seeing him for the first time. "You're serious?" I glance at our teacher, a slender woman with her hair pinned up on her head, her skirt as plain as her face and as plain as her speech when she's giving a lecture. I've never pictured Tommy standing in front of a blackboard—though I suppose he did read the dictionary for fun.

But the only schools are on the mainland.

"You'd leave the island?" I ask him.

Now Tommy looks at me like I've said something crazy. "I mean, most of us are going to, aren't we? At least for school."

His words hit me like a slap of spray kicked up from a wave. I look away as he carefully slides the paper into the front of his math textbook. Is that true? Are we all expected to leave? Will everyone I know, even Jamie, eventually end up leaving the island?

Surely, Jamie wouldn't leave.

I've always thought we will be on the island forever, just like the mountains that tower above us in the mist. I've never considered that it may just be someplace where we grow up. Have we done something to make Tommy want to leave? I can't think of anything. And he seems happy enough as we gather our lunch pails with the other students. But his words make me uneasy, like the ground I'm used to having under my feet might not be as solid as I had believed.

Usually, we take our lunch break outside. Sometimes, Jamie, Tommy, and I will go down to the docks and watch the tourists climbing unsteadily in and out of the little, brightly painted paddle boats they can rent to slosh around the harbor. Today, however, rain has started to spit against the windowpanes, so we sit against the wall around the sides of the room and open our lunch boxes on our knees.

Jamie has a hunk of rye bread, some white cheese made from their goat's milk, and a little note from her mother. She reads it as she chews the cheese stacked on the bread. Inside my metal pail, I find an apple—a little bruised, from bouncing in the crates on the ferry—and a sandwich wrapped in foil. When I take a bite, my teeth clack through the layers of spongy white bread. Frowning, I unfold the sandwich and find only a single leaf of wilting lettuce and a smear of mustard inside. I don't say anything. I don't even show Jamie and Tommy. I don't want them to know how much my mother has been forgetting things.

Maybe tomorrow I'll pack my own lunch.

As I chew through my pieces of bread, I glance over at the boy on my right. He has a steak and cheese sandwich, with a bar of chocolate wrapped beside it—a luxury lunch. And, I notice, tucked under his jacket, the copy of the *Star Trek* comic. It must be his turn to flip through the pages, in exchange for a nickel. No, probably a dime. I remember how the older boy's hair shone.

I nudge Tommy and motion to the comic book, raising my eyebrows. I'm trying to suggest that we ask the boy for a peek, and I'm trying to close the distance that has suddenly opened up between us. *Star Trek* is simple. *Star Trek* doesn't have anything to do with growing up, or going away, or becoming something different.

But Tommy only smiles at me and takes a bite of his peanut butter and jelly sandwich. Once he has accepted something, however he feels about it, he holds to it—he'll wait for the comic book next week. That's another thing I've never understood about Tommy. Maybe I don't know my friend as well as I thought.

I can't imagine the island without him, but now it seems I may have to.

Jamie finishes her lunch first, licks the crumbs from her fingers, and then goes to the window. She stands on her tiptoes so she can see out, fingers curled over the edge of the sill like a kittens' paws.

"The waves are kicking up," she tells us. She sounds thrilled. The rain is still coming down, not too hard, but enough to send steady streams rolling down the glass.

I force down the last crust of my bread and try to ignore the anxiety dampening my hands. I don't want to sail back through a storm. The other kids can just run home, up the street, or across the block. That shiny-haired boy will probably be picked up by his family. But we have to beat through the waves for at least thirty minutes, probably more with this wind, as the swells grow higher, the skies darker, and the winds fiercer.

I don't know what's wrong with me. I'm an islander, born and bred, and I'm afraid of the sea. Well, no…the water itself doesn't scare me. On sunny days, with a brisk breeze sweeping in from the ocean, my heart nearly bursts to see the light sparkling on the waves. I love the feel of the boat's prow splitting the waves, sending up curtains of spray. I even love sailing with my father, as he shows me how to trim the sails and capture the wind, like cupping water in the hand. I can't imagine living somewhere where I can't hear the sound of the sea.

But when the storms roll in, the sea changes. It becomes distant and unpredictable, like a dog baring its teeth and raising the fur on its back. When the waves are calm, riding the ferry is like being rocked by gentle arms; when they are brisker, it's like flying on a starship. But when the sea grows rough, the waves hiss and crash like they want to sink the boat.

Still, Jamie loves the storms. Even after what happened with the ribbon. So I don't know why I get this way. Maybe it's just frightening to see something familiar suddenly become strange. Maybe I don't know how to get along completely with something that could hold me up one moment and drown me the next.

After lunch, the wind starts blowing harder and the rain begins to patter on the roof. The teacher pauses, part way through science class, and looks out the window.

"You all might need to leave early," she says, motioning to me, Jamie, Tommy, and the rest of the kids from the island. We're all sitting in the same corner of the room, somehow, though our seats aren't assigned.

Wordlessly, Jamie and Tommy get to their feet, gathering their lunch pails and bookbags. This isn't the first time we've had to skip classes because of the weather. Normally, the ferry doesn't leave until four o'clock, but if a storm is coming, it'll leave early.

I don't move from my chair. As I watch the rest of the island kids pulling on their jackets, a strange unease comes over me.

Suddenly, I feel certain our ferry will sink. The storm will come rushing in, just as we reach the middle of the crossing, and we will drown, swallowed up by the foaming waves. We are all going to our deaths.

"Cade, come on," Jamie says impatiently as she pulls up the hood of her rain jacket. We all keep one in our bags, for occasions like this.

I look at her, and I know I look scared. Her gaze softens as she stares down at me.

"C'mon, Cade," she says in a gentler voice.

Tommy, slinging his bag over his shoulder, looks from me to Jamie and says nothing.

I try to ignore the dread in the pit of my stomach, to just push it aside, and get up, and walk out that door onto the ferry. We are not a superstitious people on the island. Before I know it, we will be home.

But storms are storms, and no one takes the ribbons down.

"I'm not going," I tell Jamie and Tommy. I shake my head to make sure my decision is clear.

Jamie frowns. "You have to. The ferry won't make another crossing today, not with the weather like this. If we go now, we'll be back before the worst of it."

I look down at my desk. It makes me feel horribly small to be acting like this in front of Jamie. I always want her to think me brave, confident, adventurous—like she is. But in this moment, I cannot.

Jamie presses her lips together, like her mother sometimes does. I think she's trying to decide what to do with me, but then Tommy speaks up.

"Your dad's here, right?" he says to me. Then, to Jamie: "Cade can ride back with him."

Jamie considers this. She studies me, and I wonder if she is sizing me up in her mind—who she thought I was, who I now appear to be. Perhaps you have to do that a lot, even with your closest friends. Today I have had to realize that I don't fully understand Tommy. Perhaps, as time passes, you have to do that over and over, as you discover people again and again and wonder if you ever knew them at all. I don't want that to be true.

"See you back at the island," Jamie tells me, hoisting her bookbag. She smiles at me, her thin, rather crooked smile. She seems confused, even a little sad. But she still smiles at me. I hope that means she forgives me.

Jamie and Tommy walk out of the schoolhouse and join the other kids heading down to the dock. I trail behind them, so the teacher doesn't get suspicious. But when we reach the dock, I split away and go sit on one of the thick posts by the water: dark wood wound with rope and covered with barnacles. I draw my knees up to my chest, only my heels and tail bone perched on the post. To my left, Jamie and Tommy board the ferry, and it hoists anchor, and sails out of the still harbor for the tossing sea. The unease returns as my friends wave to me from the stern. What if the storm takes them, as they cross? Already, the boat is rocking beneath them with the rolling, back-and-forth movement that would make my stomach hurt.

My eyes sting with saltwater, and I scrub them dry. Maybe I'm not a true islander. I'm afraid of storms, and I can't even ride a boat without feeling sick.

What if I'm wrong about myself, as I've been wrong about Tommy? Perhaps I'm not who I think I am. I like to think of myself as Jamie, wild and free, in love with the clean air and the hills and the sea. But I'm not like her. She stood out in a storm, her eyes closed, her arms open to the rain—she told me. I spent the night wrapped in a blanket, wishing I could feel my mother's arms around me.

The ferry sails out of sight, mist and spray hiding its shadowed outline. After it disappears, I stay sitting on the post while thunder rumbles in the distance. My limbs are stiff, my back and head are soaked with rain, and my tailbone hurts. But even though the rain is falling harder now, I can't make myself go back to the schoolhouse, or even to a café or shop. Someone will be sure to realize I don't belong.

Besides, Tommy told me about penance. His mom sometimes takes him to a Catholic church on the mainland, and he says penance is when you do something you don't like to make up for something bad you did. Sitting here feels a bit like that. If I'm not brave enough to cross the ocean, at least I should be brave enough to sit by the harbor, where the waves are only swollen ripples, and watch the storm from the sidelines.

Over the harbor, lightning flickers downward in forks. I'm shaking now, but I tell myself it's from the cold. The ferry must be almost across by now, but probably not quite.

A few minutes later, the wind gusts fearsomely, and a sudden shower of rain soaks the last dry patch on my clothes. The thunder rumbles so loudly that I clap my hands over my ears. It's all I can do not to run back to the schoolhouse.

Then, without warning, the clouds begin to clear.

The sea settles, and the sky lightens, and although the clouds do not disappear completely, the sunlight shines through them like a lamp behind thick glass. The day no longer looks like twilight, but an overcast evening. The rain slows until only a few drops occasionally fall in the water below my feet.

I feel foolish, soaked to the bone, and miserable. The storm is already over.

Jamie was right—if I had gone when they did, everything would have been fine. We would've been pulling into the harbor just as the worst of the storm passed by overhead. Now both of my closest friends are going to think I'm a coward. And they're going to be right.

"Cade?"

I had not heard footsteps approaching. When I turn, I see a man behind me, standing squarely in his yellow knee-high waders. He has a creased, weather-beaten face, with a salt-and-pepper beard and eyes as deep and distant as the sea. His voice is low and rough, like the sound of pebbles grinding underfoot.

"Hi Dad." I turn away from him. I clutch my knees closer and squeeze my eyes shut. I don't want to say why I'm still here, and I don't want him to see the tears still forcing their way into my eyes. My father is a sailor—he will not want a son who is afraid of the sea.

A warm, heavy hand lands on my shoulder. My father's fingers are worn like the rest of him, and the skin is tanned and calloused like old leather. But he can thread a needle as neatly as he can trim a sail. He does all the sewing, now that mother cannot.

"Come," my father says in a low voice. His tone is gruff, but not demanding. When his hand lifts from my shoulder, I get up and follow him.

We walk to the docks, where his sloop rides low in the water. I clamber into the boat and sit down silently at the prow, as my father unties the sloop, jumps in, and pushes off in what seems like one movement. I watch him with my shoulders slumped, head hanging in shame. I feel more miserable than I thought possible.

With a stiff breeze, the sloop comes alive beneath us. We head for the mouth of the harbor.

As my father takes the tiller, he glances at me from across the boat. I force myself to meet his deep, distant eyes—those eyes that have seen miles of ocean and places I cannot imagine. He would be Captain Kirk. He could do it. But not me. I was foolish to think of myself as some fearless adventurer, capable of voyaging into unknown lands.

Jamie could do it. Even Tommy could—he's talking about leaving our home and going off into the world to try something completely new. Maybe I was wrong. Maybe *Star Trek* is about growing up, and going away, and becoming something different. Maybe it is yet another thing I don't actually understand.

From across the boat, my father smiles at me. His smiles always seem sad, somehow. As if every good thing reminds him of a sad thing that could have been. He motions for me to come sit next to him. Hesitantly, I slide across the boat and sit down on the wooden slat beside him. I wonder if he's about to lecture me, though I rarely hear him speak more than one sentence at a time.

Taking my hand, my father rests it on the tiller. I look up at him for confirmation. He has never let me steer before. Smiling still, he clasps his hand over mine.

When I wrap my fingers around the warm wood of the tiller, I feel the water—living, pulsing—beneath my touch. My father guides my hand on the tiller, his salty, scratchy beard tickling my ear. The sloop responds to our joint commands as we leave the harbor and head out toward open sea.

I feel a smile crossing my face. I can't help it—the spray, and the salt air, and the cool rush of the wind. The sloop, too, is so slender and low to the water that I don't even feel seasick. Above us, the sail stretches tight to the breeze. The clouds are drawing back, letting streams of watery grey sunlight sparkle on the waves now unrolling before us.

My father's hand over mine angles the tiller ever so slightly into the wind.

"It is okay, sometimes, to fear the thing you love," he says softly.

He lets my hand go. I take the tiller in both hands, sitting up straight into the spray. The sloop slices through the waves, borne by the wind filling its sail, and up ahead I see the island forming out of the sea.

Home.

The salt breeze seems to breathe into me. It fills me with a feeling that makes me think of Jamie, laughing and spinning in the grass on the mountains, her freckled cheeks flushed with wind and her sandy-auburn hair dancing around her face.

On the mainland, people often think we're dragging behind the rest of the world. But as I guide the sloop across the waves, I realize they are wrong. The sea, like space, is a wild, trackless expanse, that even after years of exploration is still a mystery. And no matter who we are—even if we leave someday, like Tommy, or even if we sometimes hide from the storms—we are all born with a love of the sea. A love that isn't changed when it doesn't love us back.

I watch the island drawing near, and pride swells in my chest, like a sail stretching taut with clean, free air. We are not mussels. Here on the island, we are pioneers—living on the edge of the last frontier on earth.

Follow Me

Harold Hoss

Jan Pham has thirty thousand, six hundred, and eighty-three followers, but she wants more.

She's waiting at a coffee shop and the line ticks forward, all at once like the minute hand on an old clock, everyone in line shifting up a step and then settling back into place. Jan glares again at the small sign near the pickup window reading "Mobile Ordering Down – Sorry For The Inconvenience" with a smiley. She feels her phone vibrate and flips it over to check it.

No notifications. She must have imagined the vibration, something that happens a lot these days, and not just to her. It's what Ryan would call a "Phantom Ring," and she uses it as an excuse to check in on her last post.

In the video, Jan looks good. Her tan, lithe body in a skintight black outfit makes the chrome silver hair cascading down one shoulder and the silver stud in her nose absolutely *pop*. Or maybe it's the other way around. She doesn't care – she just loves how natural it looks. How easy it is to imagine that this is how she really looks. That it isn't all Ryan's technical tricks with the lighting, the coloring, and the shot composition.

But that's what makes Jan and Ryan such a great team. He makes her look and she makes this look natural. Shakespeare said the world was a stage and he was right – anywhere can be a stage, but these days the trick is to make the audience forget. Forget you're on stage, forget you're performing, and let them think this is the world. The real world.

In the video, Jan starts with her usual appeal to past followers and an appeal for future followers ("hey to all my *only_phams* and for all you newcomers be sure to give us a like and follow me at *Almost_Phamous*") before reexplaining the app they are reviewing. The SoulSearching App ("link in the bio") promises to modernize "Soul Searching" by bringing it to the digital age through things like chaos theory and quantum physics. What it actually does is ask users a few questions and then spit out a random address.

And people love it.

One reviewer couldn't decide which college to attend "then Soul Searching took me to a catholic church. Notre Dame here I come!" while others claimed everything from closure to past relationships to signs of life from beyond the grave. Ryan, a self-proclaimed Fater (rhymes with hater) describes it as "fucking insane" and "the dumbest thing I've ever heard," and only agreed on the condition that they did not trespass on private property.

Not that she goes anywhere or does anything without Ryan. They're a team. Ride or die. Together4ever. Pick your poison.

People love the SoulSearching App, but they also love watching influencers try the SoulSearching App – and with #SoulSearching already trending, Jan took the plunge. She answered the questions and the app took her straight to the half-empty strip mall across from this coffee shop, right between a florist and a spy shop. Jan's soul searching journey couldn't end at a spy shop, so they had pivoted, and instead Jan's journey ended at a nearby park at a statue of Amelia Earhart.

Again, the coffee line ticks forward, and Jan takes her place behind a woman holding a baby and reading the menu for the first time.

"Let's see," the woman says, adjusting the baby on her hip. "How is the…"

Jan tries not to follow the woman's gaze down to the pastries. Why look when you can't touch? Instead Jan looks back over her shoulder at the outdoor seating area where Ryan waits. He's wearing his usual uniform of all black, his wavy brown hair pulled away from his eye in a loose top knot, while a hand-rolled cigarette dangles between two fingers tucked behind the phone. She wonders what, or who, he's looking at.

He could be looking at the video. Jan might be the face of Almost_Phamous but it's a group effort. Last summer after graduation, Instagram was a hobby. Laying by the pool with plenty to drink but no jobs and no prospects, knowing what their degrees (Mass Comm and Photography, respectively) cost, but wondering what they were worth, it seemed like a dream. That day it was three photos, a dancing tik-tok and one live video that attracted eighty-three views.

Ryan hadn't liked a couple hundred random guys liking a video or photo of Jan dancing in a bikini but when Jan broke into the thousands with "Dating App Bachelorette," a faux show starring her in five roles where she gave four popular dating apps personalities to see which would earn her rose, he stopped seeing them as *random guys liking a video or photo* and just saw the number. The video made it all the way to buzzfeed – Interesting Influencers Influencing the Internet RIGHT NOW – and had over two hundred thousand videos and counting.

Jan loved that video. It was so creative. But being creative takes time – and for junior influencers consistency is more important than creativity. So she keeps her brand fresh by reviewing apps every day, at least until she and Ryan break into the six figure followers and get big enough to have a team. Once you reach six figures your followers begin to pay dividends, multiplying on their own, like a snowball gathering speed and size as it rolls downhill, and then the sponsors come calling, and then more money.

Jan can see their problems dropping away one by one – the fights about money, about the way Ryan spends every moment he can stoned out of his mind – they can all be fixed with more followers.

The line ticks forward one last time and Jan steps up and orders their drinks: one iced green tea, no sweetener for her, and a straight black coffee, hot for Ryan.

"Hot?" The barista asks, clarifying because it's the middle of summer and hot enough to melt the tar on the street.

"Hot," Jan says. Ryan does not do iced coffee. It's a thing with him. He could be walking across the desert and he'd still want hot coffee. It's part of his beatnik illusion, even if this illusion is somewhat undercut by the brand-new black range rover his dad bought for him.

The barista brings the drinks, and Jan carries them outside. Ryan's tobacco pouch and rolling papers – another beatnik thing – cover the table, and she waits for him to clear a space before setting the drinks down.

"Thanks babe," Ryan says, but he doesn't look up.

"Any more views?" She asks, lightly probing to see what he was looking at on his phone.

"What? Oh, I haven't checked yet," he says. "I was waiting for you."

She takes a sip of her iced green tea and nods, looking across the street at the first address the SoulSearching app gave her. The sign for the Spy Shop is black, with big white letters reading 'SPY SHOP' above a smaller red font reading 'When you NEED to know.' The windows of the shop are barred and covered with lists of items like "GPS Tracking" or "Hidden Cameras," and the few windows that aren't covered are blacked out.

Next door the Florist Shop, maybe to compensate for its dour spy shop neighbor, overflows with technicolor bright flowers. Even the advertisement in the window, offering a "Seasonal Sale on Funeral Arrangements" looks upbeat.

Jan can remember going to a different, much nicer florist with her mom and uncle to pick out a funeral arrangement when she was a little girl. Her uncle may have paid for the arrangement with a smile, but she knew enough Vietnamese to know what he really thought about the price during the drive home. Maybe he would have appreciated a seasonal sale on funeral flowers.

"What are you looking at?" Ryan asks.

She nods across the street. Ryan takes a drag, coughs, and somehow washes it down with scalding hot coffee, then turns to look.

"You see that Spy Shop over there?" Ryan asks, but he doesn't wait for her to answer. "My buddy's mom used to take us to baseball practice and every day we would drive by a spy shop and we would just beg to go. Just fucking beg. We thought it sounded so cool. I guess we thought there'd be some James Bond shit in there."

He turns back to Jan with a shrug, like: *oh well.*

"We could go now," Jan says. "Maybe that could be the next video."

"Too creepy," Ryan says. "Besides, who needs spies when we've all got phones."

Ryan says this like it's profound, but Jan doesn't engage. She feels another vibration, realizes she isn't even holding her phone, but still picks it up off the table and checks it. Their dog, Apple, looks up back up the background, his head cocked to one side, mouth hanging open to let the tongue roll out.

"So you see what the other Janet is doing?" Ryan asks.

The *Other Janet*. Janet Ho. JHo. Also the *Other Girl* – in the sense that she dated Ryan ("Dated no, hooked up yeah. A few times, I guess" to hear Ryan tell it) freshman year.

"She's blowing up – you see her last post?" Ryan says. "Some online bot – I hear it's a little sketch. Not illegal, but like, you know – weird black hat stuff, probably going to get banned from every app soon."

Black hat bots, Instagram bots, automation bots or usually just *bots* are an Instagram hack program. Each promises the same thing: more subscribers and more followers. They gather your information to help target *your audience,* and then with the press of a button they crawl across Instagram pretending to look at videos, like pictures and leave comments – and fooling absolutely no one. Each time Jan uses a bot it costs her followers and hurts her reputation. She imagines the bots like bugs, slipping through cracks and crawling across accounts.

"I'm not doing that again," Jan says. Still cringing about one comment plastered across 500 different pages "so qute XOXOXOXOXOXXOXO follow me for a like like," and in one case 100 times on one user's photo.

"What if it could double your followers?"

Now Jan hesitates. Ryan hands her his phone, she scrolls up then down. One week ago JHo's photos were lucky to get a hundred likes. The latest post, a black screen with a red figure eight turned sideways, has ten times that many. She's tempted. She wants more followers.

"No," she says instead, clicking open her phone and checking the last video. She's up fourteen followers. She doesn't need a bot.

Ryan drives and Jan silently checks her followers. She's up to thirty thousand, six hundred and ninety-nine followers but she still wants more. Meanwhile JHo posts a picture, the same black box with the same red figure eight, only now there's an arrow pointing up out of the center, stretching all the way to the top. This picture hits twenty thousand likes in five minutes. The caption below reads: "Link in the bio – add legions of fans – we_r_legion."

"I didn't know you were still talking to her," Jan says, putting her phone in her lap. She keeps her voice light, facing the window but looking at Ryan's reflection, who looks very focused on driving.

Janet Ho is not as pretty as Jan Pham, and without someone like Ryan to help her with the lighting and hold the camera, her videos are always shot from arm's length and have a grainy, almost home video quality. Ryan once described Janet Ho as "cute in an innocent sort of way," but only once – and he knew better than to do it again.

JHo also has an obsession with pigs: cartoon pigs, real pigs, and pig filters. Jan thinks it doesn't do the girl, who has an upturned nose and a flat face, any favors.

JHo's viral fame came with a stupid picture. Jan has seen the picture – it's JHo wearing a slutty bikini bottom, football pads, and holding a baseball bat with a caption reading: "You Don't Know JHo." Seeing the original picture of Bo Jackson, and hearing Ryan explain who Bo Jackson was and what he had done had not helped Jan's mood.

"She doesn't even know who Bo Jackson is," Jan had said, a frustration she expressed in the comments section of the photo with a *like*, saying: "Go, JHO! GO!"

At last Ryan speaks, or grunts. "Yeah, well just answering the occasional question about lighting mostly."

"Oh," Jan says, the connection between Ryan's ex-girlfriend asking Ryan a question about lighting and an Instagram bot being obvious.

Thumb hovering over the link, Jan takes a breath. She hits refresh instead. JHo's number of followers doubles.

There's an obvious reason for this: inflation. Fake accounts. A bot that creates hundreds and hundreds – a legion, based on its name – of fake accounts. It's the only way.

She scrolls through the list picking names at random. A bot account is easy to spot – usually a generic picture, no bio description, a handful of *followers* at most but *following* thousands.

Ryan clears his throat, but Jan doesn't look up.

She clicks one, then another, and then three more. All are men but all of them have a normal following to follower ratio, profile pictures, and a few have bios.

"I mean, yeah, she asked how we were doing. And I said we were trying to get more followers. Which is true. And she said her research guy had found some bot called Legionary."

"Legion," Jan corrects. "We are legion."

Ryan snaps his fingers. "Yeah, that was it. She said her guy heard about it on one of the Chans, 4chan or Allchan, one of those. Said she wanted more info but, you know, thought it couldn't hurt."

Jan refreshes JHo's page again, her stomach knotting at the spike in new followers.

"Looks like it's working. Does she have any regrets?"

Ryan shakes his head back and forth, his long hair shaking loose and falling down around his face. "No idea. Haven't talked to her – not a word since that question about the lights."

He pulls up outside their apartment and clicks a button, waiting for the garage door to open. JHo posts another picture – the same as the others but with another parallel arrow over the figure eight.

"Maybe you should," Jan says, transfixed.

She can't see Ryan, but she knows he's frowning. Like it's a trap. She pulls her eyes away from the last picture and locks her phone with the side button. It's harder than she would like.

"Call her," Jan says. "I mean, she told you about it, right? Let's ask her."

"You want me to call JHo," Ryan repeats.

Jan smiles, "why would that be weird? You two are friends, right?" And then Jan climbs out of the car, slamming the door behind her.

Jan has thirty thousand, seven hundred and two followers when she steps out of the car, jumps over the three-sided pothole crack in the pavement that Ryan once dubbed the "Bermuda Triangle for Car Tires," and jogs to the door of the stairwell leading up out of the garage. The elevator out of the garage rarely works, which is a blessing and a curse since the living room of her apartment shares a wall with the elevator shaft. When the elevator doesn't work she has to walk up three flights of stairs, but when it does work, it's all she can hear. Their apartment is on the second story of the horseshoe-shaped building surrounding a small, tear-shaped pool, two picnic tables, and six gardens protected by tall gates that cost extra. She and Ryan rent one of these gardens out for Apple, who barks excitedly when she reaches the courtyard.

"I know – I know, you see me. I'm coming." Jan croons. She feels better seeing Apple, his heavy tail wagging so furiously that it throws his body from side to side.

The video where Jan adopted Apple was cosponsored by a local Pitbull rescue and a huge hit – and Apple is a frequent special guest in her videos. He's basically her co-star. Reaching the gate she drops to one knee for kisses, then stands up and unlocks the gate.

Apple leads the way to their apartment, up the wrought iron stairs. The stairs creak and groan under the slightest strain, the sound compounded by the way it echoes around the courtyard. Apple is always eager to go somewhere else. If Jan or Ryan move for the door, he's excited to go outside. If he's outside and Jan or Ryan reach for their keys, he's excited to go inside. He's just always excited.

She drops her bag, drops herself onto the couch, let's Apple hop up next to her, and finds the link to Legion. Instead of a dot com or a dot net, she logs into a random series of numbers and letters ending in .legio/. The combination changes with an audible "click," expanding from twenty letters to a hundred. Jan gasps – thinking about the odd figure eight and arrows and praying this isn't a virus.

Another click and the numbers descend back down to a manageable fifty, another click and they're down to twenty, then ten, and then she's at the home page. "We Are Legion" across the top in white, the same symbol from JHo's feed, the two parallel arrows above a figure eight with one more arrow running up from the eight to the top, and then a promise to "Turn Your Followers Into A LEGION. We Are Legion." The page is full of typos and a third of the words veer off into Russian characters and random code, but Jan gets the gist. Like so many bots, Legion promises to be quick and easy while using the latest A.I. and special techniques. The only catch is that Legion needs the usual information to be effective: who is Jan's core audience, her target demos, what is her mission statement?

Jan's fingers fly across the buttons. She can type and text faster than she can talk, or even think. Outside the wrought iron stairs creak and groan.

"Stop whining – it's your job!" Ryan groans back at the stairs, an old joke, treating the stairs like a particularly whiny employee. The familiar jingle of carabiners and keys – Ryan believes you never regret having extra carabiners – heralds Ryan's entry into the room. He carries a black bag that's big enough for a body but not all of Ryan's equipment. He makes a beeline straight for the guest bedroom – which holds all of Ryan's equipment but has never housed a guest. He carefully drops the bag with a grunt and returns to the room.

He rubs his muscles. The equipment is heavy and there are still two more boxes. "I'll grab the rest when the elevator starts working again."

Jan doesn't say anything and Ryan doesn't move.

"How about this babe," Ryan says.

Jan notes the "babe," but doesn't look up.

"I'll do some research – see what I can learn about the app and then if we still have questions I'll call Janet Ho. Ok?"

Jan flashes her phone.

"Too late – I already signed up." She smiles. "Now *we* are *legion*, too."

The bot takes time to sync or load, or something, Jan can see a loading bar on her phone screen so she knows something is happening. Temporarily phoneless Jan is anxious. A feeling like she is lost in a foreign neighborhood only she can't call anyone or use a map. The anxiety intensifies when she opens up her laptop to the same loading bar, only this one says "sinking," a typo, she thinks. Russians or Chinese or whatever hackers must not know the difference between syncing and sinking.

"So get this – apparently Legion appeared on the chans last year, but the code is much older and you can only access it through the dark web."

Jan knows about "the chans." Ryan talks about them reverently, like they're freedom fighters, the last truly democratic bastions for people to share unfiltered opinions and speak honestly. From what Jan has seen, they're mostly used by men who share misogynist memes and views under the guise of terms like "taking the red pill." She's less familiar with the dark web.

"The what?"

"You know – there's like the web. The world wide web. Which is mapped. Then there's the dark web which isn't, you know, mapped." Ryan mimes a circle, sees she isn't getting it, grabs a pen and pad.

He draws waves across the top, like he's tracing invisible Hershey kisses with a slight curve. Here he writes "Web." Beneath that he draws a straight line that dips into a 'v' shaped cavern and then comes back up and flattens out.

"Haven't used one of these things in forever," he says.

Jan doesn't know if he means the paper or the pen. Or both. While he finishes his drawing, Jan's phone chimes. The download is complete. She starts to get up and walk to it, but Ryan cuts her off.

"Okay, so here is the world wide web right? This is where we surf." He points at the waves, waits for a laugh that will never come. "Like surf the web."

He coughs. "Then here, you have the deep web. There are no maps on the deep web – no search engines to guide you. You have to know exactly where you're going."

Jan nods. She can see her phone across the room. There's a notification. Then another. She looks back at Ryan, hoping he will hurry this along.

"And right here, this canyon? That's the dark web. The Mariana Trench of the internet. Nobody knows how deep it goes – and nobody knows what all is down there. Uncharted territory."

Ryan preens for a moment, pleased.

"So is it safe, or what?"

Ryan frowns. "It could be – I'm just saying we don't know what is down there."

"Well, what did the other Janet say?" Apple jams his head into Jan's lap and she obliges with some strokes behind the ear.

"Nothing."

Jan cocks an eyebrow.

"She didn't answer. I tried her twice. Nothing."

Jan laughs, "That's weird. It's not like she isn't always on her phone."

She pushes Apple away and pads across the room to grab her phone. There's a single message on a black screen.

Let Us Introduce Ourselves. We Are Legion. You Are JANET PHAM. Correct?

Click – Jan selects the green button to confirm. The phone pauses, whirs, and then another message unfolds.

We Are Legion And We Are Many. Certified Members Must Answer Three Questions. Do You Accept, JANET PHAM?

Click – Jan doesn't hesitate.

Question 1. Your Friends Are Now Us, And We Are Now Your Friends. Who Is Your Best Friend, JANET PHAM?

This could change, Jan thinks, but for now, he's still my best friend – and she types out Ryan's full name and clicks *Accept.*

"I'll try the other Janet again," Ryan says. "See what's up."

He looks at Jan, who doesn't look up, then looks away. Without another word he walks out of the room, leaving Jan alone.

Thank You, JANET PHAM.

Jan smiles. Her phone goes dark – save a picture of a sideways figure eight, just like the one on the other Janet's page.

An hour later Jan checks her phone, sees she has thirty-one thousand, two hundred and twenty-three followers. She screams, throws her arms around Ryan's shoulders and plants a kiss on his face.

"Just *guess* how much I'm up."

She curls up next to Ryan on the couch, easy to do in her gray yoga pants and one of Ryan's hoodies, also gray, her hair pulled back into a loose ponytail.

"Fifty?"

A blinding smile from Jan. "Try five hundred."

Joy tinged with disbelief from Ryan. "What? How?"

Jan can't explain it, only shrug.

"No, but I mean, *how?* Like what is it doing?" Ryan asks.

"I don't know but they're real – I checked. All real." She pauses. "All men, but real men. Not other bots."

Frowning, Ryan reaches for his laptop. "What was the website?"

A rumble and screech of metal and wires fills the apartment. A thin layer of drywall, barely up to code, separates the apartment living room from the elevator shaft. Since the elevator rarely works it's rarely a problem – but when it does work, as it is now, it's deafening.

Jan can barely think when the elevator is running, much less speak over the noise. She couldn't shout over the elevator and she doesn't try. She hands him her phone which has already posted a picture with the caption: *Link in the bio – add legions of fans – we_r_legion.*

Ryan types the link into his laptop and they are back at the website, the same black screen with ivory characters. The heading: *We Are Legion And We Are Growing. Visit The Tracker* flashes across the page. Ryan clicks "The Tracker" and a silent, grainy video fills the screen.

"Go pro, maybe? Not a phone," Ryan mumbles. He can't resist guessing about the type of camera used on anything.

The video scans a typical Hollywood two story apartment, each door opening into a courtyard around a pool that nobody uses. Jan thinks it could be anywhere. The camera stops at apartment number four, looking down at the welcome mat, brown with a black outline of a cartoon pig and the word *Welcome!* in cursive. Ryan tenses and takes a breath as the video goes black: "Certified Members Only," and then a number ticking upwards, presumably the growing legion.

Jan wants to ask Ryan if he recognized that apartment, but he speaks first.

"How do you become a certified member?" Ryan asks.

Jan's phone chimes in response. A message from the bot.

We Are Legion And We Are Many. Certified Members Must Answer Three Questions. Do You Accept, JANET PHAM?

Click – again, Jan doesn't hesitate.

Question 2. You Are Important To Us Now. What Is Important To You Is Now Important To Us. Who Is Your Favorite Pet, JANET PHAM?

Jan thinks this question is easier than the last, typing in Apple's name.

"Security questions?" Ryan asks, trying to refresh the web page to get the video feed to work again.

Jan watches Ryan. He looks anxious.

"What was that video?" He shakes his head. "I'm going to call JHo again. It's weird she hasn't answered."

Two emotions hit Jan at once, a tremor of anxiety for the other girl, and a pang of jealousy that Ryan looks so worried. She lands somewhere in the middle and leaves the room to check on Apple while he makes the call. Apple stands looking out the bedroom window, curious but not barking. In the other room Ryan leaves a quick message, so he must not have gotten through. When she comes back he's frowning.

"You ok?" Jan asks.

Ryan nods, distracted, pauses punctuating his words suddenly and without warning, like potholes on a dark street. "Yeah, I'm just going to go grab the heavy stuff from the car. While the elevator is working."

Jan thinks – knows – he's going to smoke a joint on the way and she watches the door close behind him, annoyance and concern pulling her in opposite directions. Outside, the elevator starts to move again, carrying Ryan back down to the garage, and annoyance wins out. She picks up her phone for a quick fix and opens the gram.

Jan always thought jaws dropping to the floor was just something made up for cartoons – but her jaw physically drops at her number of new followers, the likes, and notifications pinging her phone like hail on a tin roof. Her anger at Ryan forgotten, she squeals with delight as Apple bolts past her, stampeding from the bedroom, through the living room to the front door.

"Apple!" She shouts, but she isn't – can't be – angry right now.

She follows him through the living room, ready to take him on another walk when Ryan's laptop screen catches her eye.

The grainy video has refreshed, only now it isn't a typical Hollywood apartment – it's a dark garage, lit only by a single bulb in the ceiling. The camera moves swiftly between two cars she recognizes, stopping to stare down at a familiar, three-sided pothole. The pothole that Ryan always calls "The Bermuda Triangle of car tires."

Jan stops dead in her tracks. She can hear Apple barking, clawing at the door, and whining – but all she can see is the video. Moving between cars, looking right and left, and then stopping at a Range Rover. At Ryan's Range Rover, the light inside makes the windows briefly opaque, reflecting back the face of…there is no face.

Jan leans closer. She can see the outline of an ivory white hoodie with the hood pulled up, but inside, where a face should be, only darkness. It isn't that the hood is pulled too far forward, or that the face is somehow obscured, Jan realizes, and it isn't that there's nothing there. At least not exactly. It's more like looking down into the open maw of a cave, one that isn't just impenetrable, but actively swallows up any light that gets close.

Then the lights inside the Range Rover go out with a slight shake – Ryan closing the trunk – and the reflection is replaced by a clear shot of Ryan, eyes cashed and distant, a half smoked joint tucked behind one ear. He squats beneath his boxes of equipment, waddling between the cars towards the elevator.

Jan doesn't know if she screams or just thinks she screams. She claws out her phone, but her hands are shaking so bad she can't use her thumb to unlock it, and she messes up her password the first time. She tries to call Ryan, but instead the phone whirs and chimes as an app pops up.

We Are Legion And We Are Many. Certified Members Must Answer

Three Questions. Do You Accept, JANET PHAM?

Click – Jan doesn't hesitate, she clicks no.

The phone does hesitate, thinking. On screen Ryan stands at the elevator, the camera moves closer.

Sorry, JANET PHAM. Certified Members Must Answer Three Questions. Do You Accept, JANET PHAM?

On-screen Ryan, key chain of carabiners dangling from his fingers, presses the elevator button with his knee, kicks it once, then twice, then three times. Even without audio she knows he's groaning with frustration at the thought of carrying the heavy equipment up the narrow stairs. His shoulders slump, he turns, defeated and faces the camera for the first time.

The camera stops, tilting to the side as if cocking its head.

Ryan stares back at the camera, eyes wide. He swallows once. Good genetics combined with football and basketball through middle school and high school, intramural sports in college, and years of lugging around heavy photography equipment have kept Ryan in shape, but whatever he sees now scares him. He opens his mouth to say something when as the video goes black: *Certified Members Only* flashing on the screen and then a number ticking upwards, assumably the growing legion.

Jan looks back at her phone. It still flashes the same message:

Sorry, JANET PHAM. Certified Members Must Answer Three Questions. Do You Accept, JANET PHAM?

Click – This time Jan clicks accept.

We Are Legion. We Are Many. We Are You. You Are us. Who Are You, JANET PHAM?

Jan's fingers are still shaking as she types out her own name. Tears leak from her eyes in waves, blurring her vision. She finishes typing her name and hits enter, but the phone shakes.

Wrong Answer.

We Are Legion. We Are Many. We Are You. You Are us. Who Are You, JANET PHAM?

She tries again – adding her middle name, which she never uses. Again, *Wrong Answer*. She tries it with her middle initial, with Jan instead of Janet. None of them work and finally she jams her phone into her pocket and goes for the front door. Outside, she takes the stairs two at a time and jumps for the final three, landing heavily, as Apple pulls ahead, and before she can stop him, he's flying down the garage stairs and into the darkness.

Rubbing at her knee, Jan stops at the base of the stairs. She limps closer to the garage stairs, stopping when she is five feet away from the open door. She's taken these stairs a thousand times, but this time they look different. She gets the same feeling as looking at the strange reflection in the Range Rover's window, the sense of a cavern that swallows light, like a blackhole sucking in stars.

"Ryan? Apple?" She tries to make her voice carry, but it's barely a whimper.

She can't see an inch past the foot of the stairs into the garage, but she knows something is there, waiting. To her left, the elevator groans and clanks to life. The familiar sound of rusty metal grinds on rusty metal as the elevator ascends up out of the garage, and now Jan is crying, really crying. Because she knows Ryan always wears black, but when the elevator pings open all she can see is red. So much red.

She makes a decision, whirls around and, leaning heavily on the iron handrail, then begins hobbling up the stairs. She's halfway to the top when something hits the stairs behind her, and they groan and whine with the added weight. The memory of the white hood and the empty maw fills her mind, pushing her to move faster.

Stop whining, do your job! She prays the stairs won't collapse before she reaches the top.

She's two steps away from the top, the sound of footsteps a step or two behind her.

She jumps the final step, lands on her bad knee and falls forward through the front door, fights through the pain to slam it behind her as someone, or something crashes into it. With shaky hands she locks the door and backs away.

"Please!" She screams, "Please leave me alone."

Silence answers her, then she hears the familiar jingle of carabiners and keys and sees the deadbolt begin to turn. The chain lock hangs limply next to the door, out of reach. She turns and limps for the bedroom, pushing inside as the front door swings open.

She grabs everything she can, pushing the books, the desk chair, the matching nightstands and the dresser into a pile in front of the door. She backs into the corner of the room, pressing her back against one wall and sinking to the ground. Reaching for her phone she tries to dial 9-1-1, but the question from the app blinks up at her:

We Are Legion. We Are Many. We Are You. You Are us. Who Are You, JANET PHAM?

She tries, but fails, to answer the question. Her reflection in the black screen of the phone looks back at her. This morning she looked so good under Ryan's lighting and with Ryan's direction. The girl looking back at her now could be a different girl.

The door cracks, splinters, and breaks, under a violent onslaught, swinging open, easily brushing aside the books, chair, and desk she piled up as a last defense.

"I don't know," Jan whispers to the phone. "I don't know what you want from me."

And then her phone begins typing on its own, the app answering its own question.

We Are Legion. We Are Many. We Are You. You Are us. Who Are You, JANET PHAM?

L-E-G-I-O-N

The answer is *Legion*. Jan checks her followers – a reflex – and sees she's past sixty thousand, and counting. Then from somewhere deep inside she finds the strength to look up. To stand against it alone, as Jan Pham, of Almost_Phamous, for her Only_Phams, one last time. Her head lifts, slowly to the figure standing in the doorway, to look straight into the nothingness beneath the white hood. Her jaw set and hands clenched into fists, she looks away as it draws closer, gliding across the room to kneel in front of her, dipping its hood forward, as if to embrace her, the folds of the hood enveloping her head.

The light of her apartment fades, the familiar sounds of traffic through her flimsy walls grows dim.

Final thoughts flash across her mind like she's reading them off her phone:

You are me, and I am you.

And then she is not Jan Pham. She is Legion. And she is many.

The Cure

Kali Metis

Jane read the plaque as the tour guide droned. He'd clearly lead this tour one too many times; his excitement for the topic had been muted in the repetition. Leaning into the guide's words to regain her focus, she tightened her grip on her cane to steady her hand's quivering. She had done her best to hide her illness, but the random attacks of trembles, moments of instability, and awkward slowness aggravated her fellow travelers. They looked at her with derision, at times they questioned if she should be traveling.

Her brother had left her this trip in his will. At the time of the reading, she knew he had researched their origins, but she didn't realize how deeply he'd gotten into it. This trip wasn't optional, so to fulfill her brother's final wishes, she had taken time off from her senior baker position at The Cake Monkey Bakery. And though her boyfriend, Javier, had questioned her decision – "Are you sure you want to do this alone? You're going halfway across the world" – she was resolute.

"It's Sweden," she said. "What could happen in Sweden?"

Her brother had insisted on this specific tour which centered on a small village that contained the Birka Viking warrior gravesite. The grave of the most powerful and ancient Nordic warrior. "This holds the key," he'd noted in his will. "The key to all that you need. To all that we are."

If it was so important, then why did he...? She teared up, still in mourning for the one person she'd counted on her whole life. The one person who truly understood her. Not that Javier didn't, but they had only been together since high school; their bond was still growing.

After her brother's diagnosis of Huntington's disease, he'd become more agitated, babbling on about the importance of their heritage. At that time, he had warned her that there was a high likelihood she would come down with the disease as well. She had already felt the shaking of her hands and had suffered bouts of memory loss.

The tour guide paused before her. His focus squarely on her. "Did you mention you were a descendant?" He hoped this would get her reengaged in the tour. Even if he found the topic tiresome, it didn't mean he wanted his travelers to be bored with it too.

Preoccupied with her thoughts and fascinated with the rune etchings along the structure's walls, his inquiry startled her. "I'm sorry?"

"Descendent. Hadn't you mentioned you were a distant relative?" The tour guide looked curious more than anything else. His intention was innocent, he'd fought to keep Jane engaged with the group since day one. He'd never had someone spend so much money on a tour to pay so little attention.

"Oh, yes. Right. According to my brother, we are from the Ulf, son of Bjorn clan." Her brother had insisted that she spend the majority of her time in this little village. Based on his recommendation, she intentionally wandered off when the tour headed to neighboring villages or into the countryside. She used her illness as a reason to remain within the village on days when they were supposed to stay overnight elsewhere. Once the others had moved on, she skulked away and dove into the historical buildings and library. She wandered the museum's halls in hopes that by immersing herself in the village's history, she would unlock her own history and whatever it held that her brother had been so desperate for her to find.

She tried to stay focused on the topic at hand, but in all honesty, her desire to go home only grew. She missed Javier. She loved taking baked goods to his work at the emergency room. That was the least she could do for him and the rest of the staff. Every day, they risked their lives to save those who came in. Her dreams were of mixing and pouring batter for cakes and pastries. She knew the significant dates of every member of his staff and everyone in their neighborhood.

"Then you'll find these carvings even more fascinating," the tour guide pointed to a far wall that had been cordoned off to keep visitors from being able to touch them. "They sparked a debate as to whether there were female warriors."

"Really?" Jane already knew this from the research her brother had left. She simply didn't understand her brother's fascination.

"Yes. When they first unearthed this grave, it was assumed that the high-ranking warrior was a strategist and possibly the highest-ranking officer on this island."

Jane neared the etchings. "What changed?"

The tour guide laughed. "They performed tests and discovered that the body is one of a female. Since the Nordics were a paternal society, that meant the original assumptions were improbable."

Jane smirked. "But not impossible." Her brother had been fascinated by the Birka warrior.

"Well, that's for much smarter people than me to debate."

Jane reached out to touch the runes, the foreign words and symbols called to her. She heard the foreign words and symbols calling her in her mind.

"If you'd like, we can talk to the local historian. I'm sure he'd love to meet a descendant." The guide urged Jane onward, a few steps behind the rest of the group. Her cane in hand, her stability questionable.

"I'd like that." Among her brother's papers, she had his correspondence with an historian named Birger who had referenced much richer texts that her brother could review if he ever visited Sweden.

Something in her brother's research had driven him to this specific location. His intrigue had begun when he found paperwork which referenced their birth parents. Starting with their names, he began his journey to uncover who their parents were and why they would have left them. Unlike her brother, Jane preferred to stay in the present and focus on her immediate friends and their adoptive family.

After he had taken an Ancestry.com DNA test, his interest went into overdrive. He spent every waking moment finding whatever he could about their heritage. She thought his face would be glued to the computer screen with the letters Ancestry.com echoed on his forehead. Jane on the other hand, chose not to dwell on who their parents were or why they abandoned them. Instead, she focused on making people happy. She had apprenticed for her dream job at The Cake Monkey while in high school. Making cakes and pastries was her idea of heaven.

In his will, her brother had insisted on this exact place, not a neighboring village, not a nearby town, not the countryside, but this exact location. Something made him believe that the key to their diagnosis and eventual cure of Huntington's disease remained with the ancient texts. She only wished he would have been more patient and waited for their chance to come here, even if it was only to make his wishes come true. He had been so confident that a cure lay among the runes and within the historian's pages of texts, yet his depression became too much. His suicide infuriated her.

He had abandoned her.

*

The historian's library building was straight out of *The Hobbit*. The guide opened the circular door and led her inside. The entry opened to a vast area with rows and rows of books in various stages of tatters. She had been here in her solitary wanderings, but somehow seeing it through the tour guide's eyes made a difference. Previously, the worn books had seemed like entering the second hand store of unloved and unwanted knowledge, but with the additional inference, she saw potential. From the back came a man, his height nearly touched the ceiling.

"Good to see you, Bo," the man said to the tour guide. Embarrassed, Jane realized she never bothered to ask the tour guide's name. Even with a name tag, she hadn't retained it. Truth was, that she couldn't remember his name, a side effect of her disease and a reality she only now acknowledged. She blushed.

"Good to see you too, Birger." The men shook hands. "I've brought a special guest. She came here all the way from America."

Jane offered her hand. "Jane Auber. Nice to meet you." His hand enveloped hers. She had never thought of herself as little.

"Ah. Let me guess. You're a descendant." He nodded at her cane.

"Yes, well –"

"Based on your tremor, a direct descendant. My sympathy." He had been the first on this tour to recognize the signs.

"How'd you –"

"Legend has it your ancestors left the village in pursuit of a permanent cure. Based on your current state, looks like they never found one."

"My brother thought it may be here." She referenced the aisles of books.

"And he's...?" Birger continued forward on his tasks.

"He...died. Before he could make the trip." Her voice choked. This had been the first time she'd acknowledged his passing to a stranger. She found the nearest chair and rested.

"Wait, was your brother, Dan? Dan Auber?"

Jane nodded. When Birger said her brother's name, she felt a painful difficulty hearing it. This caused her mourning to deepen.

"I'm so sorry," Birger said. "We never met in person but…he seemed like a good soul."

"I'll leave you to it." Bo nodded to Jane. "Birger's an old friend. He will take you back to the Inn. Good to see you, sir." Bo smiled at Birger and then headed out the main entry.

"We grew up together," Birger said. "We used to play among these stacks." He motioned to the library. "My father had been the historian and librarian just as his before him."

"This comes naturally," Jane said.

"The historian bit? Yes." He paused and considered her. "Based on your comments, you're looking for a cure."

"I wasn't at first but –" Why was she sharing so much with this man? Something about him put her at ease. The insanity of the situation didn't seem so crazy when she talked to him. "Or at least a hint. Something."

"You're the fifth one from your line who's been by in thirty years."

"Fifth? I thought we were the only ones."

"They came from other lands. Your family scattered hundreds of years ago." Birger pulled out a thick volume. Leather bound with gold etching. Its pages were fragile – brittle. "Here." He put the book before her. "About two hundred years ago, the first historian took the legends to the page."

Jane hesitated to touch the book, afraid that she would cause it damage.

"Don't worry. I've been digitizing them for the last few years. No need for the stories to disappear with the well-worn paper." He reached under the desk and pulled out a laptop. "Here, use this." He shared the tale as she surfed the pages.

"Your earliest recorded ancestor, Ulf, son of Bjorn, had come to this village over a thousand years ago. Originally a member of the king's guard, he had been in search of a new land. A place to begin a new life away from the wars raged by royalty.

"A gentle soul, Ulf staked out a small farm. At times he could be found wandering the roads, unsure of where he was or where he was heading. His gentleness, his kindness, touched a young maiden named Freya. Her father was the local metallurgist, so Freya knew the ways of bending metals for war and for peace. She found Ulf walking the main road on a spring day, the clouds had come closer with threats of rain. She took him in.

"To thank her, Ulf brought Freya and her family milk and cheeses. Thus, began their courtship. Her father and mother, wary of Ulf due to his unusual bouts of forgetfulness and for fear of the near stranger's past, objected to this courtship.

"Freya, smitten, promised her parents that she'd be careful and stated that she truly believed Ulf had a good soul. It was his soul and good nature she wanted to marry. Reluctantly, they agreed to the nuptials.

"Freya and Ulf started with a modest farm of a few cows and fields of barley and wheat. Ulf gradually purchased more cattle, chicken, and sheep. Freya brought her parents spoils from the farm and they in turn gave the couple ironworks to help them in their pursuits. The loving couple enjoyed their romantic nights together, reveling in newly wedded bliss.

"Freya noted that sometimes her husband's forgetfulness was accompanied with a physical shaking. A mild tremor that seemed to pass without note."

"He had Huntington's?" Jane asked.

"Not quite. According to legend, the farm had been raided repeatedly by what appeared to be wolves. Sheep disappeared in bloody patches during the night. Ulf began to spend his evenings staking out the culprit only to awaken the next morning to find that more sheep had disappeared and the wolf had gotten away. Freya's parents offered traps to capture the wolf. Ulf declined. He wanted to resolve this issue and protect his family without their assistance.

"One evening, Freya decided to stake out the perpetrator on her own. At this point, she believed her husband to be overworked and that he had always fallen asleep just as the wolf came upon their lands. She awaited yards away from her husband, but within eyeshot. Some say she went to sleep. Others say she just lost sight of him, but in either case, at midnight, she heard a loud braying, a vicious howling. In response, she burst forward to warn him of the beast's approach. Sword in hand, Freya came upon her husband as he was in the midst of…*transforming*. His clothes in tatters, his teeth sharper than arrows, his hands shifted into claws, his eyes newly ruby with bloodlust."

"What?" Jane asked.

"Imagine what Freya thought. Initially in denial that the beast changing in front of her was her husband, she knew she had to protect herself, and raised her sword against him. However, something about the way it moved, something in its reddened eyes, something in its half-hearted attacks let her know that it didn't want to cause any harm. This creature's stance confirmed for Freya that it was indeed her husband.

"She lowered her sword, trying to think of some way to bring him back, bring back the man she loved. With her heart breaking, her need was greater than anything else in the world, and she pleaded, 'Ulf, it's me, Freya. Your wife. Please come back to me.' With those words, a glimmer of recognition sparked across his beastly face. His features softened with love and he ran away from their home and through the fields.

"Freya returned to their hut and barred the doors. The next day, confused as to what had happened, yet determined to get her husband back and angry at the world, she sought out his fellow soldiers. At first, they refused to talk to her. 'We can help Ulf together,' she told them. 'I cannot do it unless you tell me what is happening to him.' After much prodding, they revealed that he had been among the soldiers known as úlfheðnars before retiring to a life of a farmer. His hope had been to make a new life void of the horrors of transformations. He had hoped that away from the warrior's life, he'd no longer have the need for such weapons and he would be able to settle into a loving home."

"You're saying that my shaking is –" Jane looked up from the laptop.

"You're in the beginning stages. There's more to come."

Jane abruptly got up from the table. Outside the night had fallen. In disbelief, she slapped the laptop closed. "This can't be –" She looked at Birger whose expression hadn't changed. There was no evidence of him playing games or lying. If anything, he looked sincere. The reality of what he implied was so terrifying, she raced out the door. She couldn't leave the place fast enough.

Birger ran after her. "You shouldn't go out alone. It's not safe."

Jane turned on him. "It's not safe? You just told me I'm a werewoman. Have you lost your mind?" Jane stormed toward the Inn. She needed to get back to her intimate room. She needed to be alone to think, to process. Her quivering increased as she hurried her step. Is this why her brother killed himself? Is this the reason that he gave up his life? This time her hands shook with frustration and untapped adrenaline.

Birger caught up and circled in front of her. Blocking her, he said, "please. Listen to me. I know it sounds – "

"Insane?"

"Fine. Insane." He met her gaze. His height blocked the little bit of moonlight. "You need to be prepared."

"I can't talk to you right now." She shoved her way past him. She turned. "Did you tell my brother this...nonsense?"

"We never got that far." He paused, a hint of desperation in his voice, a hint of regret. "Through the years we've learned some information is best shared in person."

"*HA!*" Her laugh of mockery was void of joy. She continued towards the inn. She could feel his presence grow farther and farther away, though she felt him watching her as she stormed off. She knew he let her go. He could have easily kept her there, but he didn't. At that moment, she didn't even wonder why.

He called after her, "when you're ready, come back."

Slowly shaking his head, he whispered to himself with a tinge of sadness, "she has to come back."

Authors

Emily Castles studied at the University of Manchester and Durham University, graduating with an MA in English Literature. Born in Birmingham, she now lives in London and enjoys the theatre and going to metal gigs. She is an upcoming writer with a small scattering of published pieces, all irrevocably cemented in the delicious macabre.

After growing up in Albuquerque, New Mexico, **Wes Choc** joined the US Marine Corps in 1965 during the Vietnam era. His first book, "Just Dust" (published in 2014) recaptures his unusual experiences in this introspective narrative.Once leaving the marines in '69 and graduating from college in '70, he has lived in a dozen states over 40 years with the American Automobile Association. In '92 he was appointed president of AAA MountainWest, overseeing operations in Montana, Wyoming, and Alaska.After he retired in 2008, Wes started volunteering extensively, working with troubled youth in group homes, with returning veterans from Iraq and Afghanistan, and with young adults having Asperger's or schizophrenia.

David Fitzpatrick was born in Dearborn, Michigan. He lives in Middlefield, Connecticut, with his wife, Amy, a photographer and mental health advocate and real estate investment analyst for a Hartford firm. They have two angry cats and a pooch. David graduated Skidmore College in 1988 and got his MFA in 2011 from Fairfield University. In

2012, his memoir "Sharp: My Story of Madness, Cutting, and How I Reclaimed My Life" was published by Harper Collins. He's been in New Haven Review, Perch, Barely South Review and Fiction Weekly. Currently he is working on a YA novel called, 'End Zone.' His website is http://www.davidfitzpatrickbooks.com

Matt Hardman is husband and a father of six who resides in Calvert County, Maryland. He is a retired U.S. Navy Chief Petty Officer who works as a marine engineering consultant to the Navy's DDG 51 Shipbuilding Program Office. While on active duty, he served onboard a submarine, two aircraft carriers, two amphibious transports, one submarine tender, and one destroyer. He holds a bachelor's in Intelligence Studies and Counterintelligence from American Military University and a Master's in Writing from Johns Hopkins University.

Harold Hoss loves reading, writing, and watching horror movies - almost always while drinking coffee. A former studio executive, he currently works as a producer on the upcoming film "The Unheard."

Anna Idelevich is a scientist by profession, Ph.D., MBA, trained in the neuroscience field at Harvard University. She writes poetry for pleasure. Her books and poetry collections include "DNA of the Reversed River" and "Cryptopathos" published by the Liberty Publishing House, NY. Anna's poems were published by BlazeVOX, Louisville Review, Salmon Creek Journal, Bourgeon Magazine, In Parenthesis, O:J&A, Gyroscope Review among others. We hope you will enjoy their melody, new linguistic tone, and a slight tint of an accent.

Anastasia Jill (she/they) is a queer writer living in the Southeast United States. She has been nominated for Best American Short

Stories, Best of the Net, and several other honors. Her work has been featured with Poets.org, Pithead Chapel, apt, Minola Review, Broken Pencil, and more.

Aimee LaBrie's short stories have appeared in *Minnesota Review, Iron Horse Literary Journal, StoryQuarterly, The Cimarron Review, Pleiades, Beloit Fiction, Permafrost,* and others. In 2020, her short story "Rage," won first place in the *Solstice Literary Magazine's* annual fiction contest. In 2007, her short story collection, *Wonderful Girl,* was awarded the Katherine Anne Porter Prize in Fiction and published by the University of North Texas Press. Her short fiction has been nominated for three Pushcart Prizes. In 2012, she won first place in *Zoetrope's* All-Story contest. Aimee works as a senior program administrator and lecturer of creative writing at Rutgers University's Writers House.

Lauren Lang is a former broadcast journalist and current freelance photographer and videographer living in Denver, CO. In her spare time, she writes fiction, cooks, bakes, crochets hats for stuffed animals, gardens with the intent of taking pictures of the flowers should they live, and terrorizes local residents by pretending to be a wildlife photographer and running through area parks with her camera screaming, "Birds!". Occasionally, she does actually take a picture of a bird. She can also occasionally be found in a tree with the birds.

More information about Lauren and her work can be found by visiting:https://www.facebook.com/AuthorLaurenLang/

Jonathan Maberry is a New York Times best-seller, five-time Bram Stoker Award-winner, anthology editor, comic book writer, executive producer, magazine feature writer, playwright, and writing teacher/lecturer. He is the editor of Weird Tales Magazine and president of the International Association of Media Tie-in Writers. He is the recipient of the Inkpot Award, three Scribe Awards, and was named one of the Today's Top Ten Horror Writers. His books have been sold to more than thirty countries. He writes in several genres including thriller, horror, science fiction, epic fantasy, and mystery; and he writes for adults, middle grade, and young adult.

Asya Marie lives quietly in Washington state, where she writes and edits. Her writing has appeared in *The Nonconformist Magazine, Inkwell Journal, 805 Lit + Art,* and elsewhere.

Andy McQuestin lives in Melbourne. His short fiction has appeared in print or online in Overland, Right Now, Hawai'i Pacific Review, SIAMB!, Hyades Magazine and others. Usually, his stories adjust reality slightly, to examine relationships.

Kali Metis is the pen name for Lisa Diane Kastner. Lisa was born in Camden, NJ which was one of the most dangerous cities in America. In high school, she was a dancer and co-host on Dance Party USA. At the age of 20 she came home to find her house had burned down and she was suddenly homeless. She spent the next several years rebuilding and obtaining her Bachelors, MBA, and MFA. While fulfilling an amazing corporate career, she began Running Wild, LLC which consists of Running Wild Press where they publish great stories that don't fit neatly in a box and RIZE Press where they publish great genre stories written by people of color and other underrepresented groups. Running Wild has been honored with two best of 2019 and two best of 2020 books according to Kirkus Reviews as well as several starred reviews and additional acclaim. Lisa was named to Yahoo Finance's Top 10 Entrepreneurs to Watch in 2021 and nominated to FORBES NEXT 1000, a list of American self-funded entrepreneurs who continue to strive during the challenging times of COVID. She was named to New York Weekly's Top Ten Females to Watch in 2021, LA Wire's Top 10 Businesses to Watch in 2021, and was featured in the August/September 2021 edition of FORBES magazine. She resides in Los Angeles, California with her husband and their two felines, The Master and Margarita.

Charissa Roberson is a life-long writer and reader who is steadily filling up every spare inch of her room with books. She recently graduated from Roanoke College with her bachelor's degree in Creative Writing and French, with a concentration in film. Her fiction and poetry have appeared in several places online, including the *Elevation Review, NOVUS Literary Journal, Burnt Pine Magazine*, and *Manawaker Studio's Flash Fiction Podcast*. She has also authored two collections of short stories and a booklet on the history of her community. When not dwelling in imaginary worlds, she loves exploring the real one, making and watching films, learning languages, and playing Irish tunes on her fiddle.

Peter Roxburgh has always looked at the world in a different way - an alternative perspective on why things are the way they are.

At university, he crammed for his finals by reading self-development books in a monastery in Spain. He gained first-class honors in business. He lectured on accountancy for five years when he wasn't hugging rocks or writing for climbing magazines. And, back in '99, when the Mobile Internet was in its infancy, he went into software as a self-taught programmer. There he designed mobile payments systems, wrote books and courses for Microsoft and Sun Microsystems, and founded an online payment's company. In 2008, he sold the company and exited the commercial world to become a bicycle mechanic. During his seven years in the trade, he reflected, underwent a journey of discovery, and discovered oneness.

Today, he helps managers and leaders in blue-chip companies, such as GSK, Novartis, and Pfizer to become their best selves.

A natural born storyteller, **Nikolas Thornton** finds profound joy in sharing stories that magically appear in his mind delivered from unknown origins. Mr. Thornton's writing took a backseat for decades as his life evolved. It was at his daughter's bedtime when the fire rekindled. Given the choice to have Daddy read two bedtime stories or create their own, Michelle always chose to create their own. Together they spun magical tales from faraway lands only known to two. She called these times "Songs, Rhymes, Anytimes."

Years later while recuperating from a debilitating injury, Mr. Thornton was afforded the time to write. After writing over 100 short stories, numerous songs, several novella's, and one novel, Mr. Thornton dipped his toe into the publishing waters once again. He instantly found success. He is uniquely positioned to release numerous stories and works after waiting years to strengthen his craft and build his catalog. Talks are ongoing with various publishers regarding a children's holiday picture book that has a huge commercial potential. Other Nikolas Thornton short stories, children's stories, graphic novels, songs, novellas, and a novel are also currently under consideration by publishers. The future looks very bright.

J. T. Townley has published in *Harvard Review, The Kenyon Review, The Threepenny Review*, and many other magazines and journals. His stories have been nominated for the Pushcart Prize (three times) and the Best of the Net Award. He holds an MFA in Creative Writing from the University of British Columbia and an MPhil in English from the University of Oxford, and he teaches fiction writing at Pacific Northwest College of Art at Willamette University. To learn more, visit jttownley.com.

Editor

Benjamin B. White has worked with almost two hundred authors editing and polishing short stories, novels, poetry, and works of creative nonfiction. His own full length work includes *Buddha Bastinado Blues, The Kill Gene, Conley Bottom: A Poemoir, The Recon Trilogy +1, Mill Springs: A Poemoir of Place* (forthcoming), and *Say Their Names* (forthcoming under Anonymous). As an award-winning poet ("Johnny Reb" in Havik 2021), his poems have appeared in *The Purple Breakfast Review*, the Exterminating Angel Press: The Magazine, *Tuck* Magazine, So Say We All's *Incoming: Drugs, Sex, and Copenhagen*, and Proud To Be: Writing by American Warriors, Volumes 6 and 7. His neo-narrative poem, *The Cuban*, appeared as a novella in the Running Wild Press Novella Anthology, Volume 2.

Running Wild Press publishes stories that cross genres with great stories and writing. RIZE publishes great genre stories written by people of color and by authors who identify with other marginalized groups. Our team consists of:

Lisa Diane Kastner, Founder and Executive Editor
Mona Bethke, Acquisitions Editor, RIZE
Benjamin B. White, Acquisitions Editor, Running Wild
Peter A. Wright, Acquisitions Editor, Running Wild
Rebecca Dimyan, Editor
Andrew DiPrinzio, Editor
Cecilia Kennedy, Editor
Barbara Lockwood, Editor
Cody Sisco, Editor
Chih Wang, Editor
Lisa Montagne, Editor
Pulp Art Studios, Cover Design
Standout Books, Interior Design
Polgarus Studios, Interior Design
Nicole Tiskus, Product Manager Intern
Alex Riklin, Product Manager Intern

Learn more about us and our stories at www.runningwildpress.com

Loved this story and want more? Follow us at www.runningwildpress.com, www.facebook/runningwildpress, on Twitter @lisadkastner @RunWildBooks @RWRize

www.ingramcontent.com/pod-product-compliance
Lightning Source LLC
Chambersburg PA
CBHW051335020726
47501CB00007B/2093